BUIL

UNIVEF

William A. Pollard

RHYME PLACE
(Who stole Bo Peep's sheep?)

© 2025 **Europe Books**| London
www.europebooks.co.uk | info@europebooks.co.uk

ISBN 979-1-25697-068-1
First edition: February 2025

Edited by Veronica Parise

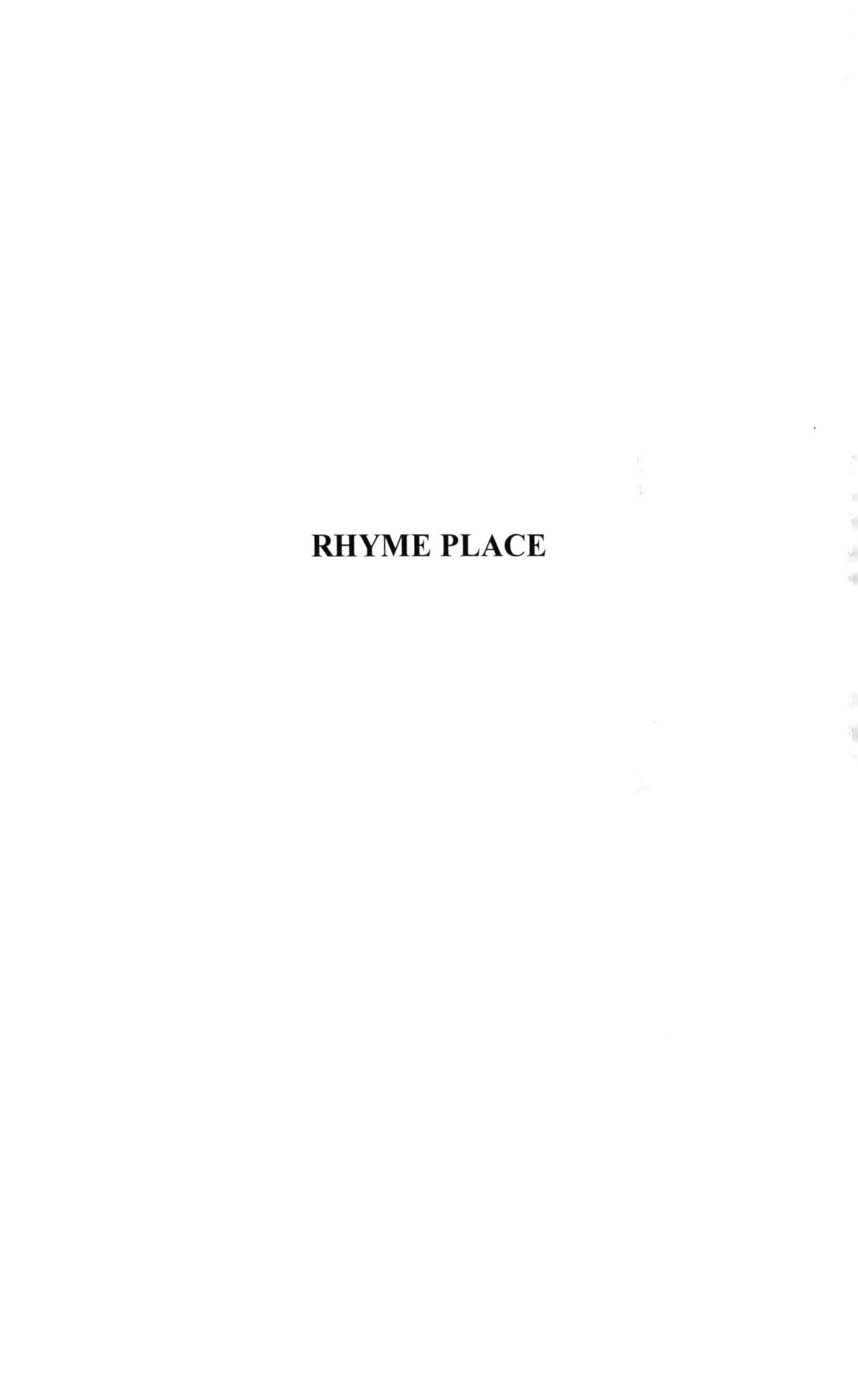

RHYME PLACE

BOOKS BY THE AUTHOR

MY ROGUE GENE
ISBN: 978-1-80074-296-3

Bill's autobiography. Full of amusing anecdotes from his past, from the time he was born up to the time he left the army after twelve years service.

Olympia Publishers
Amazon Bookstore

MY GROWN-UP ROGUE GENE
ISBN: 978-1-80439-313-0

More nonsense from Bill's rogue gene, now grown-up and still interfering with Bill's life.
This is a sequel to *My Rogue Gene*, highlighting Bill's life from the time he left the army to his life in civvy street and into retirement.

Olympia Publishers
Amazon Bookstore

BEHIND ROSE BORDERED WINDOWS
(Winner of the Golden Book Prize at the Rome Literary Awards, March 2024)
ISBN - 979-1-22014-338-7

William Colbert's wife dies. Everyone is convinced her death was an accident, including William. He has inherited a country manor in a remote part of the country, but his new life is thrown into disarray when he witnesses distressing events through the windows of the five picture postcard cottages facing his new home... Nobody believes what he has seen, until the truth about his inheritance, and his wife, is revealed.

Europe Books
Amazon Bookstore

LUCKY, OR WHAT...?
ISBN: 979-1-22014-866-5

How many people, do you think, have just wished that they had more good luck in their lives? What you don't realise is that the quicker you use up your good luck, the nearer you are to having a shed load of bad luck.
Playing an on-line game, eight finalists don't know that if they lose the game, they die. Something else they don't know is that if they win the game, they die.
Either way, they're dead...

Europe Books
Amazon Bookstore

INSIDE
ISBN: 979-1-22015-306-5

What you don't realise is that there is a whole community of tiny workers managing your insides. A really, really tiny community of people with the singular purpose of keeping your anatomy and physiology working in first class condition. They're happy looking after your insides… Until something goes wrong.

Europe Books
Amazon Bookstore

To Sophie

Table of Contents

PROLOGUE

How many of you can remember laying your head on a pillow, eyelids drooping, while you listen to Mum singing nursery rhymes to you?

Not many, I bet.

After all, we were just a few months old when Mum told us about Peter Piper picking a peck of pickled pepper, or Mother Goose squeezing out a golden egg from somewhere unmentionable.

I bet many of you have shared a few nursery rhymes with your children, though.

Nursey rhymes are nothing new. They were recorded in English plays as early as the mid-16th century, although it is understood that a French poem similar to "Thirty days hath September", numbering the days of the month, was recorded in the 13th century. As far as we know, 'Pat-a-cake' is one of the oldest surviving English nursery rhymes.

Somebody thought of combining music with nursery rhymes. The oldest children's songs for which records exist are lullabies. These are intended to help a child fall asleep and they can be found in every human culture. Have you ever tried to get to sleep while someone is singing in your ear…? It's not easy.

Anyway, we all know about nursery rhymes. We've all heard them and we've all used them, but did you know that the characters in nursery rhymes actually exist? They do, honestly… And there is a place where these characters live. It's true! Nobody knows the actual name of this place but it's really close to us all. You can visit this place, but you have to close your eyes, relax and let your imagination take you there.

You're still not convinced that it's a real place?

Okay, lie down somewhere comfortable, sink your head into a soft pillow, stop fiddling with whatever it is that you're fiddling with… Yes, put it away… close your eyes and follow me to this place.

This place, where all your nursery rhyme characters come to life.

This place, where everything is relaxed and nothing gets rushed.

This place, where little Bo Peep lost her sheep.

This place, called Rhyme Place…

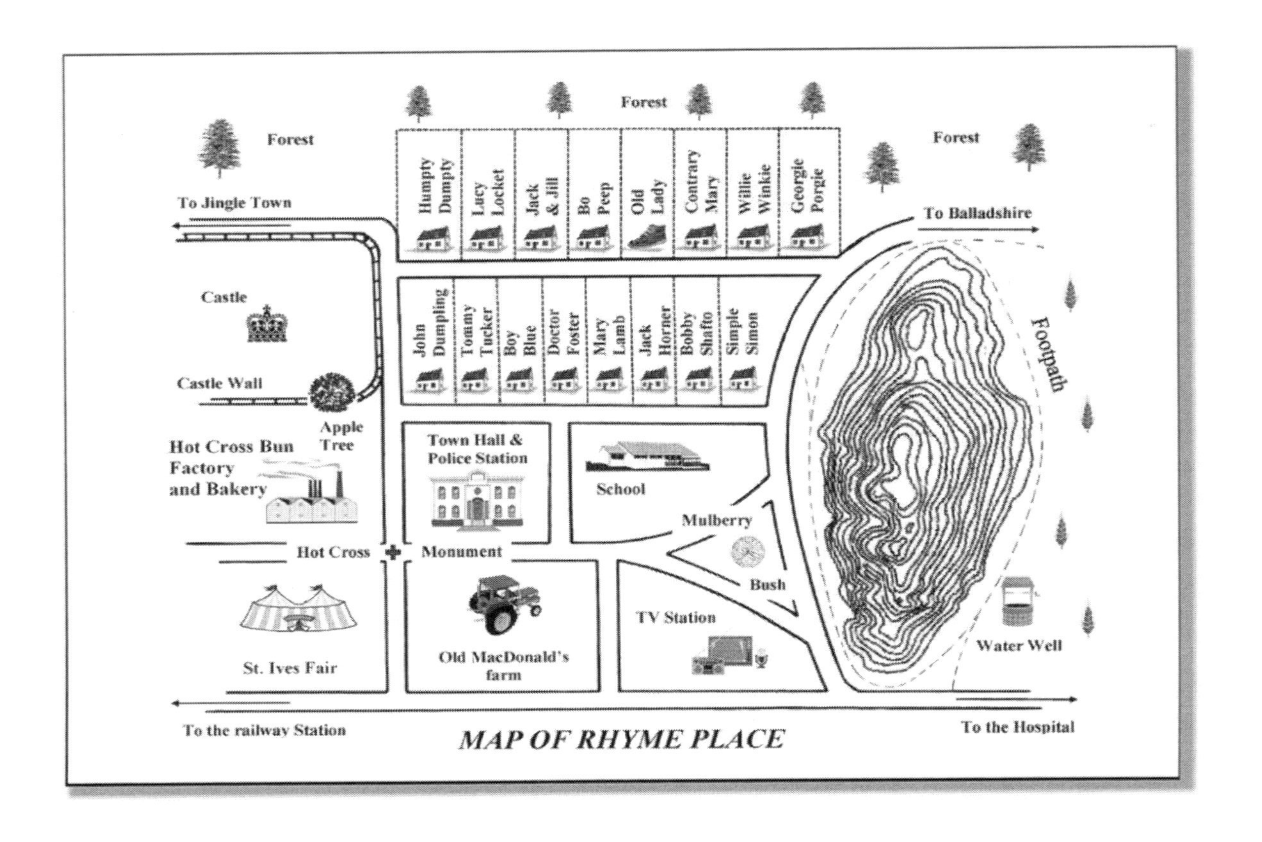

Forest
Forest
Forest
To Jingle Town
Humpty Dumpty
Lucy Locket
Jack & Jill
Bo Peep
Old Lady
Contrary Mary
Willie Winkie
Georgie Porgie
To Balladshire
Castle
Castle Wall
Apple Tree
John Dumpling
Tommy Tucker
Boy Blue
Doctor Foster
Mary Lamb
Jack Horner
Bobby Shafto
Simple Simon
Footpath
Hot Cross Bun Factory and Bakery
Town Hall & Police Station
School
Mulberry
Bush
Hot Cross
Monument
St. Ives Fair
Old MacDonald's farm
TV Station
Water Well
To the railway Station
To the Hospital
MAP OF RHYME PLACE

CHAPTER 1

Simple Simon met a pie man going to the fair.
Said Simple Simon to the pie man
"Let me taste your ware."
Said the pie man unto Simon
"Show me first your penny."
Said Simple Simon to the pie man
"Indeed, I have not any."
(England, 1764)

Week 1. Friday, p.m., at school.

It is the last day of the summer term for the children of Rhyme Place School.

Simon has, for several weeks, saved all the money he earned from his paper round. Added to this is his usual weekly pocket money from Mum, and he now has a tidy sum to spend.

He's not going to spend this stash of cash on sweets, like he usually does. It's been hard, but since he heard about the fairground coming to Rhyme Place he hasn't spent a penny of his hard earned cash.

On many occasions he was tempted to push the door to the sweetshop open each time he gazed through the shop's window, but no, he had to be strong. He had to resist the urge to delve into the pick-and-mix because he was going to need the money for his forthcoming trip to the fair.

His fortitude and patience eventually paid off. Tomorrow, Saturday, is the day that the fair comes to the village. It will take them the whole of the weekend to set up the tents and stalls and rides on the field on the outskirts of the village, but on Monday they will be ready for the onslaught of families descending on the fairground to empty their pockets of this week's housekeeping budget and hand the money over to the waiting ride attendants, standing next to their rides trying to look suave and debonaire.

As he stared out of the classroom window, Simon daydreamed about the hours of fun he is going to have at the fair. He was suddenly brought back to earth by his teacher.

"Simon!" she shouted. "You're gazing out of the window - again. Pay attention!"

"Yes, Miss," Simon answered.

"What are you gawking at?"

"Oh, nothing, Miss. I was just thinking about Monday."

"What's happening on Monday?"

"It's the fair, Miss. The fair is setting up on one of old Macdonald's farm fields this weekend and I can't wait for it to open."

"Well, you'll just have to, won't you? Now pay attention to the lesson, or you'll not learn anything. You'll grow up to be simple, Simon. You don't want that, do you?"

"No, Miss."

That's how Simon got his nickname… 'Simple' Simon.

Kids can be really cruel sometimes. As soon as one gets labelled with something derisory the rest of the kids all join in to capitalise on that child's demise, and derisory labels stick for ever.

*

Week 1. Monday, a.m.

After a sleepless Sunday night Simon washed, dressed and dashed downstairs for his breakfast.

"What are you going to do today?" asked Mum.

"The fair's in the village, Mum. That's where I'm going after breakfast."

"Oh? Have you got any money for it?"

"Yep," a huge smile on his face. "I've been saving for ages and I've now got ten pounds to spend."

"Well done. I wondered where the usual pile of sweet wrappers on the bedroom floor had gone. Do you want some more money? Ten pounds won't get you very far."

"Yes please, Mum."

Mum gave Simon an extra fiver. "Look after it - and stay out of trouble."

"Yes Mum."

"On your way home from the fair, can you pick up some more eggs from Macdonald's farm, for me?"

"Will do, Mum."

With that, Simon stuffed the fiver into his pocket to join the rest of his savings, he donned his coat and dashed out of the cottage. Mum looked on with love and pride as he skipped down the road towards old Macdonald's farm field.

*

On the way to the fair, Simon caught up with a bloke who was wearing a chef's hat on his head and an apron over the top of his plaid shirt and chequered trousers. The guy was carrying a large, heavy tray covered with a gingham cloth.

"What you got there, mister?" asked Simon.

"Pies." A brusque, irritable reply.

"Pies? What kind of pies?"

"Apple pies. Hop it, kid."

"I was only asking. No need to get the huff."

"Look, kid, this tray's heavy and I need to get these 'ere pies to the fair. So clear off and stop bothering me, or you'll get a thick ear!"

"Can I have one?"

"What? A thick ear? You'll get one if you don't stop bothering me."

"A pie."

The pie man stopped walking and breathed out a long, exasperated sigh.

"How much you got?"

"Nothing," lied Simon.

"Well, sod off."

"I bet you're a bundle of fun at parties."

"Look! If you don't get lost, kid, I'm going to put this tray down and smack you around the ear'ole. Got it?"

"Want some help?"

"With what?"

"Carrying that tray."

The pie man thought about that suggestion for a moment, then caved in to Simon's suggestion.

"Okay, if you want to help me grab hold of that side," offering the tray to Simon.

"It'll cost you."

"What? How much?"

"One pie. For that I'll help you with the tray all the way to the fair."

Another pause for thought. “Oh, alright. Get hold of the tray.”

“Pie first.”

“You cheeky sod. Here!” handing Simon one of the pies.

Simon stuffed the pie into the same pocket as his fairground money and took hold of one side of the pie tray. The two of them made their way to the fair. The pie man grumbled all the way there, but that didn’t bother Simon - he now had an apple pie to look forward to at lunch time.

Not such a simple Simon, eh…?

On the way to the fair Simon and the pie man were almost run over by a speeding truck! They managed to get out of the truck’s way just in time.

CHAPTER 2

Little Bo Peep has lost her sheep and doesn't know where to find them.
Leave them alone and they'll come home, wagging their tails behind them.
(England, c.1805)

Week 1. Monday, a.m.

The telephone on Sergeant Argent's desk rang while he was typing up a report on an incident that took place yesterday - something about a rave party at the mulberry bush that he had to break up because the party revellers had got a little bit boisterous and they had started to make a nuisance of themselves.

Picking up the telephone, he introduced himself. "Rhyme Place police station. Sergeant Argent speaking."

A tearful voice answered. "Sergeant Argent, this is Bo Peep."

"Good morning, Miss Peep. How can I help you?"

"My sheep are missing."

Cries of distress could be heard by the Sergeant.

"Oh dear. Try to calm down, Bo, while I make my way over to your place to take a statement."

"Thank you, Sergeant. I'm so worried about them. The poor little things will be so frightened."

"Yes, I'll be there as soon as I can."

"I've got hordes of television cameras and reporters all over my garden. I've absolutely no idea who told them about my missing sheep, but I've already given them a statement."

“That’s alright. Don’t answer the door to anyone else until I get there. Why don’t you put the kettle on to make a nice cup of tea and I’ll be there before it has boiled.”

“Yes. Thank you so much, the Sergeant. I’m really sorry to disturb you with this.”

“That’s okay. I’ll see you soon.”

The Sergeant put down his pencil, picked up his helmet and made his way to Bo Peep’s cottage.

*

NEWS FLASH! From Chatty Chaste on the news desk at Rhyme Place TV station.

Chatty - “This news, just in… There’s been a report of some missing sheep… Bo Peep woke up this morning to find every one of her four sheep had been stolen. Enquiries and information about this incident should be provided to Rhyme Place police station. Our chief crime reporter, Inky Irwin, is now on the scene and we’ll interrupt our Play Den programme to go over to him now.”

Cut to the outside broadcast.

Chatty - “Good morning Inky. It’s always good to talk to you. What can you tell us about these missing sheep?”

Inky Irwin - “Not a lot at the moment, Chatty. I’m told by Bo Peep that when she went downstairs to make her breakfast, this morning, she looked out of the kitchen window and all her sheep were missing from the paddock. She carried out a search of the surrounding area, but there was no sign of the sheep. I have with me the old woman who lives in a shoe, Bo Peep’s next-door neighbour. Tell us more about what you saw earlier this morning.” Inky thrusts his microphone under the old woman’s nose.

Old woman - "Well, I was just making my kid's breakfasts when I saw this man run past my kitchen window."

Inky - "And did you see where he came from?"

"No, but from the direction he was running he could only have been running from Bo's place, next door."

"Was he carrying any sheep?"

"No, but I did notice a lot of sheep shit on his wellingtons."

"Can you describe this man?"

"He looked about forty years old, with greying hair. I didn't see his face 'cos he was running too fast. He wasn't very tall."

"And did you see what he was wearing?"

"A grey dressing gown and wellingtons. The wellingtons splattered sheep shit all over my home's toe cap as he ran past."

Turning back to look into the camera, Inky concluded his report.

"Please be on the lookout for a forty-year-old man, about five foot six inch tall, wearing a grey dressing gown and shit covered wellingtons. If anyone can help police with this crime they should report to Rhyme Place police station as soon as possible. Back to you, in the studio, Chatty."

Chatty - "Thank you Inky." Chatty turns to look into the studio camera. "We'll return to this story as soon as we get any more news. In the meantime, I think little Jack Horner has been cleaned up by now, so we'll resume our Play Den programme to continue with the activities taking place there."

*

On arrival at Bo Peep's cottage the Sergeant was surrounded by the media, all eager to record what he had to say. He ushered the crowd off her garden and ordered the throng not to trespass.

"As soon as I've had the opportunity to interview Miss Peep I'll come back out to make a statement. In the meantime, please respect Miss Peep's privacy and keep off her garden."

With that, he entered Bo's cottage.

He looked into the lounge from the hallway and saw Bo Peep sat on her settee, crying. The kettle began to whistle for some attention. Bo Peep stood and turned to go to the kitchen and saw the Sergeant in the doorway.

"Sit yourself down, Miss Peep. I'll just go and answer that kettle."

Bo sat back down and the Sergeant went to the kitchen and made a pot of tea. With a tray of tea and biscuits he returned to the lounge where Bo Peep was still sobbing.

"I've made us a nice pot of tea Miss Peep, so dry your eyes while I pour us both a refreshing cup."

Bo looked up with red, tearful eyes and smiled. "Thank you, Sergeant."

After pouring out the tea, the Sergeant took out his notebook, licked the end of his pencil and waited while Bo took a sip of tea.

Have you ever wondered why policemen do that - lick the end of their pencil? It doesn't do anything. It doesn't make it any easier to write and it certainly doesn't make the graphite write more clearly. Like I said - It doesn't do anything…

Anyway, the Sergeant started his questioning.

"Tell me exactly how you found out that the sheep were missing."

"Well, like I said over the phone - I woke up this morning, got washed and dressed and came downstairs to make my breakfast."

"And what time would that be?"

"About eight a.m. Actually, it was three minutes past eight exactly when I got up because I looked at my bedside clock. I got down here at about eight forty-five."

"And then?"

"Well, I went to the kitchen, pulled up the window blind and saw they were gone. Not in their paddock."

"Is that where you always keep them?"

"Yes, unless I take them for a walk or when the weather is bad."

"When the weather is bad? What do you do with them at those times?"

"I bring them in here, in the lounge where it's nice and warm. Where else would I take them?"

"Err… *[a pause while the Sergeant looked round the room and thought of something to say]*, what happened next?"

"I ran outside and shouted for them to come back. I went to look for them, then came back here to phone you."

"Did you see anyone at that time?"

"I saw the old lady who lives in the shoe, next door… *[thinks]*, and I saw some bloke running at the top of the street."

"Which way?" asked the Sergeant, looking more interested.

"Towards Hot Cross, but he was too far away for me to recognise him."

"And that's it? Anything else?"

"Yes, I think so. I came back inside and phoned the station. Do you think the old lady next door told the TV people?"

"I don't know, but I'll be interviewing her in due course. Is there anything else I should know?"

"No, I don't think so."

The Sergeant tore off a sheet of paper from his notebook, handed it to Bo Peep with his pencil and instructed, "You write down a detailed description of the sheep while I finish this tea, then I'll be out of your way."

He then finished his tea and went to the kitchen to stare out of the window. The sheep's paddock was clearly visible. Returning to the lounge, Bo Peep handed him her notes and he quickly scanned the page;

Sheep - 4. One's only got 3 legs.
Colour - white, all of them
Eyes - 2 each sheep, brown
Hair - curly
Tails - always wagging, except when they shit
Other information - They shit a lot

The Sergeant folded the paper and carefully placed it inside his notebook.

"I'll make some enquiries on your behalf and let you know what's happening. When we catch whoever took the sheep he'll be in hot water, believe me."

"Thank you, Sergeant. I appreciate your time on this."

"No problem, Miss Peep. I'll just make a short statement to the press and then I'll be on my way."

The Sergeant exited the cottage, walked to the end of the garden path to the waiting media and had a microphone thrust under his chin.

"What can you tell us, Sergeant?" asked a dishevelled looking Inky Irwin.

"I'll just make a short statement and then I'll ask you all to leave."

A hush descended on the throng. When all was quiet, the Sergeant made his statement.

"Miss Bo Peep's four sheep appear to have been stolen. My enquiries are under way, and if anyone has any information regarding this theft I urge them to come to the station to make a statement."

With that, the Sergeant thanked the media for their time, reminded them where to send any information and began his walk back to the station.

The media stayed on site, eagerly waiting to pounce on anyone emerging from the nearby cottages.

CHAPTER 3

Mary, Mary quite contrary,
How does your garden grow?
With silver bells and cockle shells,
and pretty maids all in a row.
(England, c.1744)

contrary (kontrari) *adj.* **1.** opposed; completely different. **2.** in opposition or contrast (to): *contrary to popular belief.*

I bet you that whenever you see a picture of Mary and her sheep, you see a shy little lady, wearing a lovely bonnet and smiling a sweet innocent smile.

Appearances deceive!

The first line of the nursery rhyme gives you a clue to Mary's real character…

*

Week 1. Monday, p.m.

Sergeant Argent started his investigation by conducting a door-to-door enquiry.

The old lady who lives in the shoe, next door, wasn't at home so he decided to call in on Mary to see if she knew anything. Mary answered the door in a provocative, low-cut dress.

"Good morning, Mary. I'm making enquiries about Bo Peep's missing sheep."

"Hello, Sergeant Argent. D'you fancy a cup of tea? Or perhaps coffee?" suggestively inviting him inside.

"Err, no thanks. Perhaps another time. Have you heard about Bo Peep's missing sheep?"

"With all this commotion going on," pointing to the media, "I couldn't very well NOT hear about it. She screamed the place down this morning. Woke everyone up! Are you sure you don't want some tea and crumpet - *crumpets!* -Tea and crumpets."

The Sergeant thought it prudent not to go indoors at this precise time, especially as the reporters and TV cameras were all scrutinising his every move. It was clear that they were waiting for him to depart before pouncing on Mary's doorstep.

"I'm fine, thank you. You've got a great garden. Shall we stand out here while I ask you some questions?"

"Thank you, *you've* got a great body," said Mary, continuing to flirt.

"You must spend a lot of time keeping the garden looking this good," suggested the Sergeant.

"Yeah, it's not easy, and it's time consuming, but it's worth it. I've groped - *grown!* - grown some beautiful flowers," answered Mary.

"What about those dandelions?" enquired the Sergeant, pointing to some offending weeds.

"Missed them," replied Mary, walking down the path towards the dandelions.

She bent down to extract the dandelions from the flower bed, exposing her ample breasts down the top of her low-cut dress to the Sergeant.

Standing upright, she declared, "I've got some lovely buns - to go with some coffee," pointing towards the cottage door.

Argent was enticed by Mary's suggestion, but not enticed quite enough to drop his enquiries... Or anything else if it comes to that.

Looking embarrassed, the Sergeant continued, "Errm… what about Bo Peep's missing sheep."

"What about them?" Mary leaning provocatively against the fence.

"Well…, *[embarrassed cough from the Sergeant]* did you see anybody herding four sheep anywhere while you were out here?"

"Not really. I did see some old geezer in a dressing gown and wellies running past Bo's cottage just after she kicked off, but he didn't have any sheep… And I heard a truck driving away, but I couldn't see it anywhere.

"Where were you at the time?" asked Argent.

"Stood on my doorstep. I came out to see what all the screaming was about."

"So, do you recognise this chap?"

"No, not really. He looked familiar… And he was splattering sheep shit everywhere from his wellies, so I went back inside and shut the door, briefly. I didn't want any sheep shit all over my easily removable… Sorry, *stained* dress. I came back out when I knew he had passed by."

"Did you see where he went?"

Mary pointed towards Hot Cross. "That way, but I didn't take any real notice 'cos I had to clean all the sheep shit from my decorative cockle shells after he had run past my place. It took me an age, and some of my silver bells even took a hit."

"Do you think any of those young ladies would be able to recognise him?" asked the Sergeant, pointing to the pretty maids, all in a row.

"I don't know. You'd have to ask them."

"I will do that… What are they doing anyway?

"Queueing."

"Queueing? For what?"

"I don't know. They've come to buy some flowers… I think. They turned up just after lunchtime."

The Sergeant made a mental note that it was improbable that any of the pretty maids, all in a row, would have seen or heard anything useful to his enquiries, considering the time that they had arrived on site, but it might be useful to interview them - just in case.

"Do you want me to move them on?" suggested Argent.

"No, that's okay. They're not doing any harm. What time do you finish work?"

"Usually about six. Why?"

"Fancy a coffee?"

"… *[thinking]* Yes, okay. I'll pop round on my way back to the station after I've finished my enquiries."

"I'll put the kettle on."

Sergeant Argent had definitely succumbed to Mary's charms…

CHAPTER 4

Old King Cole was a merry old soul,
And a merry old soul was he.
He called for his pipe and he called for his bowl,
And he called for his fiddlers three.
(England, c.1708)

Week 1. Tuesday, a.m.

The following morning, a bleary-eyed Sergeant sat at his desk cogitating about last night's lack of sleep.

The telephone on his desk rang, waking him from his daydream.

"Rhyme Place police station," he answered.

"Sergeant Argent, this is King Cole. Can you please come up to Rhyme Place Castle when you have a spare moment? I'd like to discuss something of a private nature with you."

"Yes, sir. I'll come straight away."

"Thank you, Sergeant."

The call was terminated and the Sergeant picked up his hat, locked up the station and cycled his way to the castle. The castle guard, hovering outside the castle gates, held his hand up to bring the Sergeant's bicycle to a halt.

Clipboard and pen at the ready, the guard demanded, "Name?"

"You know who I am."

"Address?"

The Sergeant looked down at his uniform and, with some exasperation answered, "Rhyme Place police station. Why are you asking me these stupid questions?"

The guard looked a bit embarrassed and whispered, without moving his head or his lips, "I've got to ask these questions because the guard commander is watching from the guard house, and he'll have my guts for garters if I don't do the job properly. Address? *[loud enough for the guard Commander to hear]*"

"Rhyme Place police station *[loud enough for the guard Commander to hear]*."

"Purpose of your visit, sir?"

"The King has asked me to come and speak with him."

"When?"

The Sergeant then asked, with some puzzlement, "When did the King ask me to come and speak with him, or when does he want me to speak with him?"

"What time is your visit?" replied the guard, looking exasperated.

"Are you going to let me in or shall I let the King know that his guard prevented me from seeing him?" asked the Sergeant.

There was a slight pause while the guard thought about that threat.

"… Okay. You can pass, sir. For security purposes, please park you bike on the square, next to the parked cars."

The guard stood back to allow the Sergeant to enter the open gates with his bicycle.

The Sergeant stared at the guard with some incredulity. "What? I'm not hiding anything on my bike."

"All vehicles are to be parked on the square, sir," replied the guard, impassively.

The guard imperceptibly nodded his head back towards the guard room, eyes looking sideways, and whispered "Guard commander is watching…"

Huffing and muttering exasperated expletives, the Sergeant wheeled his bicycle to the square and leaned it up against a car. Looking back at the guard he pointed his thumb at the bike and waited for the guard to nod in approval. He then made his way to the castle.

On arrival, he was met by a butler who bid him, "Please follow me, sir. The King is expecting you but he is presently in the middle of band practice. I'll let him know you have arrived."

The Sergeant thanked the butler and followed him to the band room, where the King was sat smoking his pipe and munching on a bowl of plum pie while watching his violin trio practice their music.

Seeing the policeman enter the band room, the king stood and waved his hand at the musicians.

"Okay, that's enough for today. With a little more practice, the waltz should be ready for my banquet."

The musicians stood, collected up their music, bowed to the King and headed towards the door, smiling at the Sergeant on their way out.

The Sergeant approached the King and bowed. The King held out his hand in a welcoming gesture.

"Thank you for coming, Sergeant. I heard about Bo Peep's missing sheep. Have you got to the bottom of the incident, yet?"

"No, sir. My enquiries are ongoing at the moment, but it must be difficult to hide four sheep. I anticipate that the perpetrator has hidden them in plain sight, somewhere."

"Well, keep on top of it, Sergeant. I'm getting some noise from the village people suggesting that they are not happy about it. I want this person in jail as soon as possible."

"Yes sir. I entirely agree. I'm spending all my time on this case."

"I appreciate that, Sergeant. Do you need any help with anything?"

"Actually, sir, I could do with some men to carry out a detailed search for me. I can't cover the whole of Rhyme Place quickly enough for me to make an immediate arrest, and a few men would save a lot of time."

"No problem there. I'll have a word with the grand old Duke of York. I'm sure he can afford a few men to help with your enquiries."

"That's very kind of you, sir. I will, of course keep you updated on events as they happen."

"Excellent." The king turned to his butler. "Will you ask the Duke of York to contact Sergeant Argent as soon as possible, please?"

With a nod and a "Yes, sir," the butler bowed and exited from the band practice room.

The King continued. "Actually, I've called you here today on a matter not entirely dissimilar to that case."

"Oh? please, tell me more."

"Well, You know how my wife likes to bake tarts?"

"Yes sir, and fine tarts they are. The Queen is kind enough to have some delivered to the station whenever she makes a fresh batch. They're delicious."

"Thank you, Sergeant. I wish she would give you every one of them because I'm getting fed up with the bloody things. That's all she bakes… Anyway, I'll pass on your good words. She baked a fresh batch yesterday."

The Sergeant nodded and smiled in anticipation of receiving some more tarts. Much tastier than the sausage rolls that his desk constable gets from the baker's man.

The King continued. "When she went to the kitchen this morning they were gone. All of them. Nobody knows where…"

The King stared at the Sergeant to wait for his next words.

The Sergeant took out his note book and pencil, licked the end of the pencil and began his new enquiry.

"Do you have any idea who would do such a thing?" enquired the Sergeant.

"No, I'm afraid not."

"Well, has anybody been seen lurking around the kitchen?"

"Not to my knowledge, but I'll ask around and let you know."

"Thank you, sir. Now, has anything else been taken?"

"Again, I've not heard of anything else that has gone missing. The Queen might be able to shed some more light on the matter, and I'm sure you will get to the bottom of it. Now, I'm extremely busy trying to arrange my banquet. Do you have any more questions?"

"One last question, if I may, sir. Is it possible for me to interview the Queen some time?"

"Of course. I'm sure she will welcome a visit from you. I'll have a word today and let you know when it will be convenient for you to come here, once more."

"Thank you, sir, and I'll find who did this and let you know."

"Good man."

With that, the King excused himself and left the Sergeant to vacate the band room on his own.

On his way through the castle corridors he met the butler.

"Sergeant Argent," greeted the butler as they met, "I've spoken to the grand old Duke of York and he will contact you as soon as he can. He's busy, at the moment, with a suspected intruder."

"Oh? Where is the Duke, now?"

"I understand he's outside the castle wall, waiting for an ambulance."

The Sergeant didn't ask about the ambulance. He was confident that he would find out, soon enough.

"I'll try to catch the Duke on my way out. Now, what do you know about the Queen's tarts?"

"They're delicious. You should try some," answered the butler.

"Yes, I know. I was referring to the *missing* tarts."

"Oh, yes. Those. I can't tell you a lot, to be honest. I heard the Queen shout out from the pantry and went there to see what was wrong. She demanded to know who had taken them, but I didn't know, so I couldn't tell her."

"Did you see anyone else?"

"A few of the staff. They were hurrying to the pantry when I met them in the corridor."

Tearing a sheet from his note book, the Sergeant passed it to the butler with his pencil and asked, "Please write down the names of all those you saw."

The butler busily scribbled some names on the paper and handed it back. The Sergeant scanned the page:
The milk maid
Cook
Barry, the understudy butler
The Knave of Hearts
Tania, the King's secretary
Gerry, the horse & coach driver

The Sergeant carefully folded the paper in half, placed it in his notebook, extracted the pencil from the butler (who tried to pocket it) and dismissed the butler, saying, "Now, you will contact me if you hear anything, won't you?"

“Yes, of course, sir,” answered the butler with a bow.

On the way to the castle gates, Argent collected his bicycle — it had been moved and propped up against a different car. Approaching the open gates he was, once more, brought to a halt by the guard.

“Name…?”

CHAPTER 5

Humpty Dumpty sat on a wall.
Humpty Dumpty had a great fall.
All the King's horses and all the King's men,
Couldn't put Humpty together again.
(England, 1803)

Week 1. Tuesday, p.m.

As he exited the castle gates, the Sergeant almost collided with an ambulance.

Remembering the butler's comment about a suspected intruder, the Sergeant followed the ambulance around the outside of the castle wall until he came across a cordon of soldiers, facing outwards, surrounding a group huddled over someone laying on the ground.

The ambulance was allowed entry to the huddle of soldiers without question, but one of the men in the cordon held up his hand to halt Argent.

"Name?"

"I'm here on the King's business," answered the Sergeant.

"Name?"

With a look of exasperation the Sergeant demanded, "Where's the Duke? Fetch him here. He knows me."

"Wait here, please, sir," ordered the soldier.

The soldier did a slick about turn and dashed off to find the grand old Duke of York. A few minutes later the Duke arrived, riding his proud stallion. He dismounted and motioned to one of the men in the cordon to let the Sergeant in. "Sergeant Argent," welcomed the Duke. "It's good to see you again. We had a good time at the

King's fancy dress ball, last month - and you outdid yourself, coming dressed as a policeman. Imaginative, or what?"

"I came straight from work," replied the Sergeant, satirically.

"Oh... sorry, old boy. I thought you'd hired a costume." The Duke bellowed out a haughty laugh.

There was a slight pause while the Sergeant stared at the ground and sighed a deep sigh.

Deciding to get to the point, he asked the Duke, "What's going on here?"

"Ah...," replied the Duke, "this individual was caught trying to climb over the castle wall. My guardsman surprised him and he fell off the top."

"Has he been questioned yet?"

"Not yet, Sergeant. He only woke up a few minutes ago."

"So what's with the ambulance?"

"Yes - that. Well, the idiot appears to have broken his leg when he landed. With a bit of training he could have landed properly and rolled, but being a civvy, he's got no idea about jumping off walls. I get my men to do it all the time, especially during PT. You never know when you're going to need that kind of training."

The Sergeant ignored the Duke's self-righteous smugness and watched the injured person being stretchered into the ambulance. "I see," he said. "Has anyone seen to his wound?"

"Not really," answered the Duke. "We've tried to patch the blighter up, and we've put a temporary splint on his leg, but that's all we can do for him, and that's more than he deserves."

The Sergeant walked to the back of the ambulance. The alleged intruder had, by now, been placed in the vehicle and was being tended to by a paramedic.

The policeman entered the ambulance and asked the paramedic, "Is it okay if I ask him some questions?"

"Yeah," answered the paramedic, "he's got a broken leg and a few bruises, but he's conscious."

The chap on the stretcher was portly, about eighteen stones in weight, about twenty five years old and groaning while the paramedic replaced the temporary splint installed by the soldiers.

Bending over him, the Sergeant asked, "What's your name, son?"

"Call me Humpty Dumpty. Everybody else does," answered the patient grumpily.

"Oh? That's an unusual name."

"It's my nickname. I was given it when I was at school 'cos I'm fat."

"What were you doing climbing on the castle wall, Humpty?"

"Nothing."

"Nothing? Nobody climbs the castle wall for nothing. What were you up to?"

"Nothing, honestly. I wasn't trying to get into the castle."

"Well, what were you doing?"

"I was hungry."

"So?" the Sergeant was puzzled by this reply.

"See that apple tree sticking its branch over the top of the wall?"

The Sergeant turned to look behind him. "Yes," he answered.

"I was just going to pick those apples hanging on this side of the wall, but I couldn't reach them without climbing the wall. I wasn't doing any harm. I just fancied a couple of those apples."

The Sergeant turned and exited the ambulance. The Duke was, by now, mustering his men into some semblance of order.

"Dress back number four," the Duke ordered. "You there! Number six!" pointing to the offender with his riding crop. "Shoulders back… And straighten your arms. Look up! Stop slouching!"

Seeing the Sergeant approach, he straightened his own back and waited for Argent to come within a yard, or so, of him.

"How is the blighter?" he asked.

"Oh, he'll be alright after his leg has been seen to. He's got a few bruises, but nothing serious, sir."

"Put him in jail!" ordered the Duke.

"I'll think about it," answered the Sergeant, knowing full well that he won't. "Can I ask a favour of you, sir?"

"Of course. Anything"

"See those apples hanging over the castle wall? Can you get one of your men to pick them for me?"

"No can do, I'm afraid. They belong to the King."

"Actually, sir, they don't. They may be hanging from the King's tree, but they're hanging *over* the wall into a public space. Providing no damage is done to the wall or the tree, the public are at liberty to pick the apples. Anyway, I'm sure the King can manage without half a dozen apples. I don't think he would mind, too much. Do you?"

"Well, you know the law, sir, but I'm still not sure."

"How about I let the King know how helpful you've been, next time I see him. I'm due to meet the

Queen soon and I could put in a good word for you at the same time," knowing full well that he won't.

The Duke thought about it for a second, then turned to his Captain. "Get a couple of the men to pick those apples hanging over the wall... And only those that are on this side of the wall."

The Captain answered "Yes sir," saluted smartly and turned to organise the apple picking.

The Sergeant continued, "Thank you, sir. While we wait for the apples I need to speak to you about Miss Bo Peep's sheep."

"Yes," answered the Duke. "The King's butler has already mentioned that you need a search party. I have just the men to help you with that."

"Excellent," smiled Argent. "Is tomorrow afternoon convenient for you?"

"Absolutely. Where do you want me to muster the men?"

"I think that if we start at Bo Peep's sheep paddock, we could spread out from there."

"A good plan. We'll be waiting for you after lunch."

"Thank you, sir."

The bag of apples arrived and were thrust into the Sergeant's outstretched hand. He thanked the Captain.

The Duke mounted his steed, saluted the Sergeant, bid him goodbye and turned the horse towards his Captain. The horse let out a noisy fart about eight inches from Argent's face...

"Carry on!" ordered the Duke to his Captain.

The Captain turned to the soldiers, all stood as straight as oversized rulers and as rigid as steel columns. The Captain ordered, "The Battalion will turn to the right in threes. Riiiight TURN!"

The soldiers smartly performed a right turn and waited for the next command.

"By the left, QUICK MARCH!"

As the soldiers marched off towards their barracks, the Sergeant returned to the ambulance.

The paramedic informed him, "We're ready to take Mr. Dumpty to hospital now, Sergeant. Is there anything else?"

Before he let the ambulance go, the Sergeant took the opportunity to interview Humpty Dumpty.

"Can I ask you a couple of questions before you get taken to hospital, sir?"

Humpty, now infinitely more comfortable than he was half an hour ago, replied in the affirmative.

The Sergeant asked, "Have you heard about Miss Bo Peep's missing sheep?"

"Oh, that. Yes. I heard about that on Monday's news, after I'd got back home."

"From where?"

"The castle wall."

"You went to the castle on Monday?"

"Yes. I thought it was a good time to come here to see if there was an opportunity to get some apples."

"About what time would that be?"

"I left home early, about eight-thirty in the morning."

"Did you see or hear anything?" the Sergeant repeated.

"Sort of. While I was on my way to the castle wall I heard a scream… *[thinks]* and I heard a truck burning rubber somewhere. He must have been travelling fast."

"Then what?"

“When I arrived, there was too much activity around the place so I decided to wait until today to get those apples. I went back home.”

“Okay, you’ve been a great help, sir. I’ll let you get to the hospital, now. Something else, before you go…”

The Sergeant placed the bag of apples on Humpty’s stomach and advised, “Next time you go scrumping apples, ask before you start climbing the castle wall.”

CHAPTER 6

The Queen of Hearts, she made some tarts,
all on a summer's day.
The Knave of Hearts, he stole those tarts,
and took then clean away.
(English, c.1782)

Week 1. Tuesday, p.m.

On his way past the castle gates he was, once more, stopped - this time by a different guard.

"Sergeant Argent?"

"Yes. How can I help you?"

"The butler sent a message to the guard room to ask you to go back to the castle."

"Oh? Do you know why?"

"No, sir. I'm just the guard. We don't get told very much except what to do, and when to do it."

"Okay. I'll go there now."

"Please park your vehicle on the square, sir."

"Okay, I know."

After leaning his bike against a car, the Sergeant made his way back up to the castle. The butler was waiting for him.

"The queen is ready to see you now, Sergeant. Please follow me."

The butler accompanied the Sergeant to the queen's quarters. Lightly tapping on the door, he waited for the queen to respond.

"Enter!" ordered the Queen.

Opening the door for the Sergeant, the butler announced him and discretely closed the door behind the Sergeant.

The Queen held out a welcoming hand. “Hello, Sergeant Argent. You looked resplendent in your fancy dress at the King’s fancy dress party. How are you today?”

“I’m fine, thank you ma’am. I hope you are in good health,” choosing not to respond to the Queen’s compliment.

“Yes, generally. My joints ache and my eyesight is getting worse, but we have to battle on, do we not?”

“That we do, ma’am. Is it convenient for me to interview you about the missing tarts?”

“Yes, of course. I do hope you will let me know who did this so that I can chop off his head.”

After a second for that thought to register in the Sergeant’s brain, he replied, “I’ll certainly bear that in mind, ma’am. Have you heard anything from downstairs, at all?”

“Nothing, I’m afraid. Everyone seems to be avoiding me.”

‘I don’t blame them,’ thought the Sergeant. *‘I bet she spits fire when she’s angry…’*

He continued to question the Queen.

“In your own words, can you tell me what happened?” he asked.

“Well,” responded the Queen, “Yesterday afternoon I baked a fresh batch of tarts. When I came downstairs to give Cook my orders for the day, this morning, the tray of tarts were gone.”

The Queen raised a hanky to a crocodile tear and continued, “I’m so sorry to have let you down, Sergeant. I would have had some delivered to the station this morning, but you'll appreciate why I didn't, I'm sure." Another dab of that crocodile tear.

"Of course, ma'am. Please don't fret. I'm sure the King would miss them more than I," inwardly smiling as he remembered the King's thoughts on the Queen's tarts.

"I'll look into this for you and let you know the outcome of my enquiries," continued the Sergeant.

"Thank you, Sergeant. You're so kind. I'll get straight down to the kitchen and bake a fresh batch for you... And the King," suddenly remembering who she was!

"Thank you very much, ma'am. I can say, in all honesty, that the men down at the station all appreciate your kindness and generosity. We all think your tarts are delicious."

It never does any harm to compliment royalty, does it?

The Queen was suitably pleased.

"You know what?" she asked, "I'm going to bake a bigger batch than usual to give you and the King more to enjoy."

'I bet the King will be pleased with that...' Thought the Sergeant. "Thank you ma'am, We will all look forward to that. I'm sure the King will," he said a bow.

The Sergeant excused himself and bowed out of the room, leaving the Queen to prepare a list of ingredients for her mammoth batch of tarts.

On the way out of the castle gates, with his bike, he was again stopped by the guard.

"Name?"

CHAPTER 7

Week 1. Wednesday, a.m.

The Sergeant was in the police station, taking stock of the crimes that he had been tasked with prioritising and solving.

His first priority was the stolen tarts. He hadn't 'shelved' the missing sheep, but impressing the King was far more prestigious than impressing Bo Peep - although Bo Peep's sheep were, to him, no less important. Seeing as he has to go back to the castle to investigate the tarts more thoroughly he could, he thought, kill two birds with one stone by making sheep enquiries at the same time as the tarts enquiries.

So, what information had he collected about the tarts? He looked at his notes:

Missing Tarts:
(Tuesday, a.m.)

- The tarts went missing overnight on Monday/Tuesday. Nobody heard anything.
- Nothing else is missing, but that doesn't mean to say that something else was not stolen.
- The butler has provided a list of names* of those who dashed to the pantry when the queen shouted (Tuesday morning).
- Inside job? It must be. Security is tight around the castle, and gaining access would be difficult. Difficult, but not impossible.
- ***Witnesses** - The milk maid, Cook, Barry - the understudy butler, The Knave of Hearts, Tania - the King's secretary, Gerry - the horse & coach driver.

'*Not much to go on,*' he thought, but at least he has a list of names from the butler that he could start to interview.

Now, on to the missing sheep, and another delve into his notebook.

A map of Rhyme Place was permanently pinned to his office wall and he studied this while reading his notes:

Missing Sheep:

(Monday, a.m.)

- Bo Peep noticed the sheep were missing on Monday morning at approx. 8.45a.m. They must have been removed either overnight or early on Monday morning. Nobody saw anything. Nobody heard anything.
- Bo Peep did a quick local search Monday.
- I've got a written description of the sheep from Bo Peep.
- Chummy seen wearing a dressing gown and wellies. (Monday)
- Witness heard truck driving away. (Monday)
- There has been a TV news flash about this incident. (Tuesday) (I need to get a copy of that, 'cos I missed it)
- Possible witness - The old lady who lives in the shoe next door. (Needs interviewing)
- Possible witness - Some bloke running at the top of the street - toward Hot Cross. Not recognised by Bo Peep. (Who is this man?)

The Sergeant turned to the next page of his notebook, again scrutinising the map:

Sheep:

- Witness - [Contrary] Mary. Lives next door to the old lady who lives in the shoe.
- Didn't see anybody herding the sheep away from the paddock.
- Saw 'an old geezer' running past the old lady's shoe cottage, towards Hot Cross.
- 'Geezer' wearing a dressing gown and wellies. 'Looked familiar'
- Mary heard a truck being driven away. Didn't see it.
- Possible witnesses - The pretty maids, all in a row in Mary's garden. (Need to interview them if they are still there).

On the next page of his notebook he scrutinised the statement from Humpty Dumpty:

- Went to the castle wall to pick some apples on Monday, a.m.
- Heard scream & truck.
- Time - 8.30 - 9.00 a.m.
- Too much activity, so went back home. Decided to try for some apples the next day (Tues)

'Mmm,' thought the Sergeant, *'The tarts - I'm pretty sure this is an inside job. I'll find out when I go back to interview the staff. Sheep? - We've got chummy wearing a dressing gown and wellies and we've got a truck driving away. Who is chummy, and who is the truck driver? Did chummy steal the sheep? Where was the truck going, and what was it carrying?'*

There were so many questions, at this stage, but the Sergeant was confident that he could get to the bottom of both crimes. He already had ideas about one of them.

*

Week 1. Wednesday, late a.m.

Simon entered the police station just as the Sergeant was sharpening his pencil.

Approaching the counter, he declared, "I've come to report a crime?"

The Sergeant opened his notebook, licked the now sharp point of his pencil and answered, "A crime, you say. What crime would that be?"

"Someone tried to run me over on Monday."

"Oh? Shall we go into the back so that I can take a few details?"

The Sergeant lifted the counter leaf and ushered Simon into the interview room.

Once settled he started by asking, "Firstly, tell me your name."

"Simon. Simple Simon. Everyone calls me 'Simple Simon' 'cos I'm not very good at maths."

Making notes, the Sergeant continued, "We'll call you Simon, shall we?"

Simon nodded.

"You say this incident happened on Monday? It's Wednesday, today. Why are you only just reporting this now?"

"I wasn't going to, but this morning Mum saw these scratches on my arms and legs that I got from the blackberry bush that I dived into. She asked where I got them, and then she told me to come here to report what happened."

"Okay, in your own words, Simon, tell me what happened."

"Well, I was on my way to the fair. I met this bloke carrying a tray of pies and I offered to help him."

"And where did this happen?"

"Down by Hot Cross. You know, the crossroads where that bun factory is."

"Yes. About what time would that be?"

"About eight-fifty a.m."

"Do you know the pie man's name?"

"No, sorry, but he was a miserable old…"

The Sergeant interrupted Simon before he could go any further. "Okay, what happened next?"

"Well, we had just passed the cross at the crossroads, when this truck came round the corner and nearly ran me and the pie man down. We had to dive out of its way. The pie man crashed into the wall and demolished part of it and I finished up in the blackberry bush."

"Did you get the truck's number?"

"No. It was going too fast and I didn't get chance to see much of it before it disappeared."

"Did you see what colour it was?"

"The front of it seemed to be a dirty green. I didn't see any more of it 'cos I was too busy trying to get out of the bush. I tore my shirt, and Mum wasn't too pleased about that. She says that I should try and get a new one from the truck driver."

"I'll see what can be done. What about the pies? What happened to them?"

"Me and the pie man picked them up and dusted the dirt off them and stacked them back on the tray. The pie man said that nobody would be the wiser about the dirt. He gave me one for helping him."

"Would you be able to recognise this truck again, if you saw it?"

"I don't know. I only saw the front of it... *[thinking]*... But there was a teddy bear strapped to the grill, like you see on dustbin lorries."

"That's a useful bit of information. Now, did the pie man say where he was coming from?"

"No, but I assume he was coming from the bakery - Pies and all that..."

"I'll look into that. Okay, you've been a great help, Simon. Tell your mum that I'll look into this and let her know that I'll contact her when I've finished my enquiries," knowing that he probably won't.

"Yes, sir. Is that it? Can I go now?"

"Yes. I'll see you out."

The Sergeant accompanied Simon to the station door and then returned to his desk.

'Mmm,' he thought. *'Is this the same truck that Mary, the old woman and Humpty heard? I wonder...'*

His thoughts were interrupted by the telephone shouting out an 'answer me' chime.

"Rhyme Place police station," he said, into the handset. "Sergeant Argent."

"Sergeant, can you please come to my place as quickly as you can?" came back a troubled voice.

"Who's calling?" asked Argent.

"This is Mrs. Dumpling, John's mother. I need someone to come look at John as soon as possible."

"Oh? And why is that?"

"I can't get him to wake up!"

"Okay, Mrs. Dumpling. Call an ambulance. I'll leave the station right away.

CHAPTER 8

Diddle, diddle, dumpling, my son John,
Went to bed with his trousers on!
One shoe off, and one shoe on,
Diddle, diddle, dumpling, my son John!
(London, England, c.1797)

Week 1. Wednesday, mid-morning.

The Sergeant turned to the desk constable, PC Griller, to let him know where he was going. He instructed PC Griller to get PC Slack to find the pie man and ask him to come to the station, to help with enquiries regarding the sheep and the careless truck driver.

With a freshly sharpened pencil and his notebook in his pocket, he picked up his hat and departed for Mrs. Dumpling's cottage. After mounting his bike, he peddled as fast as his legs would go to get to Mrs. Dumpling's cottage at the top of Rhyme Place Avenue.

On arrival, he found the dumpling's front door open. He tapped lightly, announced himself and called out for Mrs. Dumpling.

"Come in, Sergeant," she answered. "I'm upstairs in John's bedroom."

The Sergeant went up the stairs and entered the bedroom. Mrs. Dumpling was sat at John's bedside, holding his hand.

"Have you called for an ambulance?" he asked.

"No, not yet. I wanted you to look at him first."

It never ceased to amaze the Sergeant the way people always thought he was the font of all knowledge. Sometimes he was asked for advice that only a doctor, or a fireman, or an electrician, or a chef, or an engineer, or a midwife can give.

However, he went to John's bedside and, on peeling back a few covers, noticed that he was still wearing his trousers. With a look of puzzlement, he peeled back some more of the sheet to find that he still had a shoe and sock on his left foot.

"What…? He's still half dressed…" he said, and turned to Mrs. Dumpling for a response.

"I know," she said. "I found him like that when I came to wake him up for work."

The Sergeant stroked his chin for some inspiration and then leaned in to get a closer look at John's face. Holding an eyelid open to look into one of John's eyes, he leaned in closer and was suddenly blasted with a serious wave of halitosis when John breathed out.

The Sergeant straightened up, turned to Mrs. D and declared, "He's drunk!"

"What?" asked a stunned Mrs. D.

"He's drunk. He's in a drunken stupor," answered the Sergeant, astounded that Mrs. D had not noticed. "Did you know this before you telephoned the station?" he asked, with a hint of anger.

"No," answered Mrs. D. "Where did he get the money to get drunk?" Anger now in *her* voice.

"I don't know. What time did he come home last night?" the Sergeant asked.

"Err, it was after I went to bed. I never heard him come in."

With a hint of an exasperated sigh, the Sergeant calmed down and calmly offered his words of wisdom. "Let him sleep it off. He'll come round in a couple of hours."

With that, he left an embarrassed Mrs. D to her thoughts.

Mrs. D didn't wait for John to wake up. As soon as the Sergeant had left the cottage she fetched a bucket of water and tipped it over John's head.

John was in so much trouble…

CHAPTER 9

Week 1. Wednesday, p.m.

They say that the grand old Duke of York has got ten thousand men. Ten thousand men? That's a bit of an exaggeration. Actually, the Duke had a garrison of thirty men. A respectable number, given the size of the village.

As agreed with Sergeant Argent, he mustered his troops at the rear of Bo Peep's cottage, next to the paddock. He stood the men at ease and waited for the Sergeant to appear, pedalling his Raleigh 'tank' of a bicycle with its three-speed Sturmey Archer gears. In my day those bikes were heavy machines that required calf muscles the size of tree trunks to pedal them forwards. Hard work! My sister had one, and she grew up with legs like a grand piano…

Anyway, the Duke brought the men to attention when the Sergeant dismounted his bike, leaned it up against the castle wall and walked towards the troops.

"Good afternoon, Sergeant," greeted the Duke.

"Good afternoon, sir. Thanks for helping out with my search for Bo Peep's sheep."

"No problem, old boy. The men needed some search and rescue training in any event. An ideal opportunity."

"Okay, shall we get down to it?" asked the Sergeant, anxious to show the duke who was in charge.

"How do you want to play this?" enquired the Duke.

"I need three men to go over the hill to see if the sheep are on the other side. The remainder of the men can spread out around the village and search the area down to Old Macdonald's farm."

The Duke smartly turned and addressed his men.

"Listen in… You there. Stop fidgeting and get your shoulders back! Hold your head up. You look like you're not enjoying yourself. Are you enjoying yourself?" demanded the Duke to one of the men.

"Yes sir," came back the required lie.

"Well, look like it!" ordered the Duke. "I won't tolerate sloppy…"

The Sergeant interrupted the Duke. "Sir? Can we get on? I need the search finished before it gets dark."

"Oh. Yes. Sorry…"

The Sergeant scribbled a description of the sheep in his notebook, tore out the page and handed it to the Duke.

The Duke turned back to face the men.

"Now, can you all hear me at the back? Good." He didn't wait for any reply. "We're here today to conduct a search and rescue for Miss Bo Peep's missing sheep."

The Duke silently read the description that the Sergeant had provided and continued, "There are four of them, and one has only got three legs. They will be wagging their tails behind them. The Sergeant wants us to conduct a fingertip search of the area to find any evidence that will help him to find the sheep and apprehend the blighter that stole them. Any questions?"

One of the soldiers thrusts his hand up to attract attention. "What colour are they, sir?"

"A good question. Well done, that man," answered the Duke. "They're white. All of them. Any more questions?"

Another soldier raised his hand. "Are there any other distinguishable features, sir?"

"Yes, They've got brown eyes and curly hair. Any more questions? Good." Again, he didn't wait for an answer.

"I want three volunteers to march up that hill smartly and see if there is any sign of the sheep on the other side."

He didn't wait for a show of hands.

"You, you and you. Step forward."

Three men extricated themselves from the body of soldiers and sprang to attention in front of the Duke.

"Now - you three. March… and I mean MARCH - up that hill to see what's on the other side. I'll be watching you and if I see any one of you slacking you'll be on extra duties forever. Got That?"

"Yes sir." snapped back all three men.

"Okay. Report back to me when you have returned from the hill. Fall out and carry on."

The three men saluted smartly, did a slick about turn and marched in step towards the hill.

The Duke then addressed the remainder of his men. "Listen in to the Sergeant for instructions."

The Sergeant stepped forward and faced the search party. "You must be observant," he advised. "The sheep have not been seen since Sunday night. They were missing when Miss Bo Peep came downstairs on Monday. So please look everywhere from here to old Macdonald's farm. Bins, outhouses, gardens, sheds. Anywhere four sheep can be hidden. And keep your ears open. Sheep tend to make some noise when they get lonely, so you might hear them somewhere. Do not… I repeat, DO NOT enter old Macdonald's farm without permission. He's a crusty old sod at the best of times, and I don't want any international incident to diffuse as a result of size twelve boots trampling over his cabbages. Any questions?"

There were none, so the Duke split the men into groups of three and sent them in all directions to search for the sheep.

"If the sheep are out there," the Duke declared, "my men will find them."

"I hope so," answered the Sergeant. "It would be devastating for Miss Peep if anything has happened to them.

*

The three "volunteer" soldiers smartly marched their way to the path leading to the top of the hill and started their ascent.

The hill is steep, and after a while the men ceased marching.

"D'you think the old fart is watching us?" asked one.

"Don't know." answered his mate. "Let's just keep going and hope he isn't… Don't look back, you prat!" he chastised the third soldier. "If he sees you looking back he's bound to call us back to bark at us for not marching."

On the men trudged. The hill got steeper the further they climbed.

"Phew! This is bloody hard work," complained one of them.

"Yeah. Just keep going," urged the leader.

Three quarters of the way to the top the three men decided enough was enough, and they stopped for a rest. They sat, just for a couple of minutes, with the intention of getting their breaths back.

Almost immediately their bums touched the ground they heard the Duke bellow, "You men - on the hill! Who said you could stop? Get off your arses and get to the top of that hill!"

“Yep, he’s watching,” declared the leader as he wearily levered himself off the ground.

The three soldiers continued their steep climb until they eventually reached the plateau.

Walking to the far edge of the plateau they looked down, into the meadow below. They didn’t see any sheep, but they did see two bodies laying prone at the foot of the hill.

The leader ordered one of the men to return to the Duke to report what they had seen while he and the other soldier went down to the lifeless bodies.

Who were the two people laying prone at the bottom of the steep slope?

To answer that we must go back to Monday morning, but before we do that we ought to look in on the Sergeant and the search party.

CHAPTER 10

Mary had a little lamb, its fleece was white as snow,
And everywhere that Mary went,
the lamb was sure to go.
He followed her to school one day,
that was against the rule.
It made the children laugh and play,
to see a lamb at school.
(American origin, 1830)

Week 1. Wednesday, p.m.

Having been sent out to find the pie man, PC Slack was unsuccessful with his search around the village.

He radioed the Sergeant.

"Sarg, PC Slack calling."

"Hello, Slack. Any news on the pie man, yet."

"No, Sarg. I've searched the village, but nobody has seen him. I went to the bakery and made enquiries with the bakery manager. Apparently, he left to go to the fair with another consignment of pies so I'm heading down there now. There's a possibility that I might meet him returning to the bakery."

"Okay, well done. If you don't see him on the way, search the fairground."

"Will do, Sarg. PC Slack out."

The radio call was terminated.

*

The leader of the hilltop search party, with his mate, started to pick their way down to the two bodies laying prone at the bottom of the hill. The third soldier started his journey back the way they had come.

The bulk of the Duke's search party had been split up into threes and were sent in all directions to search for Bo Peep's sheep. The Sergeant had brought PC Griller with him and integrated the constable with one of the Duke's three-man platoons.

*

On his way back to the station, the Sergeant encountered a distraught Mary Lamb (not to be confused with contrary Mary), who seemed to be searching in the shrubs bordering the village cottages.

He approached her. "Hello, Mary. Have you lost something?"

Almost in tears, she answered, "Yes, my little lamb."

"Oh, dear. When did you last see her?"

"On Monday morning… And it's a him."

"Oh, okay. So, where were you when *he* went missing?"

Mary sat down on the grass verge and the Sergeant sat next to her. With tears welling up, she told him how the lamb came to be missing.

"My lamb follows me everywhere. It must think I'm his mummy. It's always there, even when I go to the toilet. Anyway, I went to school really early on Monday morning to meet my friends…"

The Sergeant interrupted Mary's flow. "How come you went to school? I thought Friday was the last day of term. Aren't you supposed to be on holiday?"

"Yes, we are," answered Mary, "but my teacher still goes there even when we are on holiday, and we help her to get the class ready for the new term. I get the books that she wants from the library and take back those that we have already used."

"I see. Okay, what happened next?"

"Well, my lamb followed me, as he does, but I didn't know that. I thought my mum had stopped him going out of the cottage. So when I got there I went inside to help teacher and the lamb followed me into the classroom. Teacher wasn't pleased and she made me take him outside, so I took him to the school yard and told him to wait there and play with one of my friends, then I went back inside to finish helping teacher."

"And... ?"

"When I came back outside he was nowhere to be seen."

With tears in her eyes she continued, "I've looked everywhere, Sergeant, but I can't find him. I spent all day yesterday and today looking for him. He must be so lonely by now. I miss him lots."

The Sergeant tried to calm Mary by giving her a hug and a few words of encouragement.

"Tell you what... I'll help you look for him. We can both search for him while I look for Bo Peep's sheep. They've gone missing, as well, and they must also be feeling lonely. Do you want to help me?"

Mary perked up at the thought of having someone 'official' helping her find the lamb and she gave the Sergeant a crushing squeeze around his neck. With a nod and a "Yes" from Mary, they both set off in search of Bo Peep's sheep and Mary's lamb.

As they searched the gardens, the Sergeant made some enquiries with Mary.

"So who did you leave the lamb with, in the school yard?"

"Little Tommy Tucker. He said he would look after my lamb but he wasn't there, either, when I'd finished helping teacher."

The Sergeant made a mental note to interview Tommy Tucker.

"I'm sure your lamb is okay, Mary. You'll probably find him waiting for you at home when you get there."

"I hope so," answered a pensive Mary.

Just as they reached Mary's cottage, PC Griller's voice shouted from the Sergeant's radio.

"Sergeant Argent. Come in Sergeant Argent."

"Argent," confirmed the Sergeant.

"Serg, this is Griller. Come quick. We've found something!" shouted Griller into his radio.

"Stand by, Griller." instructed the Sergeant. "I'll just deal with something first."

"Will do," came back the answer.

The Sergeant turned to Mary.

"Mary, your mum must be getting a bit worried about you by now, so how about I keep looking for your lamb and you go inside for your tea. I promise I'll bring him back to you when I've found him. Is that okay?"

The Sergeant got another choking hug around his neck and a sloppy kiss on his cheek from Mary. "Yes. Thank you, Sergeant."

Mary skipped indoors, shouting for her mum as soon as she opened the cottage door.

The Sergeant returned to Griller's radio call.

"Okay Griller. What have you found?"

"You'd better get here fast, Sarg. They've found two bodies on the other side of the hill!"

CHAPTER 11

Oh, the grand old Duke of York,
He had ten thousand men.
He marched them up to the top of the hill,
And he marched them down again.
(Origin unknown - First noted c.1892)

Week 1. Late Wednesday, p.m.

The soldier sent by the leader of the hill party to report back to the Duke arrived while the Sergeant was searching for Mary's lamb.

Snapping to attention breathlessly, and with a slick salute, the soldier faced the Duke.

"Did you see the sheep over the other side of the hill?" asked the Duke.

"No sir. We found something else, though."

"What?"

"We found two people. It looks as though they've fallen down the hill. They weren't moving. Corporal Green and Private Greener went down the hill to take a look."

"Oh? Are the two people alive?"

"Don't know, sir. Corporal Green instructed me to report back to you before he went down the hill."

"Okay. Well done, soldier. I'll take it from here. Fall in with that search party," pointing to a group of soldiers searching behind some bins.

The Duke turned to his Captain.

"Muster the men, Captain. It looks like we are needed on the other side of the hill."

With a snappy "Yes sir," the Captain blew his whistle several times to attract everyone's attention. In true military fashion, he put the tips of his fingers on the top of his head to indicate that everyone should muster in front of him.

When the Captain was satisfied that all the soldiers had returned, he formed them into a large platoon and began to march them up to the top of the hill. The Duke took the lead riding his trusty steed.

That's when PC Griller got on his radio to the Sergeant to let him know what Corporal Green had found.

*

The Sergeant cycled down the road from Mary's cottage and looked up at the hill to see the Duke and his men marching towards the top. He assumed that PC griller was also in the throng of marching men.

There was no way in which the Sergeant had any inclination to climb up the hill. Instead, he decided to cycle along the road around the bottom of the hill and meet up with Corporal Green and PC Greener on the other side.

He set off as fast as his legs could pedal.

*

The troops laboured up the steep slope. One or two of them started to grumble at the pace that the Duke had set.

"Look at him," whispered one. "It's okay for him - he's sat on his horse and taking it easy. The bloody horse's doing all the work - and it keeps farting in our direction."

"Yeah," replied his neighbour. "Just keep going. When we're up, we're up."

“But we’re only half way up, so we’re neither up nor down.”

“I know. Won’t be long before we reach the top. Then we can relax as we march to the bottom of the hill, down the other side.”

“QUIET IN THE RANKS!” ordered the Duke. “You there! Keep up the pace. I will not tolerate slackers. Anybody would think this is hard work.”

“Somebody shoot the prat…” muttered one of the soldiers. “… and that bloody horse!” muttered his mate.

“Quiet in the ranks!” ordered the Captain.

At the top of the hill there is a small plateau. When the troops reach that, they were afforded three minutes to get their breaths back and let the tail-enders catch up. The Duke took the opportunity to look down at the two bodies, with Corporal Green and Private Greener fussing over them. Returning to the platoon, the men of which were still breathing heavily, the Duke regrouped his force.

“Stand up straight. Heads up! You…!” pointing his riding crop at a tail-ender that had just arrived, “… Stop slacking and get a move on yourself.”

Turning to the Captain he ordered, “Put that man on orders. He needs some PT to get him into shape.”

“Yes sir,” answered the Captain, knowing full well that he won’t.

The Duke gave orders for the platoon to march back down the other side of the hill and off they went, desperately trying to keep in step, desperately trying to stay upright and not trip over, and desperately trying not to push the bloke in front.

Much to the soldiers’ amusement, the Duke almost fell off his horse.

“If I see anyone so much as smile I’ll put him in jail!” he bellowed after he had repositioned himself in the saddle.

*

The Sergeant rounded the hill and turned towards the small group of people he could see in the distance.

Looking up the hill, he saw the troops slowly marching their way down. By now, they were halfway down, so they were neither up, nor down.

Arriving at the injury site, the Sergeant asked the two soldier what the state of play was.

"Both persons are conscious, now, sir. Apparently, they've been here since Monday afternoon. We found them in a poor state 'cos they needed a drink of water, but Greener went to the well to get some. They're a lot better now than when we found them."

"Right. Injuries?"

"The gentleman cannot move. I think he's got a problem with his back. I've tried to make him as comfortable as possible, but he needs urgent attention. The woman seems to have broken both her legs. She can't move either of them. That's why she couldn't go for help."

"Okay," responded the Sergeant, "let's see what they've got to say."

He looked at Jack and decided that there was no way that Jack could provide any kind of a lucid statement.

He lowered himself onto one knee to speak to Jill. "Can you tell me what happened?"

In a dazed state, Jill mumbled out just three words before she reverted back to unconsciousness.

"We were pushed…"

CHAPTER 12

Week 1. Late Wednesday, p.m. (It's getting dark)

The Sergeant stood back upright and radioed for an ambulance.

After giving his location, and brief details of the injuries, he turned towards the hill to see how the Duke and his men were progressing. They had arrived at the bottom of the hill and were marching towards him.

Seconds later, the Duke brought his men to a halt and ordered them to "Fall out."

To groans of relief, the men collapsed in a heap, puffing and blowing out of exhaustion. The Duke turned to his Captain.

"When we get back I want all those men on a fitness programme of intense PT. Look at them! Wimps, all of them."

Most of the men muttered something derogatory under their breaths.

The Sergeant decided that it was time to calm the Duke down by changing the subject.

"Do we have any medics to give these people some emergency treatment?"

"Indeed, we do." answered the Duke. "Captain, get the medic to do something for those people," he ordered.

The Captain searched out the medic and gave appropriate instructions to him.

"How can we get them off this field without causing more injuries?" asked the Sergeant.

"We have just the thing." The Duke turned to his men and instructed them to construct the stretchers.

"You have stretchers?" enquired the Sergeant.

"Absolutely. Wouldn't go anywhere without them. You never know when one of the men will get injured and needs a casavac back to civilisation."

Several men rummaged inside their backpacks, each one holding a part of a collapsable field stretcher. Two stretchers were deftly constructed.

The soldiers, under directions from the medic, then carefully lifted Jack & Jill onto each stretcher and covered them both with a blanket.

The ambulance siren announced its arrival at the gate that opened onto the field, and the Duke formed the men into four groups of three men. Each group of three men took hold of a side of a stretcher and the stretchers were both lifted in unison, to be carried to the waiting ambulance.

As soon as Jack & Jill had been loaded into the ambulance, the stretchers and blankets were returned to the Captain, and the ambulance paramedic started work on his patients.

The Sergeant looked into the back of the ambulance and enquired, "Will they be alright?"

"They're both extremely dehydrated, but I'm sure they will recover. They both need surgery so I'll get going straight away if it's okay with you."

"Of course. Griller - go with them and let me know when it is okay for me to interview them. Keep an eye on them, and don't let anyone - and I mean *anyone* - except for hospital staff, near them."

"Okay, Sarg," answered Griller as he sat next to the paramedic inside the ambulance.

The Sergeant made a note about his brief conversation with Jill, together with a reminder to interview her and Jack as soon as possible.

It was now early evening, and beginning to get dark. The Sergeant approached the Duke.

"You and the men can return to the barracks now, sir. Thank you for your help. I'm sure Jack and Jill will appreciate it when they come round. I'll put in a good word about this when I next see the King," knowing full well that he won't.

"Good man. Glad to be of assistance. It's a pity we didn't find the sheep."

"Yes, it is, but they'll turn up. I know it. Can you let the Queen know that I have a couple of ideas about her stolen tarts?"

"Will do."

With that, the Duke turned to his Captain and ordered him to form the men into a marching group - to much grumbling and swearing under the men's breaths.

"You're not going to march them over the hill again, are you?" enquired the Sergeant.

"Why not?"

"Well, it's going to be dark soon and I would hate for any of your fine men to get injured by falling down the hill."

After a brief thought, the Duke replied, "You're right! I'd already thought of that," he lied. "No, we'll take the long way round. Captain, march the men back to the barracks via the road."

"Yes, sir. Platoon! Platoon, r-i-i-i-ight turn!"

The troops did a slick right turn and off they went, with the Duke sat on his trusty steed at the front. The horse let out a noisy, whiffy fart as it passed the Sergeant's face. He screwed up his face in disgust. Several of the men gave him a wink and a nod of appreciation as they passed by. If the Sergeant hadn't challenged the Duke about the route back to barracks they would surely be puffing and blowing and heaving their bodies back up the hill by now.

The Sergeant followed the troops down the road to make his way towards the station.

*

Week 1. Wednesday evening, 9.00 p.m.

Although it was quite late when the Sergeant arrived back at the station, PC Slack was waiting for him.

"Hello Slack. Did you manage to find the pie man?"

"Yes Sarg. I brought him back here, but after about an hour he lost his temper and stormed out of the station. He was shouting something about some pies he'd left in the oven."

"Sorry. I was held up on the other side of the hill, tending to Jack and Jill and waiting for the Duke to march up the hill and down again. I'm sure that man's got a screw loose. It would have been a lot quicker to get to Jack and Jill by road."

"Oh? What's wrong with them?"

"It seems, from what Jill told me, that they were pushed down the hill, but that's all I could get from her. I'll try for some more details when they're both able to give them to me."

"Blimey, Sarg. Not what you'd expect in Rhyme Place, eh? What's next?"

"Go home and get some rest. Tomorrow, see if you can round up the old lady who lives in a shoe, the pretty maids standing in a row in contrary Mary's garden, if they're still there, and John Dumpling, and bring them all here to make a formal statement. Dumpling was drunk the last time I saw him but I'm sure he will have sobered up by tomorrow. Oh, and see if the pie man will come to the station again. If not, don't press him. I'll go to the bakery for his statement myself."

"Will do."

The Sergeant closed down the station for the night and went to bed after a cup of cocoa.

CHAPTER 13

Jack and Jill went up the hill
To fetch a pail of water;
Jack fell down and broke his crown
And Gill came tumbling after.
(London, 1765)

Now is, perhaps, an appropriate time to turn the clock back to Monday, to find out how Jack and Jill had become so badly injured.

Week 1. Monday, a.m.

Jill's slumber was disturbed by the alarm clock. It is seven forty-five a.m., and time to get Jack's breakfast ready.

After putting on a pot of coffee to percolate, Jill opened the lounge curtains and noticed a dirty green truck parked next to Bo Peep's paddock. Thinking it unusual, she stared at the truck for a while to see if she could ascertain why it was parked where it was. The truck partially hid an area of the paddock, so Jill returned upstairs to get a better view.

Peering through a crack in the curtains she looked out, past Mary Lamb's back garden to Bo's paddock. She could now see what was going on in the paddock clearly, and she dashed over to the bed, where Jack was still sleeping.

Giving him a hefty push, to wake him up, she whispered, "Jack! Jack, wake up!"

Annoyed at being so rudely woken, Jack responded, "Whaaaat? What's wrong?"

"Shhh...," whispered Jill, "There's something going on in Bo Peep's paddock. Quick! Come and have a look."

With an exasperated sigh Jack lowered his feet to the ground and made his way to where Jill was now waiting for him at the window. Sidling up to her, she stopped him from pushing a curtain to one side.

"No," she whispered, "Don't open the curtain. We don't want to let him know we are watching."

"Who?"

"Him...," providing a crack for Jack to peer through and nodding towards the paddock.

"I know that bloke," declared Jack. "He's been seen frightening little children."

"Yeah, but they couldn't make it stick, could they?"

"What's he doing?"

"Looks like he's loading Bo's sheep into that truck."

"It does, doesn't it?"

"Hang on! there's somebody with him."

Jack and Jill saw the truck driver appear from round the back of the truck and climb into the cab.

"We know that bloke, as well." declared Jill.

"What's *he* carrying?" asked Jack.

"Looks like a little lamb," Jill responded. "Maybe Bo has paid for the sheep to be taken away?" she added.

"Yeah, that's it. Bo's arranged for the sheep to be taken to market," decided Jack. "What's for breakfast?"

Drawing the curtains together, Jack finished washing and dressing, and Jill continued to make breakfast, both thinking nothing more of what they had seen.

*

Week 1. Monday, 8.45 a.m.

Breakfast over, Jill turned on the kitchen tap but no water came out.

She heard the truck drive down the road and then remembered the note pushed through the door, from Rhyme Place water department. It was an advisory note informing all occupants that the water was to be turned off this morning to enable urgent repairs to the mains water supply pipe.

She called to Jack.

"Did you remember to fill the pail with water?"

After a short pause, while Jack tried to think of a suitable reply he said, "Errm…"

Jill interrupted, "You forgot, didn't you?"

"Well…"

Another interruption. "You forgot, didn't you?" this time with a bit more anger in her voice.

"Yes," came back a rather meek reply.

Jill angrily stared at Jack for a few seconds, took a deep breath and ordered, "Get your coat on. I'll come with you to make sure it's done properly."

Jack asked, "Which way shall we go? The long way around the hill, or the short way, straight over the top?"

We'll take the shortest route to the well, and come back along the road. We don't want to spill any water, do we?"

"No, *we* don't," knowing who was going to carry the pail of water back home.

Leaving the cottage through the back door and heading towards the hill, they never heard the commotion that was to ensue when Bo Peep found that her sheep was missing. Neither did they hear the news flash later that morning, this having been sent out over the air waves as they climbed the hill.

They did, however, notice someone running up the hill before them, although the man was too far away to make out a description.

*

Week 1. Monday, 9.15 a.m.

At the top of the hill, Jack and Jill rested for a few minutes.

Looking out, over the valley below, they both smiled at the beauty of Rhyme Place. Looking back where they had just come from they saw some of the occupants running around, like headless chickens.

"I wonder what's going on down there?" enquired Jill.

"Who knows," replied Jack. "Maybe someone never read the note from the water company and they're now casting up about not having any."

The two turned to make their way down the steep slope on the other side of the hill when they heard the rustle of the bushes behind them.

Turning to see what, or who, was rustling the bushes, Jack demanded, "Who's there?"

Wellie man came out from behind and stared at Jack and Jill. They both recognised the man, but they didn't know that he had been the one they saw running to the top of the hill earlier.

"Hiya," chirped Jack with a friendly smile.

No answer from wellie man.

Jill spoke up. "We've just seen you loading Bo Peep's sheep into the back of a truck. Is she selling them?" she asked, innocently.

"You've just seen me?" enquired wellie man.

"Yeah, earlier on." replied Jack. "It was you, wasn't it?"

There was a pause while wellie man looked at the pair. He slowly walked towards the pair, both with their backs to the steep slope down to the valley floor.

As he approached Jack he said, "Nobody was supposed to see that," and with a hefty swing of his fist he punched Jack into the abyss.

Jill was so taken aback she didn't have time to grab Jack before he tumbled down the hillside. In the split second that she was trying to comprehend what had just happened, wellie man grabbed both her shoulders and gave her a colossal push. After flying through the air backwards she followed Jack's eventful journey to the bottom of the hill.

They both laid there, unconscious, until PC Green and his team found them.

CHAPTER 14

Week 1. Thursday, 8.00 a.m.

The Sergeant washed and dressed, then went to his kitchen, next to his bathroom and across the landing from his bedroom and lounge.

He lives at the station, you know, in a self contained apartment above the jailhouse and station reception. He doesn't mind living above his work. It sometimes has some good benefits. For example, he can lie in every now and then without having to worry about being late for his shift on reception, especially during the quiet times in Rhyme Place.

Recently, however, things have not been quiet. Whilst having his breakfast he read his note book and made some brief 'to-do' notes on a fresh page:

<u>TO DO</u>

The events, so far -
Missing sheep.
Stolen tarts.
Mary's lamb.
Jack & Jill's mishap.

<u>Interviews/formal statements</u> :
Bo Peep.
Old lady who lives in a shoe.
Mystery man running towards Hot Cross - find him!!!
[Contrary] Mary.
Pretty maids in Mary's garden - if still there.

Pie man.
John Dumpling.

All on the butler's list re tarts - to confirm my suspicions about an inside job.

Jack + Jill - when able to.

Continue search for the lamb.

It was looking distinctly like he had a busy day ahead of him, mainly taken up with formal statements. He accepted that he may not be able to get out and about, so he *'...must manage his time judiciously if he were to solve these crimes'* he thought.

He remembered that he had asked PC Slack to round up the old lady who lives in a shoe, the pretty maids standing in a row in contrary Mary's garden, if they're still there, and John Dumpling. Those statements will probably up take half of the morning. The remaining half would be spent searching the farm for the sheep.

'I'll contact the King to arrange when to go and take formal statements from the list of witnesses provided by the butler. This afternoon might be a good time,' he thought.

He heard the reception door, downstairs, open. *'that will be Slack,'* he mused. *'better get down there to see who is coming in today.'*

Closing his note book, he put his breakfast dishes in the dish washer and went downstairs to the reception area. There, he found the old lady and John Dumpling sitting quietly, waiting to be told what to do next.

"Good morning everyone," he welcomed the visitors. "I'll be with you in a moment. I've just got a couple of things to do before I take your statements."

Turning to PC Slack he asked, "Slack, please take Madam into the interview room and make sure there is a clean tape in the machine - Mr. Dumpling, would you mind waiting here while I interview this lady?"

"I've got things to do, you know. I'm a busy man. How long will this take?" demanded Dumpling with more than a hint of animosity in his voice.

The old lady spoke up. "I don't mind waiting here, Sergeant, if the gentleman needs to get away."

"Thank you, madam. Slack, take Dumpling to the interview room."

"What about a cup of tea?" demanded Dumpling.

The Sergeant thought for a second then turned, once more, to Slack.

"After you've taken Mr. Dumpling to the interview room, would you mind making a cup of tea for the lady?"

"Yes Sarg."

"What about me? Don't I get a cup?" asked Dumpling.

"Carry on Slack," ordered the Sergeant without responding to Dumpling's inconsiderate behaviour.

Thursday, 9.15 a.m.

Slack took Dumpling to the interview room.

Dumpling never stopped complaining all the time he and Slack were walking down the corridor and into the interview room. Dumpling wasn't happy about the time this was taking.

He complained that his human rights were being violated, he shouted that he had been discriminated against with regard to the cup of tea, he repeatedly demanded what he was being charged with and he demanded to see the duty solicitor. Once inside the interview room, and sat at the desk, he shut up and sat there with his arms folded across his chest.

As soon as the Sergeant entered the room he kicked off again. The Sergeant turned and left the room, slamming the door behind him. Dumpling continued to rant for another few moments, then became silent, once more.

The Sergeant entered the room again. Dumpling started a third outburst and the Sergeant once more left the room and slammed the door closed.

When silence again descended on the room the Sergeant opened the door and poked his head inside. This time, Dumpling took the hint and stayed silent, so the Sergeant entered and sat opposite him.

The Sergeant started the tape recorder and began his interview. “It is Thursday at nine forty-five a.m. Those present are myself, Sergeant Argent, and John Dumpling. The purpose of this interview is to question Mr. Dumpling about Bo Peep’s missing sheep.”

He saw Dumpling’s eyes dart about the room, just for a second.

“I want the duty solicitor.” demanded Dumpling.

“Why’s that, Mr. Dumpling. You’ve not been charged with anything.”

“I still want the duty solicitor.”

“Alright. You don’t need a solicitor, but I’ll ask PC Slack to bring him here. It will probably take a couple of hours.”

“What? I can’t wait a couple of hours. Why don’t I need a solicitor? Why am I here?”

“You’re helping me with my enquiries and you came voluntarily. I’m happy to get a solicitor if you really want one.”

“Get on with it!”

Taking a relieved breath, the Sergeant started his questioning.

"Where were you on Sunday night?"

"Which Sunday?"

"Look, Mr. Dumpling. The more you play games and bounce me around, the longer this will take. Now, are you going to answer my questions, or do you want me to put you in the cell for wasting police time? Which one?" The Sergeant's patience was wearing thin.

"What time on Sunday?" asked Dumpling.

"Between nine, p.m. and six, a.m. Monday morning."

"At home, in bed."

"And your mother will confirm that, will she?"

"She'd bet..." Dumpling stopped mid-sentence then continued. "Yes, she will."

The Sergeant made a note to interview Mrs. Dumpling.

"Where were you at eight forty-five on Monday?"

"At work."

"At work, where?"

"Driving."

"Driving where?"

"Around. Do you want a detailed route map?"

"Don't be facetious, Mr. Dumpling. Where exactly were you at eight forty-five on Monday morning?"

Dumpling sat tight-lipped, nonchalantly looking round the room.

"Who were you driving for, at that time?"

Dumpling still sat tight-lipped, nonchalantly looking round the room.

"You seem to have lost you memory. What vehicle were you driving at eight forty-five on Monday morning?"

Dumpling continued to sit tight-lipped, nonchalantly looking round the room.

"Okay. You can go."

Dumpling flinched. "I can go?"

"Yes."

What, now?"

"Yes."

With a smile that covered his face from ear-to-ear, Dumpling got up from his chair and left the room. On his way out he met PC Slack waiting in the corridor. Dumpling barged his way past Slack and left the building, whistling a tuneless melody on his way out.

Slack waited for the Sergeant to finish writing up his notes, then tackled him about Dumpling's release.

"He's as guilty as Hell, Sarg. Why'd you let him go?"

"Of course he's guilty… Of something, but we don't have enough on him to charge him with anything yet, Slack. We'll get him when the time is right."

"Well - you're the boss. Do you want me to send in the lady?"

"No, I'll speak to her outside."

Closing his file, the Sergeant followed Slack to the reception and sat next to the old lady who lives in a shoe.

"That man who has just left. Do you recognise him?" asked the Sergeant.

"Yes, that's John Dumpling."

"Did you see him at all on Monday morning, after you heard Bo Peep shouting for her sheep?"

"No."

"But you heard a truck driving away?"

"Yes. I didn't see where it was, though."

That's okay. Can you do something for me? Will you go home now and write down everything you remember about Bo's missing sheep, then drop that in to PC Slack, some time?"

"Yes of course," she answered.

The Sergeant let the old lady leave the station, then asked Slack about the pie man.

"Presumably, he didn't want to come in voluntarily?"

"No Sarg. He made up some excuse about not leaving his pies in the oven, but I knew he didn't have any in the oven so I decided to leave it at that and went to fetch Dumpling and the old lady."

"What about the pretty maids?"

"They weren't at Mary's cottage when I got there, and she doesn't know where they went."

"Okay, I'll just make a call to the King. Get your bike. We'll go to the bakery together, then go up to the castle, if the King agrees."

"Yes sir."

The Sergeant crossed out Dumpling's and the old lady's names from his 'To-Do' list and telephoned the King.

"Your Highness, may I call at the castle later today to interview some of the staff?"

"Yes, of course, Sergeant. Come up anytime."

"Thank you, sir."

Terminating the call, the Sergeant locked up the station and he and PC Slack pedalled their way to the bakery in the hopes that the pie man was available.

CHAPTER 15

Hot cross buns!
Hot cross buns!
One a penny, two a penny,
Hot cross buns!
(London, 1767)

Week 1. Thursday, 10.35 a.m.

The Hot Cross bun factory was in full swing when the two policemen arrived.

Leaning their bikes up against the factory wall they entered the reception. Behind the reception wall they heard the distant clatter-clatter rhythm of the bun making process. A smiley receptionist welcomed the Sergeant and his PC.

"Good morning, officers. Sales this way…, [*pointing*] and order pick-up that way… [*pointing in the opposite direction*].

"No, we've not come for some buns, we've come to interview someone. Is…?" The Sergeant was interrupted before he could finish his sentence.

"Ahh! I'll just phone for the duty officer. In the meantime, would you like a bun?"

The two policemen answered in unison, the Sergeant saying "No, thanks," and PC Slack saying "Yes, please." The Sergeant gave Slack a reproachful look and Slack lowered his head in admonishment.

Looking back at the receptionist he said, "I just need to know if…" again, he was interrupted, this time by the duty manager who had entered the reception through a side door.

“Good morning officers. Have you come to place an order for the station?”

“No, thank you,” answered an exasperated Sergeant. “I need to interview the pie man. Is he available?”

“Erm, I don’t know. Are you sure you won’t place an order? We’ve got a good offer on for today - two buns for a penny.”

The Sergeant just stared at the duty manager and waited for a reply to his question. The manager took the hint.

“I’ll take that as a no, then. I’ll show you through to the bakery, but first I must ask you to wear some protective clothing. Please, follow me,” and the manager walked towards the door he had just used to enter the reception.

The two policemen followed. On their way past the receptionist PC Slack mimed for two buns, behind the Sergeant’s back. He whispered, “I’ll pick them up on my way out.”

With a smile as white as the flour that the factory uses, she nodded in approval.

The Sergeant stopped and turned. “Make that four buns, and Slack will pay for them.”

*

Feeling a little self-conscious wearing the white coat, white wellies and fetching white hairnet that the factory manager had insisted they wear, the two police officers were shown through the factory to the bakery. It was much quieter here than the factory, and the bakery had that warm bread smell that we all enjoy.

The manager handed the policemen over to a different receptionist. This one was identical in every way to the one in the bun factory. Even down to the style of hair band holding back an identical hair style. Identical face, identical height, identical white smile, and identical clothes. *Everything* identical!

"Good morning, officers. Sales this way..., [*pointing*] and order pick-up that way... [*pointing in the opposite direction*]," chirped up the receptionist.

"No. Don't want any pies, buns, bread, cakes, rolls, sandwiches, tarts - or anything else that might be on offer. We've come to see the pie man. Is he in?"

"Oh...," answered the receptionist, dejectedly. "I'll just phone him."

There was a small conversation between the receptionist and the person she called, during which the policemen were announced, followed by the occasional 'Yes' and 'No'. She replaced the telephone handset.

"I'm sorry, he's not in."

The Sergeant stared at the receptionist for a second, then picked up the telephone handset.

"What's his number?" he demanded.

"I..., I don't think I should give it to you," she answered, hesitantly.

"Number?"

She caved in under the Sergeant's cold stare. "Extension two-three."

The pie man answered the phone almost immediately the Sergeant dialled the extension number. "I've told you, I'm not in! Send those coppers away!"

The Sergeant responded in a matter-of-fact tone, "Would you prefer to talk to me in handcuffs, down at the station, seeing as you're not in right now?"

There was a pregnant pause. The Sergeant heard the pie man utter something unrepeatable under his breath and then the click of the call being cut off as the pie man replaced his handset. The Sergeant did likewise and stood looking at PC Slack.

Slack raised his eyebrows, in question, at the Sergeant. "Is he coming?" he asked.

"I reckon. We'll give him a couple more minutes before going to arrest him."

The side door to reception creaked open and the pie man stormed into the room.

Angrily, he asked, "What do you want?"

"You know what I want, but to make it absolutely clear I want to interview you about Bo Peep's missing sheep. Now, do you want me to take this statement here, or down at the station…?"

The pie man thought about what the Sergeant had just asked, then answered, "I've told the constable that I don't know anything about any missing sheep."

"Shall we sit down? Then you can tell me while I make a few notes?" looking back at the reception sofa.

With a deep sigh to indicate a large measure of irritation the pie man sat next to the Sergeant on the sofa. Slack stood by the door in case the pie man decided to make a run for it.

Taking out his notebook, the Sergeant began his interview.

"Name?"

The pie man ignored the Sergeant's question and advised Slack, facetiously, "You should wear that hat more often - it suits you."

Slack was just about to open his mouth to respond with something inappropriate but the Sergeant quickly stepped in.

"Name?"

"Pie Man."

"Age?"

"About thirty-five."

"About...?"

"Thirty-five."

"Address?"

"Is this entirely necessary? I've got lots of pies to make for the fair."

"Address?"

"The bakery. I've got a flat over reception."

"Now, I'm told that you were almost knocked down on Monday. Is that true?"

"Yes."

"Where and what time?"

The pie man was, by now, resigned to the fact that the Sergeant was not going to let him go, so he mellowed slightly to answer the questions.

"Just by Hot Cross. I don't know what time it was, precisely, but I had just left the bakery to deliver some pies to the fair, so it must have been between eight forty-five and nine, a.m."

"Was anyone with you at the time?"

"No... Yes! [*suddenly remembering*] That young kid with dark hair. What's his name?"

There was a slight pause while the Sergeant gave the pie man time to think.

"Simon! That's him. Simon. I gave him a pie for helping me carry the tray."

"Go on," prompted the Sergeant.

"Well, we had just passed Hot Cross, when this truck came charging round the corner. It nearly rammed us both! We had to dive to one side to avoid it, and my pies went flying all over the road. Me and the boy picked them up, dusted them off and put them back on the tray."

"And then?"

"Well, nothing. We carried on to the fair and I delivered the pies to the food van, parked opposite the swinging ship. It's a good pitch, that - in front of the swinging ship."

"Oh? Why?" chipped in PC Slack.

"Well, you sell a few pies, the punters go on the swinging ship and they spew up when they get off. Empty stomachs, they buy a few more pies."

"Do you remember the colour of the truck?"

"Yeah, a dirty green. It had shit dripping from its tailgate."

"Did you hear any sheep as it passed by?"

"Nah. It all happened in a flash. I was too busy trying not to get knocked down. The kid was really unlucky - the truck missed him but he dived into a thicket of blackberries. Poor sod came out all cut and bruised, with his shirt torn."

"Did you get a chance to see the driver?"

"Nah. Too fast."

"Is there anything else you noticed?"

"Nope."

"Anything at all?"

"Nope."

"Did you see anything on the engine radiator?"

"Nope."

"Did you get the truck's number?"

"Nope."

"Okay, sir. That's all, for now. We'll leave you to your pies, now, but we may want to speak to you again."

"Okay. No probs. Just try to make it a bit later, will you, when I've finished baking and I'm waiting for the pies to cool? About ten thirty-five in the morning would be about right."

The Sergeant silently recollected that that was about the time he had arrived at the bakery...

Back outside, the Sergeant and PC Slack recapped on the discussion.

"That certainly ties in with what Simon told you," offered the PC.

"Yeah, but I get the feeling that he's not told us everything he knows."

"I got that, as well. Do you think he had anything to do with the missing sheep?"

"Don't know, but I'll get to the bottom of it, I'm sure. Let's find somewhere to have some snap, then we'll get on to the farm to see if old MacDonald knows anything."

The two men cycled to the park and sat watching the people go in-and-out of the fairground as they ate their lunch - two buns each that Slack had bought from the factory reception, and a pie each that the pie man had just donated as they left the bakery... Delicious!

CHAPTER 16

Old MacDonald had a farm, E-I-E-I-O,
And on his farm he had some cows, E-I-E-I-O,
With a 'moo moo' here, and a 'moo moo' there,
Here a 'moo', there a 'moo',
everywhere a 'moo moo',
Old MacDonald had a farm, E-I-E-I-O.
(This traditional English version was first recorded and released on the Edison label in 1925)

Week 1. Thursday, p.m.

After lunch the two policemen made their way to old MacDonald's farm. As they were mounting their bikes PC Slack reminded the Sergeant that they still had to interview the castle staff.

"No, I hadn't forgotten that, but I thought I would call in to the farm to have a nose around. We might come across that dirty green truck..."

"Or even some sheep." interrupted Slack.

"Yeah. It can't be easy to hide some sheep, can it?"

"And don't forget Mary's lamb," reminded Slack.

Cycling towards the farm house they looked around the fields owned by MacDonald. There were no sheep, but there were plenty of cows. The cows appeared to be heading towards the farm house, as if they had some purpose going there. In the distance, the policemen heard Macdonald calling them - *'cup, cup, cup, cup.'*

"That must be him," the Sergeant said to Slack as they cycled up to the farm house. "It must be milking time."

A queue of cows snaked into a barn from an open gate. Both the Sergeant and Slack inwardly wished they had some wellies strapped to their bikes because the farm yard was awash with slimy, runny cow shit. Rather than contaminate their shoes they slowly cycled right up to the barn door, thinking it better to hose down their bikes than their shoes. MacDonald was busying himself with the cows.

"Mr. MacDonald?" alerted the Sergeant to their presence.

The farmer looked up, saw the two policemen, put down his milking stool and approached the officers.

"What do you want? Can't you see I'm busy?" demanded the farmer, angrily. Some of the cows looked up from their troughs of oats in surprise.

I've come to ask you about Bo Peep's sheep," answered the Sergeant.

"So?"

"So, do you know anything about them going missing?"

There was a pause as the farmer thought of something to say. He then sighed in exasperation and said, "No. Don't know nothing!" Again, an angry response.

"Well, is it okay if we look round the farm to see if any have strayed onto your land?"

"You got a search warrant?"

"No. I was hoping you would co-operate with us."

"No warrant - no search. Now get off my farm!"

"Look, sir, we haven't come to make any trouble. You don't need to help us with the search, we can do that ourselves. All we're asking is that you co-operate a little and give us permission to make a search. Just the two of us. Nobody else. We won't cause any damage and you can get back to your milking while we look round."

"No warrant - no search."

The Sergeant's patience was beginning to slip.

"What have you got to hide, Mr. MacDonald?" asked PC Slack.

"Nothing. Now please let me get on with my work."

"We're not stopping you from working, sir," replied the Sergeant. "If you've got nothing to hide there should be no reason to prevent us carrying out a search."

In a brusque manner, the farmer ordered, "Off you go, and don't forget to close the gates on your way out."

The farmer was definitely NOT going to back down, so the two policemen exited the barn, mounted their bikes and headed back down the road. Rounding a bend, the Sergeant waited for Slack to catch him up and then flagged him down to a stop.

"Slack, why don't you take a look around, but DON'T get caught. I'm pretty sure he's hiding something. I need to know what, whether it's the truck or the sheep. I'll wait back at the station for you."

"What about the castle staff?"

"They'll wait. We can't go up to the castle like this, anyway," replied the Sergeant looking at their cow shit splattered bikes and trousers. "I'll straighten things with the King. I'm sure he will understand."

"Okay, Sarg. See you back at the station."

The Sergeant left PC Slack to do his thing and returned to the station.

*

Week 1. Thursday, mid-afternoon.

Arriving back at the station, the Sergeant phoned the King to apologise and fix up a time to interview the castle staff the following morning.

He then phoned Judge Fairly to ask for a warrant to search old MacDonald's farm. Having discussed the farmer's attitude, Judge Fairly agreed that a search of the farm was merited. The Judge promised to deliver the warrant to the Sergeant personally, which wasn't as helpful as it may seem, at first glance, because the Judge's office was just one floor up in the same building.

Handing the warrant over, the Judge asked, "Do you need any more help with the search? I can arrange for a couple of men from Jingle Town to join in."

"Thanks for the offer, sir. I think I can manage the search with my officers, but it would be really helpful if you could arrange for someone to take over from Griller at the hospital. He's been guarding Jack and Jill since they were admitted."

"No problem, Sergeant. I'll get on it right away."

"Thank you. sir."

The Judge hurried back upstairs to arrange for a relief for Griller. The Sergeant radioed PC Griller, still guarding Jack and Jill at the hospital.

"Griller, I've arranged for someone to relieve you at the hospital. Return to the station as quick as you can."

"Yes Sarg. Do you want me to wait here 'til the relief arrives?"

"No, Jack and Jill should be okay for a while, but let the hospital staff know about your relief, and let them know that you are leaving. Ask them to keep an eye on their patients. How are they, anyway?"

"Jack still hasn't woken up, and Jill wakes up intermittently for a few very brief moments. I've been unable to interview either of them."

"Okay. See you when you get here."

Slack entered the station just as the Sergeant's radio conversation with Griller was terminated.

“Slack, tell me you found that truck.”

“No Sarg, didn’t find the truck, but I did hear a lamb bleating from one of the barns. I couldn’t get close enough to see anything, though, ‘cos MacDonald, Little Boy Blue and John Dumpling were hovering around.”

“Dumpling was there?” asked the Sergeant.

“Yes Sarg. MacDonald was giving him some orders and pointing towards the fields, but I wasn’t close enough to hear what was being said. I almost got caught sniffing around, so I decided to leave.”

“Okay. Well done Slack. I’ve now got a search warrant and when Griller gets here we’ll all go and see what MacDonald’s got to hide.

Slack put the kettle on for a cup of tea while they waited for Griller to arrive.

CHAPTER 17

Week 1. Thursday, mid-afternoon.

Griller approached the nurses' station and collared a passing nurse.

"I've been called away. Is there anybody available to watch over Jack and Jill until my relief gets here?"

"How long do you think that will be?" asked the nurse.

"Well, I understand that arrangements have been made for some officers to come from Jingle Town. Maybe ten or fifteen minutes?"

"Okay. I'll ask someone to stand in for you. Is the person who did this still out there, then?"

"Yes, I believe so, but we're on the lookout for him and I'm sure he'll be apprehended soon. Do you know how long they are going to be unconscious?" asked Griller, nodding toward the room that Jack and Jill are in. "We really need to interview one of them."

"Who knows. It could be tomorrow, it could be next week. We don't really know. Coma is a complicated thing to predict."

"Okay, I must go. Please keep an eye on them."

"Of course."

Griller departed from the hospital and made his way to the police station.

Unbeknown to him, someone was watching Jack and Jill's room from a short distance.

*

Back at the police station, things had suddenly become chaotic.

The telephones were constantly ringing and a crowd had gathered outside. The Sergeant left PC Slack to try to answer as many calls as he could while he went outside to see what the crowd was shouting about.

Opening the station door he was confronted by a mass of people facing the Town Hall, and chanting, "Leave our bush! Leave our bush!"

The Sergeant walked up to a woman at the front of the crowd and asked, "What's all this about?"

"They're going to destroy the Mulberry bush to make room for a chicken processing factory for old MacDonald. If they do that we'll have nothing to dance round."

"Really? I didn't know about that."

The Sergeant dashed back inside and ran upstairs to the planning department. Crashing through the planning department door he faced the chief planning officer over the counter.

"What's this I've just heard about MacDonald removing the Mulberry bush to build a chicken factory?"

"Is that what all the noise is about downstairs? I was just on my way down to see what the crowd wanted," asked the planning officer.

"It is. What about the factory?"

"We had the application dropped into our letter box about three months ago, and notices were sent round to every occupant of Rhyme Place at that time. With no objections having been received by us, it was approved yesterday. We've not even had chance to put out a notice about its acceptance. That's why you don't know, yet."

"Well, I do know now." retorted the Sergeant as he dashed out of the department to go downstairs to try to calm the crowd down, with the planning officer hot on his heels.

*

NEWS FLASH! From Chatty Chaste on the news desk at Rhyme Place TV station.

Chatty - "We interrupt our Romper Corner programme to bring you this news, just in... A large crowd of angry demonstrators has gathered outside Rhyme Place Town Hall to protest about the destruction of the Mulberry bush. They are noisily chanting 'Leave our bush!' We understand that the police are in attendance, and that Sergeant Argent is attempting to get control of the throng... I'm now getting a message through my ear-piece that a second protest crowd has encircled the Mulberry bush to prevent builders from getting anywhere near it. Our roving reporter, Snoopy Satchel, is on the scene. Snoopy, describe, for us, the scene down at the Mulberry bush..."

Cut to the outside broadcast unit.

Snoopy Satchel - "Well, Chatty, a crowd of about forty people from the outlying villages has, as you can see, encircled the Mulberry bush. They are holding hands and chanting, 'Leave our bush!'

"We can see builders in the background who are attempting to break the circle with the intention of up-rooting the Mulberry bush to prepare the land for construction of a chicken processing factory. Fights between the builders and some of the protesters are beginning to break out but the builders are greatly outnumbered and have, so far, been unable to breach the cordon. At the moment, it is too dangerous for the camera crew to venture anywhere near the bush so we have been unable to interview anyone. I've asked for a statement from the council and old MacDonald, but as yet both parties have declined to comment. We'll let you know the minute we get somebody to talk to us. In the meantime, back to you in the studio, Chatty..."

Chatty - "Thanks for that, Snoopy. Stay out of trouble...," a finger pressing her ear-piece closer to her earhole.

Snoopy responds with a very firm "Absolutely!" and Chatty returns to the camera and continues.

"Well - there you have it. There has been a lot of discussion in the past about whether to keep the Mulberry bush, but it seems that it is far more popular than anyone realised. We have asked for a statement from old MacDonald, but so far he has declined to comment. We will keep you informed of developments on this issue as they occur, but for the time being we'll return you to the Romper Corner."

*

Back at the police station, Griller managed to barge his way through the crowd to reach the station door. The Sergeant instructed him and PC Slack to go down to the Mulberry bush, via the station back door, to calm things down there. He then went back outside to confront the protesters. Standing on the steps of the Town Hall, he held up his arms to ask the crowd to quieten down. After a few moments, silence descended.

The Sergeant lowered his arms and said, "Thank you. Now, I have just sent my two PC's down to the Mulberry bush to take control of things there. In the meantime, I have asked the council's chief planning officer to make a statement."

The planning officer stepped forward. "There have been many discussions between our office, old MacDonald and, indeed, the various towns' residents. The planning application was made to us about three months ago, and with no objections, council approval was granted yesterday. Appropriate notices are being prepared for distribution right now."

Somebody from the crowd shouted out, "We don't want a chicken factory. We want our Mulberry bush."

The crowd roared in approval, stamped their feet and clapped loudly.

The planning officer held up his hands.

As soon as silence descended, once more, he continued. "I'll request an emergency council meeting to debate this and you are invited to attend. There is room for twenty people, only, in the council chamber, so entry to this debate will be on a first come, first served basis. Please give your names to the police station. Thank you."

With that, he turned round and returned to the Town Hall door.

There were lots of jeer's and angry protests from the crowd and the Sergeant once more faced everyone, holding his hands up to command silence.

"Anyone wishing to attend the debate can leave their name at my reception desk and the list will be sent upstairs to the planning department. In the meantime, please disperse quietly."

Nobody moved. There were lots of mumblings, head nodding, head shaking and finger pointing from the protesters… but nobody moved.

Someone re-started the chant, "Leave our bush! Leave our bush!"

Satisfied that the crowd were not in a destructive mood, the Sergeant made his way to the Mulberry bush to join his two PC's.

He took the search warrant with him.

CHAPTER 18

Here we go round the mulberry bush,
The mulberry bush, the mulberry bush.
Here we go round the mulberry bush,
On a cold and frosty morning.
(England, mid-1700s)

Week 1. Thursday, mid-afternoon.

Events at the Mulberry bush took a turn for the worse. Although the ambient air temperature is what one would expect in the height of summer, the temperature at the Mulberry bush had certainly risen to an all time high.

PC Slack tried hard to maintain order, but with feelings running high, and tempers exploding, his efforts were hopeless. All he could do was to stand back and allow the protesters and builders to bash each other to pieces.

Those protesters not fighting smashed up the path around the bush and threw the fractured pieces of concrete at the builders. In answer, the builders that were not fighting or, indeed, injured by the concrete fragments, threw the fragments back at the protesters.

The fighting and senseless fragment throwing resulted in many serious injuries. Someone had telephoned for an ambulance, but even this was attacked in the melee and had to withdraw. The paramedics stood around, waiting for a break in the free-for-all. As a consequence, many injured bodies lay on the ground, blood pouring from heads, noses and cheeks, broken bones waiting for some treatment. Anyone unable to get out of the way was trampled on - or kicked - by those fighting.

But the cordon held fast because the builders were vastly outnumbered by the protesters and unable to get at the Mulberry bush. This didn't stop the builders cracking a few heads with a readily available concrete fragment. Nor did it stop the protesters breaking a few bones with the vast array of weapons brought by them.

The Sergeant arrived on site. He was horrified at the scene before him.

Griller had attempted to break up a fight but was now on the ground, being kicked by the two men he had been trying to stop fighting, as if they were both now on the same side.

The Sergeant ploughed in, kicking and punching his way to Griller, and broke a fighter's nose in the process. He helped Griller to his feet and both backed away from the riot to join PC Slack.

Now, one thing that the Sergeant has learned, is 'always be prepared'. He didn't carry a gun - he wasn't allowed to - but in the saddlebag attached to his bike he always carried the next best thing… A string of about ten firecrackers. Lit and thrown into a Saturday night free-for-all, the firecrackers sounded, to the unsuspecting, like gun fire - a sound guaranteed to make people stop what they are doing and look round in surprise.

Out came the firecrackers, out came the Sergeant's box of matches and the burning fuse was thrown into the centre of the riot. The effect was much as anticipated. Thinking that guns were being fired the rioters all stopped punching, kicking and throwing stuff and dropped to the ground in submission. Like a huge cloak falling out of the sky, silence descended.

The Sergeant stepped forward and calmly asked everyone, "Have you all finished? Had enough? Or does anyone want to be accompanied to the station handcuffed to my bike?"

Nobody moved, except to wipe blood from flattened noses or split lips or cracked heads.

The Sergeant continued. "Good. Now, all you builders - move away and stand back at least twenty yards. Griller make sure they limp into a heap somewhere."

Griller moved forward to 'assist' any builder who needed to be reminded about the Sergeant's threat.

"Slack, notify the paramedics that it's okay to begin tending to the injured. You lot!" pointing to a couple of able bodied men, "give PC Slack a hand to get these people to the ambulance."

Turning to a paramedic he asked, "Have you radioed for more ambulances? You're going to need them."

"Another four are on their way. Should be here in a few minutes," answered the paramedic.

"Good," replied the Sergeant. "Now listen in, you lot!" he shouted to every one of the rioters. "You should be ashamed of yourselves. You ALL deserve to spend some jail-time locked up, but you should ALL count yourselves extremely lucky that I don't have room for everyone, otherwise you would be hauled before Judge Fairly quicker than you can scratch your arses. So I'm not going to arrest anyone for this stupid, mindless incidence... But if any one of you makes the wrong move you can bet your trousers that I'll be busy with my handcuffs. Does ANYONE want to say anything?"

He paused for just a couple of seconds to wait for a reply. No one dared to answer.

"Good!" he declared. "Now, those of you still able to walk, help PC Slack and the medics carry the injured to that ambulance then get off home where you belong. I don't want to see any of you back here for at least seven days. Is that clear?"

Still no answer.

"I'll take that as a yes, then."

The Sergeant stood around to wait for the back-up ambulances to arrive. He and his men then assisted the paramedics in loading these up and sending them off to the hospital.

The field around the Mulberry bush was now empty and peaceful. The Sergeant turned to his men and gave then some encouragement.

"Well done, men. You made me proud. Shall we now go and search Old MacDonald's farm for some sheep?

CHAPTER 19

Little Boy Blue come blow your horn.
The sheep are in the meadow,
the cows are in the corn.
Where is the boy who looks after the sheep?
Under the haystack, fast asleep.
(First reference to this rhyme made by George Homans, 13th Century)

Week 1. Thursday, late afternoon.

The three policemen cycled up to the farm.

Arriving at the farm gate they dismounted, removed their cycle clips from their trousers, and made their way up the farm track to the farmhouse. Griller's face looked a bit beaten up from the pounding he received during the riot, but that just made him look even meaner than he usually looked.

As they approached the farmhouse, PC Slack came to a sudden halt and whispered, "Listen!"

Bending their heads to direct ears towards the discussion taking place, Griller confirmed, "That's old MacDonald shouting about something. The noise is coming from that barn…," pointing towards one of the outbuildings.

The three officers quietly crept up to the barn door to better hear what was being said.

MacDonald - "You stupid lout!" A slap, followed by a groan, was heard. "How the bloody Hell did you lose them?" bellowed MacDonald. "All you had to do was to load them back into the truck, you incompetent fools!"

Plaintiff voice - "Somebody left the doors open. They must have just walked off."

PC Slack, whispering - "That's John Dumpling."

The Sergeant - "Yeah." He was peering through a crack in the doors. "There's someone else in there. I can't quite make him out."

MacDonald - "And you! Why didn't you warn anyone that they were escaping? Why do you think I gave you that horn, you prat!?"

Mystery voice - "How did I know this fool was going to bunk off and have a kip somewhere? I left him to look after them while I went to get my sandwiches."

MacDonald - "Well you shouldn't have. You know this idiot has got one brain cell less than a worm. I might have known that giving you two the simple job of looking after something important would be a stupid thing to do on my part. Get up..."

The policemen heard a kick and another groan.

PC Slack, still whispering - "That sounded like little Boy Blue."

The Sergeant - "It was. MacDonald has just kicked Dumpling's arse and told him to get up."

MacDonald - "You two had better get out there and find them. I don't have a clue as to what I'm going to say to the pie man. If he welches on this deal it's coming out of your pay. Got that?"

Dumpling - "It's not my fault the doors were left open."

MacDonald - Stop snivelling and get out. Find them, or get lost for good. And you...!" pointing to Dumpling, "Forget about that coat I promised to give you."

MacDonald, Dumpling and Boy Blue turned to make their way out of the barn. The three officers quickly and quietly scurried back to the farmhouse and stood in front of its doorway. When the three men exited from the barn, the Sergeant rapped on the farmhouse door and stood back, as if they had just arrived.

MacDonald shouted, "What do *you* want?"

The policemen turned to face him.

"We've come to carry out a search of the farm for Bo Peep's sheep," waving the search warrant at the farmer.

MacDonald snatched the warrant from the Sergeant's hand, read it and replied," Well, you won't find them on my land."

He turned to Dumpling and Boy Blue. "You two. Get out there and do your job. Don't come back unless you find what you've lost."

Dejectedly, Dumpling and Boy Blue made their way to the farm gate.

The Sergeant asked, in a matter-of-fact tone, "Problem?"

"The idiots let my cows escape. They're fools, the pair of them. I should never have given them the job of looking after my stock. Now, what else do you want from me. Whatever it is forget it, 'cos I won't give it to you."

"It's very kind of you to help us with our enquiries, sir," answered the Sergeant, sarcastically. Turning to his two PC's he ordered, "Slack - you search the fields. Griller you search the outbuildings."

Turning back to MacDonald, he said, "And I'll search the farmhouse," with a satirical smile on his face.

MacDonald just growled, turned, and went into the farmhouse.

The Sergeant called Slack back and, with his back to the farmhouse, whispered, "You're not going to find anything in the fields, but I do want you to see what

Dumpling and Boy Blue are up to. Don't let them see you following them."

"Yes, Sarg. Do you think he was shouting about his cows, or the sheep?" asked Slack.

"I don't know, but I'm sure I'll find out soon enough."

Slack nodded, turned and ran to catch up with his quarry.

Just as the Sergeant was walking back to the farmhouse, PC Griller appeared from a barn holding a lamb. The Sergeant hurried towards him.

Again with his back to the farmhouse, the Sergeant whispered, "He's watching us through the curtains, so don't say anything - are there any sheep in there?"

A single shake of Griller's head acknowledged the Sergeant's question.

"Okay, look down and answer - is there any indication that the sheep were in there?"

Looking at the ground, and trying not to move his lips, Griller answered, "There's nothing but straw bales right now, but the floor is covered in sheep shit."

"Okay. You go and give Mary's lamb back to her. I'll search the farmhouse on my own, but I doubt I'm going to find anything incriminating. When you've handed the lamb over, go up to the castle to ask the King if he would be good enough to summon these people to his dining room tomorrow morning for me to interview them," handing Griller the list of names provided by the butler.

"Yes, Sarg," and Griller disappeared towards the farm gate.

The Sergeant rapped on the farmhouse door, once more. Without waiting for an answer he entered the building. He then made a search of the farmhouse for anything that might tie the farmer to the missing sheep. As anticipated, he found nothing. Before leaving, he approached the farmer who was in his kitchen eating a sandwich.

"We just found a lamb in one of your barns," he announced.

"What lamb?" an innocent face on the farmer.

"The one you've just seen Griller holding."

"Not mine," came back a terse reply.

"Well, whose lamb is it?"

"Don't know. Doesn't belong to me. Never seen it before."

"What was it doing in your barn?"

"I don't know. Probably shitting all over the place. I cleaned that barn out this morning," lied the farmer.

"How did it get there?" asked the Sergeant, patiently.

"I just told you. I DON'T KNOW...!" shouted MacDonald. "Maybe it crawled under the door."

"You know that's not possible, sir. There's not enough room. Now, where did you get that lamb?"

"One of the boys brought it in. I told him to take it back, but he must have forgotten."

"You do realise that I'll be interviewing those two, don't you?"

"I don't care. Do what you want. It's got nothing to do with me."

"Who brought the lamb into the barn?"

"Forgot..."

"Frankly, Mr. MacDonald, I don't believe you. I think you know more about Bo Peep's sheep than you care to tell me, but I'll be back - and the next time I'm confident that you'll walk out of here wearing my bracelets."

"Get out! You've got nothing on me. You'll not GET anything on me - and my solicitor will be in touch with you about the slanderous allegation you've just made."

"Please don't go anywhere, sir. I may need to ask you a few more questions."

"Knock yourself out, Sergeant. Just make sure my solicitor is present when you ask those questions. Now, for the last time - GET OUT!"

The Sergeant was now almost one hundred percent convinced that MacDonald was embroiled with the missing sheep. He was also convinced that Dumpling and Boy Blue were MacDonald's accomplices.

But who else was involved?

CHAPTER 20

Cut back to Thursday, mid-afternoon (Week 1).

Back at the hospital the telephone on the emergency reception desk chirped.

Nora, the desk nurse, lifted the receiver. "Emergency department…" she declared and waited for an answer.

"Nora, this is Marg. Have you seen what's on the television?"

"Hi Marg. I thought you were off-duty."

"I am. Have you seen what's on the television?"

"Hang on, I'll just switch it on."

Nora reached up to the television, high on a shelf above the emergency reception desk, and stood back to see what was on. She joined the news flash from Chatty Chaste about a quarter of the way through it. Snoopy Satchel was giving his report.

Alarmed at the riot that was taking place at the Mulberry bush, she abruptly ended the call from Marg and dialled the personnel department.

"We're going to need all the staff that is available. There is a riot at the Mulberry bush and from what I've seen on the TV there are quite a few casualties."

As soon as the call was terminated the paramedic contact radio, sitting on the desk, shouted for attention.

"This is a code red!" advised the paramedic, who was stood next to the Sergeant at the Mulberry bush. "There's a riot here at the Mulberry bush and we need at least another four ambulances. Please also send any spare doctors or nurses that may be available."

Nora picked up the telephone receiver and dialled the personnel department again.

“It’s Nora, in emergency, here. I’ve just requested emergency backup from all available staff. Please divert four nurses and two doctors to the mulberry bush immediately.”

Over the Tannoy system she put out a request for all available nurses to attend the emergency department and she busied herself organising the department for what may well be a huge influx of patients.

The first of the ambulances arrived. Staff hurriedly wheeled two semi-conscious patients into the emergency reception, and a flurry of activity around them materialised.

The day promised to be a busy one for the hospital staff.

*

The mystery person, hiding in full sight wearing a white coat and with a stethoscope hanging round his neck, saw an opportunity to seek out Jack and Jill. Much of this small hospital sprang into organised chaos with news of the impending influx of patients, and he knew that Jack and Jill’s observers would be diverted away from them.

Approaching a nurse’s station he asked which room they were in. With this knowledge, he made his way to the lift but was stopped by a nurse in the corridor before he could reach it.

“Doctor, all available staff are needed in the emergency department. We are expecting many injuries to arrive shortly and the emergency staff need a boost,” the nurse advised.

“Yes, I’m just on my way there now,” answered the mystery impostor.

He turned and started to walk down the corridor. After a few steps he stopped and looked behind him. The nurse he had just been talking to had disappeared round a corner so he hurried towards the lift once more. From nowhere the same nurse appeared carrying a kidney dish and towel.

"The emergency department is that way," she said, pointing down the corridor.

"Oh, yes. Of course. I was just going to see a patient on the third floor, but it will wait."

The mystery impostor feigned a 'just remembered' look on his face and turned towards the emergency department. This time he knew that he would have to go there in case the nurse followed him.

She did, after waiting for a few seconds to see what he would do.

You'll recall that Judge Fairly had requested a back-up team to take over from PC Griller, up at Jack and Jill's private ward.

The back-up team of three PC's arrived just as our mystery impostor walked into the emergency department, followed, a few seconds later, by the nurse who was watching him closely.

The nurse walked up to one of the back-up team and asked him to follow her.

Hiding behind a large column, she whispered, "You see that doctor, over there?" pointing to mystery man. "I don't think he's a doctor."

The young PC diverted his eyes away from the nurse to peer round the corner of the column at the mystery man. "Why do you think that?" he asked, quietly.

"Well, I've just found him wandering around the corridor. He didn't seem to know where the emergency department was - and he told me he was going to see a patient on the third floor. We only have two floors..."

The PC thought about the nurse's comments for a second or two, then nodded.

"And another thing...," the nurse continued, "...our doctors *never* hang their stethoscope around their necks. They always carry them in their pockets."

"Are you absolutely sure that he's not a doctor?" clarified the PC.

"The wellies covered in shit are a give-away...!"

The PC gave another nod. "Okay," he said, "leave him to me. Don't let on that you've spoken to me."

With that, the nurse smiled and nonchalantly walked from behind the column. The PC continued to observe the imposter while talking to a colleague with his radio. After a couple of minutes standing around and looking in all directions, the imposter was confronted by another nurse.

"Doctor, will you take a look at the patient in cubicle three? I think he may need an x-ray of his arm."

"Yes, of course"

Looking round for cubicle three, the imposter made a bee-line towards it, drew back the curtain and entered the cubicle. Picking up the mill-board from the end of the bed, and pretending to read the notes scribbled on it, he approached the patient. He didn't realise that he was being watched.

"Good morning, Mr. Smith. I'm just going to take a look at your arm."

Without waiting for approval the imposter squeezed the patient's arm and lifted it from the bed, to much groaning in pain from the patient. Putting the arm back down, the imposter unravelled the stethoscope from around his neck and pressed its diaphragm onto the patient's arm. Paying absolutely no attention to what the patient had to say, the imposter looked around furtively, checking to see if he had been rumbled. To his surprise, he saw two police officers stood at the entrance to the cubicle, watching him. He tried bluffing his way out of the cubicle.

Shouting to a passing nurse, he suggested, "Nurse, can you take this man to x-ray."

The nurse approached and replied, "Yes, doctor?" She took the mill-board from him and looked at the sheet clipped to it.

She continued, "You haven't completed the x-ray authorisation, doctor…"

Before she could hand the mill-board back to the imposter the two PC's made a move towards him. He suddenly bolted for the door, but one of the PC's was much quicker than him. There was a scuffle as the two PC's tried to handcuff the man, but he broke free, kicked one of the PC's in the stomach, punched the other in the face and dashed for the exit door. On his way out he barged into a group of nurses, paramedics and hospital visitors, all of whom were unceremoniously knocked to the ground. The PC's by now, had recovered and were in hot pursuit, but the pile of bodies in front of them hampered their chase and the imposter was able to escape through the doorway.

Carefully trying not to injure anyone, the two policemen eventually made it to the door. Dashing outside they looked in all directions for the imposter, but were unable to locate him.

The only movement visible was a dirty green truck, heading out of the hospital grounds. It was too far away for either of the policemen to note its number.

CHAPTER 21

Little Jack Horner
Sat in the corner,
Eating his Christmas pie;
He put in his thumb,
And pulled out a plum,
And said, "What a good boy am I!"
(English, 1765)

Still Thursday, mid-afternoon (Week 1).

The pile of people, barged into a heap at the entrance doorway to the hospital by the imposter, managed to unravel themselves, sort themselves out, dust themselves down and continue their journeys into the hospital.

Mrs. Horner stopped the policemen as they re-entered the hospital.

"How can I help you, madam?" asked one of the PC's.

"My name is Horner - *Mrs*. Horner. That man…," answered Mrs. Horner, pointing towards the door, "…the one you just chased out - I think I know him."

"You do? Can you give us a detailed description?"

"I can, but I must go to visit my son, first."

"Oh? Your son is in the hospital?"

"Yes. That's why I came, today. He's very poorly."

"Oh dear. What's wrong with him?"

"Well, yesterday I noticed that one of my Christmas pies was out of its 'use by' date, so I peeled back the foil cover and noticed that it had some funny black spots on the top. Assuming it had gone off, I put it on the kitchen counter to take out to the bin later that day."

"And…?"

"And my son, Jack, scoffed it while I was making the beds. He's a greedy little sod, you know. He eats anything and everything. He'd eat the curtains if I didn't watch him. Anyway, he got food poisoning from the pie and I had to bring him in to hospital last night. I was just on my way to visit him when that man crashed into us and barged us to the floor. It wasn't a very polite thing to do…"

One of the policemen interrupted her. "You say you can put a name to him?"

"Yes, I think so."

"I'll go with you to visit your son, Mrs. Horner, and wait outside his ward for you to come and give me a statement. Okay?"

"Yes. That will be fine."

Mrs. Horner and the policeman made their way to the lift. The other policeman radioed the conversation in to the station and made his way to Jack and Jill's ward.

*

Week 1. Thursday, late afternoon.

Let's now catch up with the Sergeant.

You'll recall that he and his Station PC's had broken up a riot at the Mulberry bush and then gone on to search the farm. The Sergeant had attempted to formally interview old MacDonald, but the farmer wasn't very co-operative, so the Sergeant decided to bide his time and gather more evidence before arresting anyone. He received a radio call from one of the backup PC's.

"Sergeant Argent? It's PC Peecie here. Me and two other PC's have been sent to the hospital by Judge Fairly to guard Jack and Jill."

"Hello Peecie. How are they?"

"They're still being kept under heavy sedation by the doctor, but he says he will stop the medication soon. Both patients are sleeping peacefully. I'm calling to report an incident, here at the hospital."

"Fire away," requested the Sergeant.

"Well, an imposter, disguised as a doctor, was found in the emergency department. We tried to apprehend him, but he got away."

"Do you know what he was after?"

"No, Sarg. I can only guess that he may have been trying to get to Jack and Jill, but I don't know for sure."

"You say he got away. Were there any witnesses?"

"Yes, Sarg. A Mrs. Horner. She approached PC Polite and told him she could recognise him."

"Get a statement from her as soon as you can and bring it to the station. Did you get a description?"

"Only as far as wellies covered in shit. The statement is in hand. PC Polite has accompanied Mrs. Horner to visit her son and will take her statement as soon as he can."

"Well done. Get that statement and a full description to me as soon as possible."

"Will do, Sarg."

As the Sergeant departed from the farmhouse, having been 'asked' to leave by old MacDonald, PC Slack emerged from the trees and dashed up to him.

"Sarg! I've just found the truck!"

"Oh? Tell me more…"

"I was following Dumpling and Boy Blue through the forest and they emerged into one of MacDonald's fields. There's a road running by the side of the field and the truck pulled up in front of Dumpling and Boy Blue. The pair went around to the driver's side and they chatted about something. I was too far away to hear what was being said, but the truck drove off. I decided to forget about Dumpling and Boy Blue and I ran through the trees to follow the truck. I found it parked up in the forest."

"Well done, Slack. Good thinking. Did you get a look at the driver?"

"Unfortunately no, Sarg, and when I came across the truck he had disappeared. I searched the truck, but it was empty except for a load of sheep shit in the back. There was nothing in the glove box, and nothing to confirm who owns it except the registration number."

PC Slack showed the Sergeant his notebook, opened at the page where Slack had made a note of the vehicle registration number.

"Good man…," complimented the Sergeant, "…get back to the station and find the owner of that truck. I'll go take a look myself. With a bit of luck I might catch chummy returning to it.

PC Slack dashed off and the Sergeant headed towards the truck.

CHAPTER 22

Georgie Porgie, pudding and pie,
Kissed the girls and made them cry,
When the boys came out to play,
Georgie Porgie ran away.
(Kentish Coronal, 1841. This version c.1884,
The Oxford Dictionary of Nursery Rhymes 1951)

Week 1. Thursday, late afternoon.

Following the directions given by PC Slack, the Sergeant found the truck parked up in a forest clearing.

The bonnet was still warm, indicating that the engine had been used recently. The colour tied in with what witnesses had seen - a dirty green colour - and Simple Simon's observation of a teddy bear tied to the front grill was spot on.

The sheep shit in the back of the truck convinced the Sergeant that this was definitely the truck used to transport the stolen sheep.

But who was driving, who does the truck belong to, who gave orders for the sheep to be stolen and why, and who is the ace card in this pack of criminals? These were the questions rolling around in the Sergeant's head, but he was confident that they would be answered in due course. It was all down to collating the evidence.

There was nothing in the glove box except a grubby, handwritten plan of Bo Peep's cottage, sheep paddock and access road. The Sergeant wondered what purpose this drawing had in all this business. Somehow, he had to get a sample of writing from the person that had drawn and labelled this plan. If the plan *was* connected, in any way, to the theft of the sheep then it would not only prove the connection between the truck and the sheep, it would also prove the connection between the sheep and the person who drew the plan.

After carefully putting the drawing inside his notebook, the Sergeant made his way back towards the station. On the way, he decided, he would call in to someone's cottage to take another statement.

*

Week 1. Thursday, late afternoon.

Back at the station, PC Griller was behind the reception desk.

He had returned the lamb to Mary [Lamb] and was 'thanked' by a very, very grateful Mrs. Lamb… Extremely grateful!

The station door opened and Daisy Petal entered the station in tears, still wearing her school uniform.

Daisy is nine years old and goes to Rhyme Place Junior School, an annex between Rhyme Place Infants' School and Rhyme Place Senior School. Everyone just refers to 'Rhyme Place School' when talking about any of these three institutions.

A concerned PC Griller walked from behind the reception desk and sat down on one of the visitor's chairs, inviting Daisy to sit next to him.

"What's wrong, Daisy? You look as if you've just found a penny and lost sixpence."

Daisy smiled a sniffly smile at the PC, took a deep breath and replied, "It's that Georgie Porgie…"

"Oh? What's he done to make you cry?"

Without taking a breath, Daisy blurts out, "He keeps creeping up behind us and then he kisses us on the cheek. He shouldn't do that, should he? It's wrong. He just runs away when the boys come out to play, so they don't ever see him and so they don't ever stop him doing it."

"Oh dear. We'll have to see what can be done about that, won't we?"

"Yes. You should put him in jail for the rest of his life and never let him out again," demanded Daisy.

"Well, he's a bit young to be put in jail, but I'm sure we can have a word with him to make sure he doesn't do it again."

"Can you? It's not fair. He gets away with it every time and we can't do anything about it..."

Tears began to form in Daisy's eyes once more and Griller wrapped his arms around her in sympathy, and gave her a caring squeeze. She reciprocated with a really tight hug.

PC Slack entered the station and smiled at Griller's embrace of Daisy. "Hiya Grillo [*Griller's nickname*]. Didn't know you had your girlfriend here," he jibed, with a wink and a smile.

Daisy pulled away from Griller and faced Slack. "I'm not his girlfriend! I'm too young to be his girlfriend!" she announced, angrily.

"Slack sat in another visitor chair. "You're a girl, aren't you?" he asked.

"Yes," came back the anticipated answer.

"And you're his friend, aren't you?"

Daisy looked up at Griller's smiling, rubbery face and asked, "Are you my friend?"

"Of course I am. I'm everybody's friend. Shall we go and have a word with your mum? Then I'll go talk to Georgie Porgie's mum. I've got an idea that will make him stop doing what he does to upset you. I don't like my friends being upset."

Daisy gave Griller a massive smile and another hug and they both stood to leave the station.

On the way out, Griller instructed Slack, "When the Sarg gets in, can you let him know that the King will see him first thing in the morning?"

"Will do," acknowledged Slack.

*

Griller and Daisy strolled down to Daisy's cottage, hand in hand. On the way there, they met up with the Sergeant.

"Hello Griller. Hello Daisy. What's what?" looking down at Daisy.

Griller just said two words. "Georgie Porgie."

"Him again!" replied the Sergeant. "Somebody ought to do something about him constantly annoying the girls. What's wrong with the boy?"

"He's naughty!" chipped in Daisy.

"He is, that," said the Sergeant. Looking up at Griller, he asked, "Did you manage to see the King?"

"Yes. He'll muster those on the Butler's list tomorrow and wait for you in the dining room at about ten-thirty in the morning. The Queen asks if you would be kind enough to call into the kitchen when you've finished."

"Will do. Off you go - and Daisy, we'll try to make Georgie Porgie stop upsetting you."

"I know," she declared smugly. "My friend is taking me home to talk to Mum about him, and then he's going to talk to Georgie Porgie."

"Well," replied the Sergeant, "I'd better let you and your friend go, then, hadn't I?"

With a polite "Thank you" from Daisy the pair continued their journey.

The Sergeant continued his journey to the shoe house to interview the old lady.

*

Daisy's mum was stood in her doorway when Daisy and the PC arrived.

"Daisy, where have you been? I was getting worried about you," welcomed Mum with a hug for Daisy.

The PC spoke up. "Everything is okay, Mrs. Petal. Daisy and me have just had a chat down at the station. I thought I had better bring her home to let you know where she's been."

"Is she in any trouble?" asked a concerned Mum.

With a chuckle, the PC said," No, of course not. I'll let her tell you all about it. Okay Daisy?"

With a frown, Daisy described why she had gone to the station, and finished with, "My friend [*pointing to Griller*] said he's going to talk to Georgie Porgie about it and stop him doing it."

Mrs. Petal smiled at Griller and said, "Thank you Constable. Daisy has clearly taken a shine to you. It's not everyone that she considers to be her friend."

"She's a good kid, Mrs. Petal, and she's not just my friend - She's my BEST friend," looking down at Daisy and squeezing her hand.

Daisy wrapped herself around Griller's leg with a smile that almost made her face disappear.

Extricating himself from Daisy's arms he confirmed that he would talk to Georgie Porgie's mum in the morning and he made his way home, waving to his new friend, Daisy, as he departed.

CHAPTER 23

There was an old woman who lived in a shoe.
She had so many children, she didn't know what to do.
She gave them some broth without any bread;
Then whipped them all soundly and put them to bed.
(English, c.1784)

Week 1. Thursday, late afternoon.

Arriving at the shoe house, the Sergeant heard pandemonium inside.

Children - lots of children - were fighting, screaming, singing, shouting, running around, and the TV was in competition with the commotion, trying hard to be heard. The Sergeant wondered if this was the right time to call. Dusk was beginning to cover the town and cottage lights were beginning to be switched on. He recalled that earlier, that day, he had asked the old woman who lives in the shoe to write out a statement about what she saw in respect of the missing sheep. As he was passing, he thought now would be a good time to collect the statement from her.

Gingerly, he knocked on the door… No answer.

He knocked again, this time a bit louder… No answer.

He tried to get some attention for a third time, this time hammering loudly on the door… Still no answer.

It was obvious that the racket inside was eclipsing his door knocks, so he opened the door, poked his head inside the hallway and bellowed, "QUIET!"

The children were immediately silent. After a second, or two, even the volume on the TV was turned down to a whisper. The silence was more deafening than the noise it suppressed. The old woman poked her head round the doorway of the kitchen to see who had bestowed some semblance of order inside the home.

"Phew! That worked," she said, walking into the hallway towards the policeman. "Hello Sergeant Argent. Sorry about the commotion. It's a Hell of a job getting these kids into bed, but once they're in it's nice and quiet. Don't stand out there, come on in. Make yourself comfortable in the lounge - if you can find somewhere to sit down. I'll just finish bathing this little one and I'll be with you shortly. Want a cup of tea?"

"No thanks," replied the Sergeant, and stepped into the shoe.

The children in the immediate vicinity all viewed the policeman with suspicion and made a hole for him to walk down the hallway.

As he made his way towards the lounge the old woman, now back in the kitchen, shouted, "Get off the settee and make room for the Sergeant to sit down."

As the Sergeant entered the lounge several children bounced off the settee and stood in the middle of the room, staring at him. Sitting down, he looked at all the faces pointed in his direction. A couple of the children continued their game of snakes and ladders.

One of the children, a girl, asked, "Have you come to take Michael away?"

With a furrowed brow, the Sergeant replied, "What's he done?"

"He keeps drawing pictures on Mum's walls."

"Oh? Which one?"

"That one," pointing to a wall.

"No, which picture?" asked the Sergeant, scrutinising the many pictures that had been crayoned onto that particular wall, some old, some fresh.

The girl went up to the wall and put her finger on a crude drawing of a cottage with a couple of children in the garden and a huge sun beaming down on them.

The girl continued, "Mum told him that if he didn't stop drawing on the wall she would get the police to take him away. Have you come to take him away?"

"Where is Michael?" asked the Sergeant.

Several of the children shouted his name. One of them dashed out of the lounge, presumably to go and bring him to the Sergeant. A reply from upstairs came back, "What!?"

One of the children poked his head round the doorway and shouted back, "You've got to come downstairs - NOW!"

Footsteps were heard running along the corridor and down the stairs. The children in the lounge continued to eyeball the Sergeant with suspicion. Michael appeared, looked at the Sergeant and stopped in his tracks. He stood, staring wide-eyed at the Sergeant.

The Sergeant stood up and towered over the children.

Walking over to the drawing he pointed to it and asked, "Did you draw this picture?"

Michael didn't answer. He just nodded slowly.

"Did your mum tell you not to draw on the walls?"

Another slow, silent nod.

The Sergeant stroked his chin, nodded and muttered, "Mmm," as he returned to the settee and sat down. "Come here," ordered the Sergeant, patting the settee next to him.

As Michael walked towards the settee, head hung low, the girl piped up, "He's come to take you away, Michael."

The Sergeant saw the terror in Michaels face as he sat down and he felt Michael shaking.

"Why don't you do as your mum says?" he asked, gently.

Michael looked up with pleading eyes and answered, "I love drawing, but we can't afford any drawing paper. I tried drawing on the pavement outside, but my drawings just get washed away by the rain. I haven't got any where else to draw."

"Tell you what," said the Sergeant, rummaging in his pocket and pulling out a five pound note. "How about you clean of all your drawings from your mum's walls, and I'll give you this fiver to buy some drawing paper tomorrow. On your way back from the shops, call into the station to show me what you've bought and I'll get one of my PC's to give you a box to put your paper in. Will you do that?"

The little boy sniffed, wiped his nose with his sleeve and nodded furiously. He jumped up, but before he could go anywhere the Sergeant grabbed his arm.

"You're not going to draw on your mum's walls again, are you?"

"No, sir."

"Promise?"

"Yes, sir."

The Sergeant turned to one of the girls. "If Michael breaks his promise, you come down to the station to let me know and I'll come and take him away. Okay Michael?" The Sergeant waved his handcuffs at Michael.

"Yes, sir," nodding furiously, his eyes darting between the handcuffs and the Sergeant.

With that, Michael dashed out of the lounge to collect a bucket and cloth to clean off the drawings.

"Don't forget the ones upstairs," reminded the Sergeant.

"Yes, sir… No, sir," answered the child.

The Sergeant was confident that Michael had got the message. He was sure that Michael would not draw on mum's wall's - ever again. He looked up to see the old woman standing in the lounge doorway, cradling a young child and smiling.

Speaking to the children, the Sergeant suggested, "How about you all go and get yourselves ready for bed - quietly, without making any noise. With a bit of luck, your mum might even tell you a bedtime story."

The children all quietly lined up to leave the lounge and go and get ready for bed. Michael turned and smiled at the Sergeant as he went about cleaning off the drawings from the walls.

"Thank you," the old woman said. "I'm afraid they need a father figure. I can't give them the type of discipline that they need."

"How come you've got so many children living here?" enquired the Sergeant, inwardly noting the diversity of colour and appearance in the children.

"They're not all mine. They're all foster kids from the nearby towns. I'm the only one with a place big enough to house them. I'm not making a very good job of bringing them up, am I?"

"You're doing fine. I've not had any complaints and I've not had any of the children brought to the station for any wrongdoing, so you must be doing something right."

"Yeah - well..." The old woman shrugged her shoulders. Changing the subject she confirmed, "I've done the statement you asked for. I assume that's why you've called round."

"Yes, that's correct," taking the folded statement from the woman. "I'll just go through it while I'm here."

After reading the statement he asked her to sign and date it. The statement was an exact replica of the discussion the woman had with Inky Irwin, the news presenter, on Monday morning. The Sergeant followed up with a couple of questions.

"Do you recognise the man running past your window?"

"No. He looked a bit familiar, but I'd hesitate to put any name to him."

"Did he speak to anyone as he passed by?"

"I didn't see him speak."

"Okay, I don't need to take up any more of your time."

The Sergeant rose to his feet. By this time, the children had all changed into their jimjams and had returned to the lounge. The room was now quite crowded with all the children taking up every inch of spare floor space and chairs, several occupying each chair.

The Sergeant addressed them. "Now, your mum needs a lot of help and you older children can give her that help instead of fighting or watching the television. You can help by cleaning up and making the beds and looking after the younger ones. If you organise yourselves properly you'll be able to spread the load of chores between yourselves AND still have time to play games and watch the TV. Okay?"

Several of the children nodded and looked around, as if summing up the list of chores that they could do. The Sergeant pointed to the one that looked to be the oldest.

"Why don't you sit down with your mum and make out a list of chores that you can help her with? Then you'll have something to plan out between you all. You're in charge. Okay? And all you other children - follow her lead and help out, or I'll come and take you away. Okay?"

A few nods were nodded. The Sergeant reinforced his suggestion. "OKAY?" he repeated.

This time there were a few more nods and a couple of the children answered "Yes sir."

"Do we all understand?" asked the Sergeant, forcefully.

An outbreak of nods ensued, and the children all straightened up and took on an optimistic look.

Asking the eldest child and the old woman out into the hallway he spoke so that all the children could hear. "If anybody doesn't behave themselves just let me know and I'll be back to take them away."

In a more hushed whisper, he said to the old woman and the girl, "If you need anything, just let the station know and I'll see what can be done."

The woman thanked the Sergeant and the girl hugged him lovingly.

He looked down to her and said, "You know where you can find me."

"Yes, thank you," she answered with a smile.

He shouted to Michael. "And don't forget the ones in the kitchen, Michael…"

"No, sir."

It was now quite dark outside, so the Sergeant decided go back to his apartment above the station and relax for a while.

CHAPTER 24

Bobby Shafto's gone to sea,
Silver buckles at his knee;
He'll come back and marry me,
Bonny Bobby Shafto!
(Found in the Henry Atkinson *manuscript*
from the 1690's)

Week 1. Friday, early a.m.

After a peaceful night's sleep the Sergeant bounced down the stairs from his apartment and entered the station. PC Slack was already on duty behind the reception desk.

"Mornin' Slack. Any problems?"

"Mornin' Sarg. No, no problems so far."

"Good. Keep it that way."

"Yes Sarg. I've got a message from Griller. Last night he asked me to let you know that the King will see you this morning, and that the Queen wants you to look in on her."

"Yeah, got that. I met him myself, on my way back here."

"Oh, okay. What's on for today?"

"You stay here and man the desk. I want Griller to come with me to take some statements. Where is he, anyway?"

"He phoned in earlier Sarg. Said he's got an errand to run then he'll be back here."

"Did he say what errand?"

"No Sarg. He asked if you could wait here for him. Shouldn't be long."

"Okay, let me know when he arrives, will you?"

"Yes Sarg."

The Sergeant went to his office to read up on his notes.

*

Yesterday afternoon Griller had made a mental note to visit Georgie Porgie's mum. On the way to the station he called into her place. Mrs. Porgie answered the door with a frown on her face.

"What's he done now?" she asked.

"It's not too bad Mrs. Porgie. He's been running around annoying the girls at school. I thought I would call in this evening to have a word with him."

"Yes, please do. I'm at a wits end trying to make him behave. Do you know what he did the other day?"

"No. What?"

"He tied a firework to the tail of Mrs. Shafto's cat and watched it run around, terrified. It cost me an afternoon trying to pacify Mrs. Shafto but she eventually settled down after a cup of tea and a couple of tarts. Since her Bobby went to sea, the cat is the only thing she's got for company."

"Well, I'll see if I can calm him down a bit. I'm guessing it is just boyish pranks, but if he's not careful he'll finish up in some serious trouble. I have an idea but I need your blessing, and I need a large portion of your trust in me."

"If it works you've got it. Tell me more."

Griller laid out his plan to make Georgie behave himself. With a smile, Mrs. Porgie declared, "If that doesn't work I don't know what will."

"See you after school tomorrow?" asked Griller.

"I'll put the kettle on, ready for you." answered Mrs. Porgie.

"Before I go, can I ask you a couple of questions on a different matter?"

"Of course. What is it?"

"You mentioned tarts, earlier."

"Yes, do you want one now?"

"No, thank you. I was just wondering where you bought them."

"From a bloke who had set up a stall outside the railway station."

"Can you remember what he looked like?"

"Yes."

Mrs. Porgie described the street seller while Griller made some notes. When she finished, he bid her goodbye and left for the station with a grin on his face. He had just received some information that will be useful to the Sergeant.

PC Griller entered the station and PC Slack sent him to the Sergeant's office straight away.

The two men greeted each other and the Sergeant noticed Griller's smug face.

"What?" asked the Sergeant.

"Oh boy! Have I got some good news for you," declared a beaming Griller.

The Sergeant sat up and waited for the news.

"I've just been to see Mrs. Porgie. She bought some cheap tarts from a street pedlar down by the railway station."

"And…?" There was a hint of expectation in the Sergeant's voice.

"She's given me a full description AND the name of the guy selling the tarts."

The Sergeant grinned from ear to ear. "I'm pretty sure I know who it was. Give me his description, first, and I'll tell you his name."

This game was played out by Griller and the Sergeant, both smiling at the anticipated outcome of their conversation.

"Let's go up to the castle to give the King some good news, but first, we have to ask a few more questions."

On their way out, PC Slack stopped the Sergeant and said, "I've just had a call from Mrs. Dumpling about a disturbance at her place. Do you want me to see to it?"

"Yes, please," answered the Sergeant. "Call me on the radio if you need any help. Griller and myself will be up at the castle."

"Will do Sarg."

The station was locked up and the three policemen went about their business.

CHAPTER 25

Little Tommy Tucker
Sings for his supper.
What shall we give him?
White bread and butter!
(English, c.1744)

Week 1. Friday, still a.m.

PC Slack strolled down the road towards Mrs. Dumpling's cottage.

He didn't see any disturbance in the area, but he did hear the angelic voice of little Tommy Tucker percolating from Tommy's open bedroom window. Tommy was singing a haunting, but beautiful, melody made famous by a well known pop artist.

As he approached the cottages a window was opened and Mr. Dumpling - John's Dad - poked his head out.

"WILL SOMEONE SHUT THAT DAMNED KID UP?" he bellowed.

PC Slack stopped in his tracks.

Mr. Dumpling had another go at Tommy's singing. "QUIET, YOU NOISY LITTLE BRAT! IF I HAVE TO COME ROUND THERE TO SHUT YOU UP I'LL RIP YOUR TONSILS OUT. NOW SHUT THE HELL UP!"

The singing continued, much to the annoyance of Mr. Dumpling.

Dumpling's window was slammed shut and he disappeared into the room, emerging from the cottage a couple of seconds later sporting a grubby, off-white vest and grasping a rolled-up newspaper. He saw Slack, abruptly ceased his purposeful pacing towards Tommy's cottage and stood glaring angrily at the policeman.

The PC spoke first. "Where do you reckon you're going with that?" nodding at the rolled-up newspaper.

"To stop that kid's God-awful noise!" declared Dumpling.

"And what were your intentions when you got to his house?" asked the PC, calmly.

Dumpling thought for a second, looked down at the rolled-up newspaper and appeared to calm down. "To stop that kid's God awful noise," repeated Dumpling, this time without shouting.

Tommy's bedroom window opened and Mrs. Tucker looked out. Her appearance at the window enraged Dumpling.

"YOU!" he shouted. "Can't you keep that kid of yours quiet for just one minute? Just listen to him. He never stops that wailing for a second."

The window was hastily closed and the singing stopped.

"Calm down, Mr. Dumpling," instructed Slack.

Dumpling stood in the middle of the road, looking like he was about to explode into millions of pieces. Tommy's cottage door opened and Mrs. Tucker appeared, holding a rolling pin. The PC moved up to stand in between her and Dumpling. Dumpling slowly raised his rolled-up newspaper in a threatening manner.

Slack had to take charge of this little neighbourly disagreement before it got out of hand.

Holding his arms outstretched to stop the two neighbours getting to each other, he ordered, "Calm down Dumpling… And Mrs. Tucker, go back inside. I'll come to you in a minute."

Mrs. Tucker backed off with the words, "You obnoxious little man. Haven't you got anything better to do than to bully my Tommy?"

"Haven't you got anything better to do than to play the piano all day?" retorted Dumpling.

Slack intervened, once more. "Mrs Tucker, I won't ask you again. Go inside! And Mr. Dumpling - you do the same!"

The two warring neighbours glared angrily at each other before they both turned and headed towards their respective cottages. Slack followed Dumpling.

Arriving at Dumpling's cottage door Dumpling turned to face the policeman, now stood behind him.

"What?" he demanded.

"I'd like to come in to discuss matters with you," the PC replied.

"There's nothing to discuss."

"Yes, there is. There is the subject of your threatening behaviour, for a start."

Dumpling thought about the PC's comment for a second then went inside his cottage, leaving the door open for the policeman to enter. Without waiting for an invitation, Slack sat in an easy chair opposite Dumpling, who was busily rustling his newspaper as if to read it.

"Put the paper down, Mr. Dumpling, and tell me what this is all about."

After a moment's thought, Dumpling explained his anger at the singing.

"I work nights in a factory over in Jingle Town. I get home at about eight a.m., and all I want to do is get some sleep. As soon as my head hits the pillow that bloody kid starts his wailing, with his mum on the piano. I'm sick of it, PC Slack. Absolutely fed up with hearing that bloody boy singing all day, every day, with his mum banging out the same tune day-in-day-out."

Dumpling threw down the paper and folded his arms. He sat there, silently waiting for Slack to speak.

"What were you going to do with the rolled-up newspaper?"

"Absolutely nothing. I didn't even realise I'd still got it in my hand when I went outside. I was so angry. What have I got to do to get some sleep after a hard night's graft in the factory? It's been like this for weeks."

"I'm sure you have a good reason to be angry, but that's no reason to threaten people - even with a rolled-up newspaper."

"Yeah, you're right. I'm sorry. It won't happen again," surrendered Dumpling.

"Tell me about the factory. What does it make? What do you do there"

Dumpling straightened up and looked pleased at Slacks' interest in his job.

"Well, we manufacture children's toys and books. We've got masses of work on right now. There are hundreds of children's authors wanting their book printed, and they all want them printed yesterday. Every shift is a full-on stretch. I work a ten hour shift, starting at nine p.m. each night, then I have to come home to next door's racket."

His shoulders slumped again at the thought of Tommy's singing.

An idea then came to Slack, like a light bulb that had just been turned on inside his head.

"It must be pretty boring sitting in front of a machine all day. Does management do anything to kill the boredom?"

"They've got piped music, but it's the same CD all day and the day shift tend not to listen to it. They've got some kind of request procedure for the music, but nobody ever takes the trouble to ask for any special piece. I think they've just got used to listening to the same old stuff and they now just ignore it - like you do in a supermarket."

"Is there a spare room in the factory that Tommy could go to sing in?"

"Actually, there is..." Dumpling's light bulb inside his own head lit up. "You reckon Tommy would go there to sing?"

"I don't know. Shall we go round to his cottage to ask?"

After a few seconds of consideration, Dumpling stood up to leave the room and let out a loud, deep breath. Slack followed him out. As they reached Mrs. Tucker's front door the PC held Dumpling back.

"Perhaps I should knock," he suggested, placing himself between the door and Dumpling.

A purposeful knock on Tucker's door achieved the desired result. Mrs. Tucker opened it and her eyes opened in wide surprise to see Dumpling stood behind the PC.

"What does HE want?" she demanded.

"He's come to apologise, haven't you Mr. Dumpling."

There was a short pause while Dumpling thought about Slack's surprise ambush on him, and he muttered, meekly, "Sorry..."

"You what?" demanded Mrs Tucker, clearly intent on showing everyone who was boss.

Dumpling coughed, then answered in a more positive tone, "I'm sorry I threatened you."

Slack decided it was time to take charge, once more.

"Mr. Dumpling has an idea that I'm convinced will improve the relationship between you both. Can we come in to talk about it?"

Mrs. Tucker looked at the two men long and hard, then opened the door wide to let them in.

"Take your boots off before you step into the hallway."

The men wrestled with their footwear to comply, and then stood upright for Mrs. Tucker's inspection. After looking down at the men's socks - both of the men had his big toe poking through a hole in one of his socks - she just nodded and walked into her lounge.

"Sit down, somewhere," she ordered. When everyone was comfortably sat, she continued, "So, what's this idea then. It had better be a good one or you're both out of the door."

Dumpling glanced between Slack and Mrs. Tucker, obviously waiting for Slack to make the suggestion. Slack took a deep exasperated breath and said to Dumpling, "Well - tell her about your idea."

Dumpling's brow furrowed. "Idea?"

Slacks eye widened in disbelief, "Yes, Mr. Dumpling. Your idea about where Tommy can sing."

"Oh, yes. Mrs. Tucker, we've got a smashing room at the factory where Tommy can come and sing to the workers all day if he wanted. It's even got a piano in it. We could pipe his singing throughout the factory. I'm sure the workers would welcome a break from the tedious CD that management keep playing…" He waited for a response.

Now, this took Mrs. T by surprise. She didn't expect Dumpling to be so nice.

"Would you like a cup of tea?" she asked.

Both men answered in the affirmative and she disappeared in to the kitchen.

Tommy appeared in the lounge doorway.

"Hello, PC Slack - Hello Mr. Dumpling."

"Hello, Tommy." Both men spoke in unison.

Tommy looked down at the floor and scraped something invisible from the carpet with his foot. "I'm sorry you don't like my singing, Mr. Dumpling."

This took Dumpling by surprise. "It's not that I don't like it, Tommy. You've got a smashing voice - and you sing like an angel. It's just that I need to get to sleep when I get home and I can't if you're singing loudly all the time."

"Oh. I didn't know," volunteered Tommy. "I've got a talent competition coming up and I need to practice, but I don't have anywhere to go to practice. I love singing and I want to be a proper singer when I grow up. Mum always gives me something special for my supper after I've practiced."

His eyes returned to the floor.

The two men, Dumpling in particular, saw, in Tommy's manner, the regret that he had for causing so much trouble and both Dumpling and the PC also stared down at the ground, not knowing what to say next. Tommy's mum appeared with a tray of tea and biscuits. Easing Tommy into the lounge with her knee, she placed the tray on the table and poured out the tea.

"Mr. Dumpling has got an idea about your singing, Tommy. Do you want to hear it?" asked Mum.

Tommy just nodded, his eyes still focused on a spot directly in front of his shoes.

Dumpling once more explained about the spare room at the factory, the boring CD and the piano, then asked, "What do think Tommy? You'd have a live audience to practice to."

"Can I, Mum?" His eyes had now come alive at the thought of singing to a live audience. "Can I?"

Mum looked at Dumpling, then Tommy, then back at Dumpling. “Do you think the boss will object?”

“I am the boss…” replied Dumpling.

Turning back to Tommy who, by now, was bobbing up and down in eagerness, Mrs. Tucker said, “I’ll have to look up the bus timetable so that we know what bus to catch.”

Tommy smiled a huge smile.

Mrs. T smiled a huge smile.

Dumpling smiled a huge smile - in the knowledge that he would now be able to get some sleep.

PC Slack also smiled a huge smile as he departed from the cottage, leaving Tommy, Mrs. Tucker and Dumpling to finish their cups of tea while talking pleasantries over the biscuits.

CHAPTER 26

The Queen of Hearts, she made some tarts, ...

The King of Hearts called for the tarts,
And beat the Knave full score.
The Knave of Hearts brought back the tarts,
And vowed he'd steal no more.

Week 1. Friday, a.m.

The Sergeant and PC Griller approached the guard at the castle gates.

"Name?"

The policemen looked at each other and both shrugged their shoulders.

"Griller, you help this guy to fill in his questionnaire and I'll continue up to the castle," instructed the Sergeant.

By-passing the guard, he went to lean his bike up against a car parked on the square.

The surprised guard dodged between the Sergeant and Griller, not knowing whether to impede the Sergeant or question Griller. As the Sergeant got further away, the guard decided to confront Griller. On his way past the guardhouse the Sergeant waved at the guard Commander, who was watching the activities down at the gates with interest. Waving back to the Sergeant, in approval, he folded his arms and continued his scrutiny of the gate guard.

Having parked his bike, leaning it up against a Rolls Royce stood on the square, the Sergeant met Griller on his way to park his own bike.

"Better not use the same car to lean your bike on," advised the Sergeant. "Rolls Royce's are for the Sergeants only. Lean it up against that Mini."

"Right you are Sarg."

"You go and start interviewing the people waiting for us while I go and speak to the Queen. DON'T interview the Knave, and DON'T let him leave the dining room."

"Yes Sarg… No Sarg… Okay, Sarg."

The two men parted company.

*

The Sergeant met the butler as he walked through the corridors to the Queen's chamber.

"Good morning, Sergeant. I presume you have come to see the Queen. I'll accompany you and announce your arrival."

"No. No need for that. I'm sure I can announce myself. However, would you be good enough to give a statement to PC Griller about the missing tarts? He's interviewing the staff in the dining room?"

"Yes, of course, Sergeant."

The Sergeant continued to the Queen's quarters and lightly tapped on the door.

"Enter," came back a reply.

Entering the chamber he bowed in respect, then stood upright. "Good morning, your Highness. I understand you want to speak to me."

The Queen was having her hair done by one of her maids. A pretty maid… One of the pretty maids standing in a row in contrary Mary's garden. The Queen spoke to her.

"That'll be all for now, Felicity."

Turning to the Sergeant, the Queen asked, "How do you like my new hair style?" oscillating her head from side-to-side to show off her new hair style.

"It's excellent, Ma'am. It makes you look ten years younger - although you never do look old in the first place."

It never does any harm to compliment royalty, does it?

"Oh, Sergeant. You're the perfect gentleman. I do hope you are flirting with me," she smiled cheerfully.

The Sergeant blushed profusely. "Absolutely not, Ma'am. What would the King say?" smiling back.

The Queen turned to Felicity. "Felicity, my dear. I told you that it would be a good idea to change my hair style for something new. See? The men are admiring it already."

"Yes, Ma'am," answered the maid.

"If you've finished, you can go now."

"Yes, Ma'am. May I just have a quick word with the Sergeant before I leave?"

"Of course, my dear."

The Queen busied herself in front of her mirror as the maid approached the Sergeant.

"Sergeant, I understand that you are investigating Bo Peep's missing sheep."

"Yes, Ma'am, I am. Have you got any information that you would like to pass on to me?"

"I don't know. It may be nothing."

"Well, you tell me what you want to tell me, and I'll decide if it's nothing. Okay?"

The maid thought for a moment, then spoke. "When you went to see contrary Mary on Monday afternoon, do you remember seeing me queuing to buy some flowers?"

"Yes," answered the Sergeant, "I went to Mary's cottage to ask about the missing sheep."

"Well, I think I may have seen somebody stealing the sheep on Monday morning."

The Sergeant thought about interviewing the maid there and then, but thought better of it when he noticed the Queen tapping her fingers on her desk in irritation. The Queen clearly wanted to continue her business with him.

Licking the tip of his pencil and making a brief note in his notebook, he said to the maid, "Tell you what. Why don't you come down to the station this afternoon to make a formal statement?" Turning to the Queen he asked, "Is that okay with you. Ma'am?"

The Queen returned a bored look and answered, "I suppose so." Her patience was now beginning to wear thin as she waited for some attention.

"Okay?" asked the Sergeant, looking at the maid.

"Yes, Sergeant."

The maid curtsied, departed from the Queen's chamber and closed the door behind her.

"How can I help you, Ma'am?" asked the Sergeant.

The Queen went to a cupboard and took out a brown paper bag with the King's cypher on it.

Handing the bag to the Sergeant, she said, "I made a fresh batch of tarts yesterday. I've instructed cook to send some down to the station for your staff, but I've put twelve in this bag especially for you."

Bowing to the Queen, the Sergeant took the bag and replied, "That's very kind of you Ma'am. I sincerely hope you've got some left over to give to the king," remembering how much the King enjoys the Queen's tarts. "I'd hate to think that you need to make another batch for him because you've given all your delicious tarts away."

It never does any harm to compliment royalty, does it?

"Oh, he won't mind. Anyway, baking tarts helps me to pass the time. It can get pretty boring up here at the castle, sometimes," placing her hand on the Sergeant's arm.

An alarming thought jumped... No, crashed into the Sergeant's head. *'Blimey! SHE's FLIRTING with me!'*

He took a discrete step back, and bowed after thanking the Queen for the tarts. Backing out of the chamber, he quietly closed the door behind him and made his way to the dining room.

Pc Griller had finished interviewing all the staff except the Knave.

"Is this going to take long?" asked the Knave.

His eyes darted around the room shiftily, as if he was looking for something or someone to appear.

"I'm sure the Sergeant will be with us shortly," answered a dispassionate Griller.

"I've got things to do, you know," pleaded the Knave.

"I'm sure you have, sir."

The discussion was brought to an abrupt end as the door to the dining room opened.

The Sergeant entered with the words "Sorry to keep you waiting, gentlemen."

The Knave looked even more nervous than when he was alone with Griller. The Sergeant sat opposite him.

"Griller, will you see if you can find another bag for these things - a bag without the King's cypher on it?" placing the bag on the table.

Taking hold of the bag, Griller answered, "Yes Sarg," and left the room.

"Now...," continued the Sergeant, looking directly into the Knave's eyes. "Where were you when the Queen's tarts went missing on Tuesday morning?"

"Er, busy."

"Busy where?"

A Pause, then, "Busy cleaning shoes in the kitchen. Ask the cook."

"I'm sure that PC Griller has already asked her."

The Knave suddenly changed his mind.

"Wait! No! I've just remembered. I was in the corridor, on my way to the kitchen to clean the shoes."

"And then?"

"And then nothing. I went to the kitchen and cleaned the shoes. Ask the cook."

"What did you do after you had cleaned the shoes?"

"Can't remember. I think I went out somewhere."

"Where?"

"Can't remember."

Griller entered the dining room carrying a different bag.

The Sergeant continued his interview. "On Tuesday morning, where were you when the Queen cried out?"

"In the Kitchen."

"But the Queen was in the pantry - which is in the kitchen. You couldn't have been in the kitchen with her because the butler met you in the corridor."

"Oh, yes. Now I remember." The Knave was beginning to sweat. "I was just returning from the stables and I heard the Queen scream. As I ran down the corridor towards the kitchen I met the butler."

"Okay. What were you doing yesterday morning?"

"Yesterday morning?"

"Yes, yesterday morning."

Once more, the Knave looked around the room, nervously. "Er, down town."

"Where down town?"

"Shopping, I think."

"You seem to have a poor memory, Knave. Let me help you out, a little. What were you doing down by the railway station?"

The knave sat there, dumbstruck. He knew that he had been rumbled and he decided that being quiet and not answering any questions might get him out of trouble.

Wrong!

The Sergeant poked him some more. "Let me help you out a bit more. What were you doing behind a market stall down by the railway station?"

The Knave's shoulders dropped in silent resignation.

"Lost your tongue? Shall I tell you what you were doing?"

The Knave just stared at the Policemen.

"You were selling the Queen's tarts weren't you? The tarts that you stole on Tuesday morning. Has your memory returned yet?"

The Knave just nodded and lowered his head onto his chin in submission.

"Put him in the cell, Griller."

The knave stood, to be accompanied to the cell and asked, "What will you tell the queen? She'll surely have my head on a pole for this."

"Why did you steal the tarts?" asked Griller.

"I just fancied some. They look so nice. You know, the Queen never gives us, the staff, any perks. She's as tight as a screw cap on a bottle of lemonade, yet she never thinks about giving any of the staff something nice. I didn't think she would miss a few tarts. Anyway, they tasted awful. I ate just half of one, threw the other half out the window for the pigeons, then decided to sell the rest. The pigeons didn't even like them. I saw that half chewed tart still sat on the grass when I went out the other day, untouched by the birds."

Griller and the Sergeant looked at each other and sighed.

"Sit down," ordered the Sergeant. "Look," he continued, "I'm not going to take any action against you - this time - but you're going to have to do something to earn your freedom."

"Anything. What?"

"We're going to take these tarts to the King…," passing his bag of tarts to the Knave, "…and you're going to admit what you've done. We'll let the king decide what to do with you."

The Knave breathed a sigh of relief and took hold of the bag.

"Thank you, Sergeant," he said, shaking the Sergeant's hand vigorously.

"Don't thank me yet. We still don't know what the King will do. Shall we make our way to him?"

Before leaving the dining room, the Sergeant turned to Griller.

"Griller, go back to the station and wait for me there with Slack."

"Yes Sarg."

The Sergeant and the Knave made their way to the King's chamber. The Sergeant instructed the Knave to "Wait here," before knocking lightly on the door and waiting for the anticipated command.

"Enter!"

Both the King and the Queen were in residence.

After bowing before them he opened the conversation. "Good day, your Highness. Good morning, Ma'am. Please forgive me for disturbing you, but my enquiries about your missing tarts, Ma'am, have been completed and the perpetrator is waiting outside the door."

"Who is it?" asked the King.

"The Knave, sir, and I can assure you that he is more than regretful for his actions."

The Queen spoke up. "Off with his head!" she demanded.

The King quickly reminded the Queen, "No, no, my dear. We don't do that any more, do we?"

"Oh… I forgot," she replied.

The King shouted to the Knave. "Knave! Get in here!"

The door opened slowly and the Knave entered the chamber.

Standing by the door, the Knave bowed to the King and Queen and then lowered his head in disgrace.

The King ordered the Knave to step forward. "What have you got to say for yourself?" he asked.

"Well, sir, I confess to stealing the Queen's tarts on Tuesday morning."

The Knave immediately looked down at the floor after speaking.

The Queen once more demanded, "Can't we chop off his head, just this once?"

"No dear," interjected the King, "you know that we don't do that to the staff any more."

The Queen shrugged her shoulders in disappointment.

"What have you got there?" asked the King.

The Knave handed over the bag of tarts that the Sergeant had given him and promised never to steal again.

"What shall we do with him, Sergeant?"

"The Queen jumped in with "Put him on the racks!"

The demand was ignored by the King and the Sergeant.

"Well, sir, Griller and myself have interrogated the Knave quite extensively, and we're both of the opinion that he is ashamed of what he has done. I don't think that the crime is worth disturbing Judge Fairly, but I do know that Griller will be the first to put handcuffs on him if he steals again. I'm sure the Knave is repentant."

"How is Griller?" asked the King. "I heard about him returning that lamb to young Mary. A first class chap, what?"

"He is, sir. One of my best men."

"You've only got two."

"Yes, sir, and the other one, PC Slack, is a good policeman, as well. What do you want to do about the Knave?"

"Oh. Yes. The Knave."

The King turned back towards the Knave.

"I've listened to what the Sergeant has said in your favour, and as you appear to have replaced the missing tarts I'm going to give you a punishment befitting your actions. If you act like a naughty schoolboy, then you must expect to be treated like one."

"Clap him in irons!" interjected the Queen, again ignored by all.

The King gave out his sentence to the Knave. "I think a few weeks of community service will be sufficient. A bit of weeding and dog walking and clothes ironing will teach you a lesson, but don't neglect your normal duties here in the castle. If you steal again the Queen knows where there is a very sharp axe. Okay?"

The Knave bowed, thanked the king for his consideration and backed out of the chamber, well and truly reprimanded.

The Queen huffed in disappointment…

CHAPTER 27

Lucy Locket lost her pocket,
Kitty Fisher found it.
Not a penny was there in it,
Only ribbon round it.
(English, early 19th century. First recorded by James Orchard Halliwell in 1842)

Week 1. Friday, mid-morning.

Bowing with every step, the Knave reversed out of the King's chamber and closed the door behind him. The King smiled at the policemen.

"Thank you, both, for getting to the bottom of the missing tarts. I would never have guessed that the Knave had taken them, and I would never have heard the last of it from the Queen," laughed the King. "Well done."

"Thank you, sir," responded the Sergeant, with a bow of his head.

The Queen stepped forward and handed the Sergeant the bag of tarts that the Knave had passed on to the King… The tarts that the Queen had originally given to the Sergeant and the ones that the Sergeant had given to the Knave.

"Thank you, Sergeant, for all your hard work. Please give these tarts to your team with my thanks to them for solving this crime. If I had my way the Knave's head would be inside this bag instead of the tarts!"

"No, dear," interrupted the King, "You know those days are over. We really MUST respect the staff's lives."

"Yes, dear…," answered the Queen with a sigh, eyes looking up in submission.

The Sergeant and Griller bid their farewell and departed from the castle.

Down at the square/car park the Sergeant found his bike lying on the ground in the slot that the bike's leaning post, the Rolls Royce, had previously occupied. Griller's bike was still propped up against someone's Mini. Retrieving their bikes, the two policemen approached the gate. The guard Commander had come out of his hut and was approaching them.

"The King's driver asks you NOT to lean your bike up against the King's car, sir. He asks if you could find another car to lean it on. Perhaps the butler's car...," pointing to a rusty old banger parked in a space away from all the other cars, as if it was in isolation for being so rusty.

The Sergeant just nodded and caught up with Griller, waiting outside the castle gates.

"Back to the station," he said and they both pedalled away from the castle gates.

*

It's still Friday, mid-morning (Week 1).

Back at the station, PC Slack had returned from Tommy Tucker's cottage and was catching up on a few reports as he stood behind the reception desk. The Station door opened and Kitty Fisher entered.

"Hello, Kitty," he welcomed. "What brings you here today?"

"I was just on my way to the shops and I saw Wee Willy Winkie throw this purse into some bushes. I thought I ought to hand it in because it looks expensive."

She passed the purse over to Slack.

Inspecting it closely, Slack said, "Doesn't feel like there's any money in it. Shall we take a look inside?"

Opening the drawstring he looked inside the purse and pulled out a length of decorative ribbon.

"Nope," he continued, "just this ribbon. I was hoping it had someone's name or address in it."

He re-tightened the drawstring and put the purse into a brown bag.

"I'll pop it into Lost & Found to see if anyone claims it. If no-one does claim it within six weeks I'll give you a call to come and pick it up, and it's yours."

Kitty replied, "It's an expensive purse, so I'm sure that someone will claim it."

"Maybe, but I'll let you know either way, Kitty. Thanks for bringing it in. I'm sure someone will appreciate your good turn."

Kitty left the station, and Slack put the purse into the Lost & Found locker. He then phoned the TV station to ask to speak to Chatty Chaste. She answered as soon as the TV station receptionist put her through to Slack.

"Hiya, Slack. How's things? Any decent news for me?"

"Hi Chatty. I'm phoning to ask you for a favour."

"For you - anything, but it'll cost you a dinner at my place - followed by a coffee…"

"I thought you'd never ask, especially as I stood on the cat's tail last time I was at your place. That put the damper on things, didn't it?"

"Just a bit. Anyway, What's this favour you want from me?"

"What looks to be an expensive purse has just been handed in to the station. I wondered if you could put out a call to anyone that wishes to claim it to contact me at the station."

"That's an easy favour. I'll make sure the cat isn't anywhere near the bedroom when you come round."

"It's a deal. I'll be round after my shift ends at about six, p.m., and forget the dinner."

"See you later..."

PC Slack and Chatty Chaste have been 'friends' for some time, now.

*

NEWS FLASH from Chatty Chaste on the news desk at Rhyme Place TV station.

Chatty - "We'll be back to Cooking In The Kitchen in just a few moments after we've taken a short break," tapping the papers together on the desk in front of her.

She then continued, "Before the break, however, I've just got a quick message for you... An expensive purse has been found and handed in to Rhyme Place police station. PC Slack is anxious to find the owner of this purse and he can be contacted at the police station any time between eight a.m. and six, p.m. Please don't try to contact him after six, p.m. because I do know that he will be extremely busy with other things. Now it's time for the break, so don't go away - Cooking In The Kitchen will be back with you shortly."

CHAPTER 28

Week 1. Friday, p.m.

Earlier, the Sergeant and PC Griller had returned to the station - with a bag of tarts.

The remainder of that morning was quiet, so all the policemen were now catching up on some long overdue paperwork. The Sergeant took a call from the hospital.

"Sergeant Argent? It's the ward nurse here at the hospital. PC Slack asked me to let you know when Jack or Jill woke up."

"Which one is awake?" asked the Sergeant.

"Both of them. We discontinued the sleep medication last night because they both showed some improvement and they regained consciousness at about twelve fifteen today. They should be ready for you to see them tomorrow morning, after breakfast."

"That's good. Slack and myself will be there around about ten, a.m. Is that okay?"

"Perfect."

The Sergeant turned to his PC's and told them about his telephone conversation with the hospital.

"Griller, tomorrow morning, when we go to the hospital, perhaps you could get Wee Willie Winkie in here to ask him what he knows about that purse. I'd be interested to know why he didn't hand it in."

"Will do, Sarg."

"You've got a call to make today, haven't you?" the Sergeant asked Griller.

"Yeah, I promised Mrs. Porgie that I would meet Georgie from school today."

"Okay. You'd better get along there. They'll be chucking out, soon."

Griller picked up his hat and departed from the police station.

The station doorbell rang. Slack answered it. Standing outside was a pretty maid - one of the pretty maids that were queuing in contrary Mary's garden. The same pretty maid that the Sergeant had met up at the castle. Slack invited her in.

Approaching the desk she reminded the Sergeant that he had asked her to make a statement about the missing sheep.

"Come into the interview room," invited the Sergeant, "and I'll take your statement there."

They both disappeared into the interview room.

*

Griller waited outside the school gates until chucking out time.

A flood of schoolchildren poured out of the school as if a dam wall had just failed, laughing, skipping, holding hands and singing. Griller had closed one of the school's double gates to restrict the flow of kids out of the school yard. Eventually, Georgie Porgie came into view.

The policeman watched him dashing round the yard, trying to kiss the girls. Many of them were able to swat him away with the words, "I'm telling teacher…," but a few burst into tears as he ran away from them.

Eventually, Georgie noticed the policeman standing at the gates, watching what he was doing. The sight of Griller made him suddenly look innocent and he made his way to the gates. Griller was having none of that.

"Georgie," he said, as Georgie arrived at the gates, "come with me."

The children all stopped walking and fell into silence as Griller took Georgie by the arm and marched him away from the gates.

Across the road, he faced Georgie and asked, "Why were you dashing round kissing the girls and making them cry?"

Georgie knew he had been rumbled, and chose the silent route of answering questions.

"Lost your tongue, have you?"

Still no answer. Georgie just stared at the pavement.

"Well, perhaps you'll answer my questions down at the station," declared the PC and proceeded to take Georgie by the arm and march him towards the police station.

"My mum will be angry with you for not letting me go home," proffered Georgie.

"Really? How about I give her a ring when we get to the station to let her know where you are?"

No answer.

With all the children looking on and chattering about Georgie's 'arrest', Griller marched the boy to the station. One of the children went back into the school to tell teacher.

*

Back at the station, the Sergeant finished interviewing the pretty maid, thanked her for coming in and opened the door for her to leave.

Placing the pretty maid's statement in the missing sheep file, he smiled a self-assured smile. He now had a name that he could put to the sheep thief.

Slack noticed the Sergeant's smile and asked, "Good news?"

"Yeah, I'll say"

*

The station door opened and Griller and Georgie entered the station.

The Sergeant gave Griller his instructions for the next day.

"Tomorrow, when you pick up Wee Willie Winkie, put him in the interview room and don't let him out. If he makes a fuss, put him in one of the cells."

"Will do. What about asking about the purse?"

"I'll ask. Just hold him."

"Okay."

The Sergeant then asked, "What have we got here, then?"

"Georgie Porgie, Sarg. He keeps kissing the girls and making them cry."

"Oh?" The Sergeant strode up to Georgie. "Is that so?"

No answer, just a stare down at the floor.

"Oh dear," said the Sergeant. "It seems that Georgie is trying the silent answer routine. Put him in the cell, Griller. Maybe that will loosen his tongue."

Georgie's head shot back and he looked, wide eyed at the policemen.

"My mum will get you into trouble if you do."

"Really? Shall we give Mrs. Porgie a phone call, Slack? Griller, put him in the cell."

"No! Don't do that! I'll talk," blurted out Georgie, tears now forming in his eyes.

"Take him to the interview room," instructed the Sergeant, "and stay with him until Mrs. Porgie gets here."

"Yes, Sarg."

Sitting Georgie in a chair across from the interview desk, Griller sat in a chair in the corner of the room and kept his eye on Georgie, who was now crying his eyes out. Georgie's knees felt like rubber, so he was glad of the chair that he had been told to sit on.

Mrs. Porgie entered the station about half an hour later.

"Good afternoon, Mrs. Porgie. Georgie is waiting for us in the interview room."

She smiled at the Sergeant. "Is PC Griller around?" she asked.

"He's sitting in with Georgie. Shall we go and see how they are?"

Mrs. Porgie and the Sergeant entered the interview room, much to the relief of Georgie. He stood and ran into his mum's arms.

"What have you been up to?" she asked.

"Nothing, mum."

"Nothing? People don't get arrested by the police for doing nothing, do they?"

Georgie just looked into Mum's face. He wiped the tears from his cheeks with his sleeve.

The Sergeant spoke up. "PC Griller tells me that he witnessed this naughty boy kissing the girls and making them cry. Is that right, Georgie?"

Georgie looked at his mum and answered, "I was only messing about, Mum. One of the boys at school dared me to do it. I didn't mean any harm, honest."

"You do know that it's wrong, don't you?" Mum asked.

"I didn't mean to upset anybody. We all thought it was a laugh, that's all."

"Supposing I put him in the cell until Judge Fairly can see him?" asked Griller.

Tears, once more, streamed down his face. "No, Mum. Don't let them do that. I won't do it again, I promise," he sobbed.

Mrs. Porgie looked at Griller and asked, "What shall I do with him Mr. Griller. He's naughty a lot of the time and he won't do what I tell him."

Griller pulled up his chair and sat opposite Georgie. "Is that right, Georgie? Are you naughty at home?"

"Yes, sir, but I promise not to be naughty again. I promise."

"And you're going to keep that promise?" asked Griller.

"Yes, sir."

"Well, Georgie. I can't let what you've done go unpunished, can I?"

"No, sir."

"Okay. Here's what we're going to do..." The policeman took out his notebook, licked the end of his pencil authoritatively, and wrote something down.

Handing the paper to Georgie he instructed, "Read that out so we can all hear it."

Georgie took the paper, read it. Then, reading from the paper, he spoke. "I, Georgie Porgie, do promise to stop annoying the girls at school, and I promise to apologise to every girl that I've upset. I promise to help my mum around the house, I promise to work hard at school and do all my homework, and I promise to stop being a naughty boy."

He put the paper down, on the desk.

Griller gave him the pencil and instructed, "Now sign your name at the bottom of the statement - in your best handwriting."

Georgie concentrated on writing his name, then handed the pencil back to Griller. Griller swept up the paper and warned Georgie, "I'm going to hang on to this, Georgie, and if I hear about you being naughty, or not keeping any of these promises you know what will happen, don't you?"

"Yes, sir."

"What?"

"You'll put me in a cell until Judge Fairly can see me."

"That's right, Georgie. I'll be watching you…"

"I'll keep my promises, sir."

Georgie was allowed to leave the station with his Mum, his head hanging low in shame. On the way out, Mrs. Porgie nodded a thank you to Griller.

When they were gone Griller screwed up the declaration and threw it in the bin.

"I don't think we'll be hearing from him again," he said to the Sergeant.

CHAPTER 29

Friday evening (Week 1).

The three policemen were about to lock up for the night when the doorbell rang. Slack went to answer it.

Opening the door, he was confronted by Lucy Locket and her mum. The policeman stood to one side to let the two women in.

Tidying up some files, the Sergeant looked up and welcomed Lucy and her mum. "Good evening, Mrs. Locket. What can I do for you?"

"We've come about that purse that was found. We heard the TV broadcast about it this morning and it belongs to me," declared Mrs. Locket.

"Slack, can you get the purse out of Lost & Found, please?"

The PC dashed off to retrieve the purse.

"He'll just be two ticks," advised the Sergeant. "Perhaps you can describe the purse for me?"

"Yes, it's a brushed leather purse in a pink embroidered bag with a green drawstring to close the bag. The purse, itself, is a single pocket purse with a silver clasp. It's about four inches wide."

Slack returned carrying the evidence bag with the purse safely sealed inside it, and handed it to the Sergeant. Carefully opened the evidence bag and inspecting the purse, the Sergeant saw that it was exactly as Mrs. Locket had described.

Showing it to her, he asked, "Is this your purse?"

"Yes, that's the one," she exclaimed, "there should be a length of ribbon and a lot of loose change inside."

Slack spoke up. "When it was handed in, Mrs. Locket, there was just this piece of ribbon tied round the bag," taking out the ribbon from inside the purse and showing it to Mrs. Locket.

"There was no money inside?" she asked.

The Sergeant answered, "Afraid not. How did you come to lose it?"

Mrs. Locket turned to Lucy and instructed, "Tell them what happened, Lucy. It's okay, dear, you're not in any trouble."

Hesitantly, Lucy explained how she lost the purse. "Well, I had just been to town to buy that ribbon for Mum. I put the change from Mum's five pound note in the purse and I put the ribbon and the purse in the bag…"

The Sergeant interrupted, while taking notes. "How much change?" he asked.

"There was three pounds and fifty-five pence. The ribbon cost one pound, forty-five pence."

"Go on," prompted the Sergeant.

"Well, as I was walking down the road towards our cottage, this man came from behind me and snatched the bag from my hand. He twisted my little finger as he pulled the bag from my hand and it really hurt."

Lucy showed the Sergeant her little finger. There was nothing to see, but the Sergeant sympathised, anyway.

"That's a lot of money for someone so young…," he said to Mrs. Locket.

"Yes, I know," she replied, "but I only had a five pound note at the time. I didn't expect her to be robbed."

"No, I guess not," answered the Sergeant. "I'm afraid that I need to hang on to this for a while because it is evidence of a crime that has been committed. I'll let you have it back as soon as possible, but it may be some time."

Looking down at Lucy he asked, “Do you know who took it?”

“Yes. It was wee Willie Winkie.”

A hush descended on the room as the three policemen looked at each other.

The Sergeant turned to PC Griller. “I think you had better get Willie Winkie in here as soon as possible. Don’t let on what for, just bring him in… In handcuffs, if necessary.”

Griller nodded in agreement. The Sergeant turned back to Mrs. Locket.

“Mrs. Locket, thank you for bringing Lucy in to speak to us. Would you and Lucy be good enough to give a statement to PC Slack in the interview room, before you leave?”

“Yes, of course,” came back a response.

Slack accompanied Lucy and her mum to the interview room.

The Sergeant turned to Griller and said, “I want this man brought in, Griller. I don’t care what you have to do. Just bring him in.”

“Yes Sarg. First thing tomorrow morning.”

CHAPTER 30

Doctor Foster went to Gloucester
In a shower of rain.
He stepped in a puddle
Right up to his middle,
And never went there again!
(English, 1844)

Week 1. Saturday, a.m.

This morning is a miserable morning. It is cold, and windy, and the rain was almost horizontal as it pounded the windows in Rhyme Place. It was doubtful that anyone would be going out, today, much to the annoyance of the fairground community. Their takings, today, will most probably be non-existent unless the weather improves.

By the time PC Slack had arrived for duty at the police station, PC Griller was on the hunt for Wee Willie Winkie. The driving rain made it extremely uncomfortable, but Griller gritted his teeth and ploughed on.

The station doors were flung open by Slack as the Sergeant was donning his wet weather gear to go to the hospital. Slack kept his poncho on and he patiently waited for the Sergeant to wrap up against the inclement weather.

Doctor Foster was blown through the station door and he quickly turned and slammed the door shut. Watched by the two policemen, he approached the reception desk.

"I'd like to make a complaint!" he declared, angrily.

Slack got a piece of paper, licked the end of a pencil that was removed from his top pocket, and asked, "A complaint, you say, sir? What would that be?"

"I want to complain about the state of the footpath outside my surgery."

The PC looked silently at the Doctor, waiting for him to continue.

"Is the highways department open yet?" demanded the Doctor.

"I'm afraid not, sir. Opening times are nine to five, weekdays only, closed Saturdays and Sundays."

The PC rummaged under the desk and fetched out a four page form for the Doctor to fill in. Pushing this across the counter, the PC continued, "If you'd care to fill out this complaint form, sir, I'll get it upstairs to the highways department on Monday morning."

In a frustrated tone, the Doctor asked, "Do I have to fill this in? Can't you just go upstairs and tell them about the problem?"

"Afraid not, sir. They do like their forms to be filled in. What is the problem, anyway?"

"I left my surgery this morning to go to Gloucester and I tripped over a bloody pothole in the middle of the pavement. It's a danger to pedestrians. I've got better things to do than to tend to people who have got bruising because they have tripped over some stupid pothole that should have been repaired long ago!" He took a breath. "I've now got a tear in my trousers and I'm going to have to change them. It's going to make me late for my appointment!" he shouted, angrily.

"I'll certainly pass on your comments when I take your completed complaints form upstairs on Monday, sir."

"And another thing…," Doctor Foster barked, "It's about time Bo Peep did something about her sheep."

"Sheep?" The PC's ear pricked up. "What about the sheep?"

"They're roaming about all over the place, shitting everywhere people want to walk. It's a disgrace. She should be made to clean it all up throughout the town."

PC Slack was now beginning to show some interest in the Doctor's rants.

"Where, precisely are these sheep, sir?"

"All over the place. There's at least two of them eating my flowers in the front garden."

Slack pushed the complaints form back over the counter towards the Doctor, asked him to "just complete the relevant sections," and invited him to sit at a low table in front of the reception chairs.

The PC turned to face the Sergeant who was in his office with his head buried deep in a file. "Sarg, Doctor Foster has seen Bo Peep's missing sheep."

"Really…?" he came out of his office to sit next to the Doctor. "Good Morning, Doctor. Whereabouts did you see the sheep?"

The Doctor looked up and answered, "They're all over the high street. Somebody's going to have an accident if those sheep are not penned, especially as they're dropping sheep shit everywhere. It's beginning to stink the place out."

"Okay, calm down, Doctor. I'll see to it immediately."

"I should think so…," demanded the Doctor.

The Sergeant picked up the telephone receiver and dialled the hospital.

"Hello, this is Sergeant Argent down at the police station," he advised. "You've got a couple of PC's there looking after Jack and Jill."

"Yes, Sergeant. Do you want to speak to them?" answered the duty nurse.

"Can you ask PC Peecie to come to the phone, please?"

He heard the clunk of the phone being put onto the desk. After a couple of minutes PC Peecie picked it up.

"Peecie here, Sarg."

"Peecie, can you come down to the station straight away. We've got some sheep to round up."

"On my way, Sarg."

The Sergeant then dialled Bo Peep's number. While he waited for an answer he asked Slack, "Has PC Griller found Wee Willie Winkie, yet?"

"Don't know, Sarg."

"Okay, get on the radio to him and ask him to meet us in the high street."

"Yes Sarg."

Bo Peep answered the Sergeant's call. "Hello Sergeant Argent. Is this a social call?"

"Unfortunately not, Miss Peep. I think we may have found your sheep. I'm getting a few men together to round them up and we'll herd them into your paddock."

"Oh, heaven… I'll open the paddock gate for you."

"No need for you to turn out in this weather, Miss Peep. I'm sure my team will manage."

"You're so kind, Sergeant. I'll put the kettle on for a nice cup of tea for you and your men when you get here."

Putting everything away and locking up the cupboards and internal doors, the Sergeant asked the Doctor, "Would you mind leaving the form in the tray on my desk and closing the door on your way out, Doctor. I'll release the lock, so the door should lock automatically when you close it."

"Yes, of course, Sergeant."

The Sergeant and PC Slack made their way to the high street.

The rain had eased, slightly, and the two policemen went to meet PC Griller and PC Peecie to round up some sheep.

CHAPTER 31

Little Bo Peep has lost her sheep…

Leave them alone and they'll come home,
wagging their tails behind them.

Week 1. Saturday, a.m.

The Sergeant and PC Slack met Griller and Peecie on the way to the high street. The rain stopped watering everything and the sun poked its face through the clouds.

"Couldn't find Willie Winkie, then?"

"No, Sarg," answered Griller, "I reckon he's been given the nod that we want to talk to him and he's now gone to ground."

"He'll turn up."

The four policemen sauntered to the village high street and came across two of Bo Peep's sheep feasting on Doctor Foster's flowers.

"Let's find the other two before we disturb these two," decided the Sergeant, and the policemen split up to comb the streets of the village.

Griller was the first to find one of the loose sheep. Shooing this towards the Doctor's house, he shouted to his colleagues, "Got one! On its way to the garden."

The sheep dodged from left to right, but had nowhere to go in the narrow street except towards the main road. Slack met Griller and the sheep as they emerged into the main street and helped shepherd this towards the Doctor's garden.

The Sergeant heard PC Peecie shout, "Got the three legged one. Bringing him in." This particular sheep wasn't as agile as the sheep that Griller had found, so didn't take much shepherding.

When Griller and Slack arrived at the doctor's garden they found it empty. The two original sheep were nowhere to be seen.

"Didn't you close the gate?" asked Griller.

"No, thought you'd done it."

Muttering profanities, Griller and Slack eventually managed to guide their sheep into the garden. Griller closed the gate and made sure it stayed closed. Peecie appeared with the three legged sheep. This was also steered into the garden. The Doctor's garden was, by now beginning to look like Old MacDonald's farmyard - all ploughed up by the sheep's hooves, no flowers, lots of sheep shit.

Peecie commented, "He's going to have some nice flowers when that lot's been dug in," nodding towards a pile of sheep shit.

Griller replied, "He had some nice flowers before the sheep arrived…!"

"Oh, well," interjected Slack, "I'm glad I won't be around when he gets home."

So, there were two sheep in the Doctor's garden, once more, and the three policemen went on the hunt for the other two.

"Found 'em!" shouted the Sergeant. "We're in Mrs. Tucker's back garden."

The three PC's dashed round to the Tucker's back garden to retrieve the sheep and bring them to join the two in the Doctor's garden. With all four sheep now in the Doctor's garden, the policemen talked tactics on how to get them to Bo Peep's paddock.

The Doctor appeared and looked in horror at the ploughed-up mess of a front garden. He went ballistic, stamping his feet and shouting about the state of his garden and all the sheep shit in it.

Slack didn't help much by commenting, "At least you'll have lots of rhubarb…" much to the amusement of his colleagues.

PC Peecie joined in the merriment by commenting, "Nah, sheep shit is better for cabbages than rhubarb."

Griller then added, "He'll get first prize at the village fair for years!"

The policemen burst into fits of uncontrollable laughter. The Doctor just stood and gawked at them, lost for words.

The Sergeant brought the PC's back down to earth. "All right, you lot. Let's get these sheep back to Bo Peep's paddock, shall we?"

Turning to the Doctor, he said, "Don't worry about your garden, Doctor. I'll have a word with Bo Peep and see if there's any way she can help you out with this," pointing to the garden.

Someone in the street behind the policemen piped up, "We'll do it…"

The policemen and the Doctor turned to see Bo Peep, contrary Mary, the woman from the shoe house and Mrs. Tucker facing them and smiling, all grasping an assortment of garden forks, trowels and spades.

Contrary Mary added, "I'll bring some of my flower cuttings for you to plant, Doctor."

The Doctor made some appreciative noises and then stood back for the Sergeant to open his garden gate. Before doing so, the Sergeant looked at his watch and said to the PC's, "I've got to get along to the hospital now, chaps. I'm sure you'll be okay getting these sheep back to Bo's paddock without me."

The women all chipped in , "We'll help."

The gate was opened and the townsfolk began shepherding the sheep back to Bo Peep's paddock, little Tommy Tucker and Simple Simon bringing up the rear with buckets and spades to pick up the sheep droppings that had been deposited onto the street.

The Sergeant made his way to the hospital to interview Jack and Jill.

CHAPTER 32

Ding dong bell,
Pussy's in the well.
Who put her in?
Little Johnny Green.
Who pulled her out?
Little Tommy Stout.
(English - earliest recorded reference
by John Lant c.1580)

Week 1. Saturday, late a.m.

All four sheep safely returned to Bo Peep, the Rhyme Place residents and PC Peecie set about repairing the Doctor's Garden. Bo Peep stayed with the sheep to settle them down in the paddock. PC Griller decided to call in on Mary Lamb, "to see how the lamb was getting on…"

Slack returned to the station to write up his reports on the morning's activities. As he wrote in the day's report book, the telephone rang.

"PC Slack, this is the vehicle licensing department, upstairs."

"What can I do for you chaps?" asked Slack.

"Nothing. I've got that information you asked for, and wondered if you could come upstairs and get it off my desk."

"Oh? What information was that?"

"On Thursday afternoon you asked me to identify the owner of a green truck - remember?"

"Oh! Yes! That! I forgot all about it. I'll be up there right away.

*

The Sergeant cycled to the hospital. On arrival, he parked his bike up against a bollard in the car park, next to a parked 4x4, and walked to the hospital reception desk.

"Good morning, Sergeant," smiled the receptionist.

"Good morning. I've come to talk to Jack and Jill, if it's okay."

"Ah, yes, Sergeant. I think they are both awake."

The receptionist phoned Jack and Jill's ward and spoke to the ward nurse. Replacing the telephone receiver, she confirmed, "It's okay for you to go up to the ward, Sergeant. They're both talking to PC Polite."

The Sergeant made his way upstairs to Jack and Jill's ward. PC Good was sat outside the ward, reading a newspaper. Seeing the Sergeant, he quickly buried the newspaper behind him and stood to face the Sergeant.

"Everything is all quiet here, Sarg."

"I've noticed…" looking at the screwed up newspaper.

The Sergeant knocked on the door and entered the private room. PC Polite immediately stood up from the chair that was positioned next to the door and faced the Sergeant.

"Everything is all quiet here, Sarg."

The Sergeant nodded and sat in the visitor's chair in between Jack's and Jill's beds.

Facing Jill, he spoke up, pencil and notebook at the ready. "Good morning Jill. How are you both, today?"

"We're okay," answered Jill. "We woke up yesterday."

"Yes, I was told, but I decided to wait until you were both well enough to provide a statement."

Handing his pencil and notebook over to PC Polite, he asked the PC to take the notes.

"Do you remember what happened?"

"I'm not sure," answered Jill. She continued after some thought, "I doubt that Jack will be able to tell you much," looking at Jack.

The Sergeant turned towards Jack. "Over to you, Jack. What can you tell me about your accident?"

"Well, not a lot, really. Jill and myself arrived at the top of the hill and I think I was pushed. I remember flying for about three seconds, then everything went black when I landed and banged my head. I honestly don't remember anything else."

"So you don't remember who pushed you, or why?"

"No, sir."

Turning round to face Jill, the Sergeant asked, "Okay, Jill. From the beginning. What were you doing at the top of the hill?"

"On Monday, Jack and myself went up the hill to fetch a pail of water. As you know, the well is on the other side of the hill, so we decided to go the quickest route straight over the top of the hill."

"Is that the same well that little Johnny Green dropped the cat in?"

There was a look of puzzlement on Jack's and Jill's faces as they turned to look at each other.

"Johnny Green?" asked Jill.

"Yes," reminded the Sergeant, "the one that little Tommy Stout rescued the cat from."

"Oh, that one - Yes that's the well we were going to."

"... And?"

"It's just like Jack said. The same bloke suddenly appeared out of the bushes and pushed us both over the edge. The next thing I know we were being woken by a nurse, here at the hospital."

"Why would he push you both over the edge?" asked the Sergeant.

"I don't know," answered Jill, hands turned upwards in puzzlement.

"Is there anything else that you remember - something that would have a bearing on what the guy was doing up there?"

Jill paused for another thought. "No, I'm sorry. Apart from what I've told you, everything else is a blank."

"You don't remember the grand old Duke of York and his men carrying you to the ambulance?"

"No. Nothing…"

There was a long pause as Jill tried to remember what actually happened, but nothing came to mind.

The Sergeant looked at PC Polite and then asked Jill, "I have an idea that might help you to remember some more detail. Are you willing to give it a try?"

"Anything," answered Jill. "The sooner we get to the bottom of this, the sooner we will know what happened to us."

The Sergeant explained his idea to Jack and Jill and they both willingly agreed to it. He left the room to find a nurse.

Approaching the ward reception desk, he asked the nurse, "Is Jack and Jill's doctor available?"

"I think so. I know he had to go to Gloucester early this morning, but I'm sure he's back. I'll just page him," the nurse answered.

Her voice boomed out over the Tannoy system. "Doctor Foster. Please come to the reception desk."

Putting the microphone back down, she asked the Sergeant to wait for a few minutes. The Sergeant sat in one of the visitor chairs. After about five minutes, Doctor

Foster clattered through the swing doors and walked up to the reception desk.

"Yes, what is it?" he asked brusquely.

This guy thinks he is an important guy - a really important guy!

The nurse pointed to the Sergeant who was now stood behind the Doctor. Turning round, the Doctor demanded, "What is it Sergeant? I'm far too important to be disturbed from my rounds!"

"Good morning Doctor. It's nice to see you again," holding out a hand for shaking. The hand was ignored.

"Get on with it, Sergeant. I hope it's not about those sheep, again. I've had enough of those. It will be months before my garden is looking like it did."

"Partly, sir. I want to try an experiment with Jack and Jill, but I need some help from you chaps."

"Experiment, you say? We don't experiment on patients, Sergeant. We get them better so that they leave the hospital and stop all this bed-blocking."

This guy really does not want to do anything that will divert him away from his routine!

"It's nothing that requires medication or invasive treatment, sir. It will cost nothing, except a specialist's time, and it may well go to solving a few crimes that put Jack and Jill in hospital, not least attempted murder."

The Doctor thought for a moment and then asked, "What is it you want to do?"

"Well, sir, you're more than aware that they both presently have a - what shall we say...? A restricted memory."

The Doctor interrupted, "Correct. I can't release them until they return to normal..."

It was the Sergeant's turn to interrupt. "No, sir. I'm in the same boat in that I can't release my PC's until you release Jack and Jill. Anyway, I thought that if they were hypnotised to give me the answers that I need, it might speed up the process a little bit, and…"

He let the sentence hang in the air to give the Doctor space to think about the suggestion. After a few moments of chin rubbing and head scratching the Doctor spoke up.

"I don't suppose it will do any harm, Sergeant, but I insist on being present."

"Of course, sir. I've asked them both if they would be willing to go through with it, and they both agree that it could be a way to accelerate their recovery."

"Alright. If they agree to it then there is nothing I can do to stop them. What do you want from me?"

"I don't suppose you know anyone who is good at this kind of thing, do you, sir?"

"I have just the man in mind. He's also a Doctor in this hospital. I'll have a word with him and arrange a session for this afternoon. Three o'clock okay with you?"

"Perfect."

The two men shook hands - much to the surprise of the Sergeant - and Doctor Foster went away to arrange for Jack and Jill to be hypnotised.

CHAPTER 33

Week 1. Saturday, late a.m.

Back at the station PC Slack opened the door of the vehicle licensing department, upstairs from the police reception desk. Waiting at the department reception desk was Bently Carr, head of the department.

"Hiya Slack. How's things?"

"Not bad, Bently. Lots happening at the moment, what with Bo Peep's missing sheep and Jack and Jill's accident."

"Yeah. Heard about those on the news." Bently opened a file he had brought with him and read the information inside its cover. "I looked up the owner of that vehicle number you asked me to find. It's a green Ford Transit, registered to old MacDonald. Tax *and* insurance ran out on it a few months ago, so if you find it perhaps you could get it towed away. We've sent several reminders to old MacDonald, but he just ignores them."

"Okay. I think we know its whereabouts, so I'll get Mike, the Mechanic, to put down his guitar and pull the truck into the yard. Thanks for that, Bently. I owe you one."

"No probs."

Slack returned to his desk downstairs and radioed the Sergeant.

"Got the identity of the owner of the truck, Sarg."

The Sergeant responded, with a smile, "I bet it belongs to old MacDonald."

"Right, first time. How did you know that?"

"Oh, just a hunch. I'm at the hospital right now and won't be able to return 'till later this afternoon. While I'm here will you and Grills try to locate Wee Willie Winkie? I want to question him about Lucy's purse"

"Yep, will do Sarg."

*

Week 1. Saturday, 3.00 p.m.

It's time for Jill to be hypnotised.

Jill was chosen for this because Jack had suffered some minor brain damage during his fall and Doctor Foster didn't think he was up to being hypnotised. The Sergeant, Doctor Foster, another Doctor called Harry, and a nurse trooped into Jill's room.

Doctor Foster was the first to speak. "Hello, Jill. You know why we're all here, don't you?"

"Yes, Doctor."

"Are you sure you want to go through with this?"

"Yes, of course. I need to know what happened to Jack and myself, and if this is the quickest way to find out then let's go."

The Sergeant smiled and stood in a corner, well out of the way.

Doctor Foster introduced Harry, the hypnotist, and the nurse, and told Jill what he expected to happen.

"While you are being questioned, under hypnosis, we will be recording everything you say," pointing to a tape recorder being prepared by the nurse. "Is that okay with you," he asked.

"Yes, of course," answered Jill.

Harry turned to the spectators.

"While I do this I must insist on absolute silence. Only speak if Jill speaks to you, and then as briefly as possible. Is that clear to everyone?"

All the spectators nodded.

Given the go-ahead, the nurse stepped forward and placed a kidney dish on Jill's bed. Taking the needle and a swab from the dish, she swabbed Jill's arm and injected a mild sedative into it. After a few moments Jill sat back against her pillows and her head started to loll forward. The nurse carefully guided Jill's head back on to the pillow and then withdrew to man the tape recorder. The hypnotist took hold of Jill's hand and spoke softly.

"Jill… Jill, open your eyes."

A bleary-eyed Jill forced her eyelids up and she looked around the room, trying to focus on her surroundings.

She smiled a drunken smile and said, "Wow! Best party ever…"

With a chuckle, the hypnotist answered, "No, Jill. You're not at a party, you're in a hospital bed. Remember?"

"Oh, yes. Hello, Sergeant…" Jill smiled at the Sergeant, as if this was the first time she had met him.

The Sergeant smiled back. "Hello Jill."

The hypnotist continued. "Jill, I want you to close your eyes but do not let yourself go to sleep. Stay awake, with your eyes closed. Do you understand?"

"Yes."

"Okay. Now, I want you to think about a feather, Jill. A feather floating in the air. Can you see it, Jill?"

"Yes. It's lovely. Free. I'd love to be able to do that."

"Okay, Jill. I want you to watch the feather slowly fall to the floor. Is it falling yet?"

"Yes, really slowly. It's lovely. I'd love to be able to do that."

"Yes, Jill. We know. Now, as the feather falls to the floor, you will slowly go to sleep. You will sleep, but you will hear my voice. Are you ready to sleep?"

"Yes. It's lovely. I'd love to..."

Harry the hypnotist interrupted Jill's sentence. "Is the feather near the floor yet, Jill. Are you almost asleep?"

"Yes."

"On the count of three, Jill, you will be fast asleep because the feather has landed on the floor. One... Two... Three..."

Jill sighed a deep sigh and laid there, her breathing slow but regular. Doctor Foster put his stethoscope to the crook of Jill's arm for a few seconds, then turned to the watching people in the room.

"She is ready for your questions, Sergeant."

The Sergeant handed over a paper with his questions pre-loaded onto it. Harry the hypnotist looked at the questions then turned back to Jill.

"Jill, can you hear my voice?"

"Yes."

"I'm going to ask you a few questions. Are you up to answering them?"

"Yes."

"Start with the time you got out of bed on the day you went up the hill, and tell me what happened. Imagine it's all a dream, Jill. Tell me what's happening in the dream."

"Well, I went downstairs to get a cup of coffee for Jack and me and I saw a truck next to Bo Peep's paddock..."

"What colour is the truck, Jill?"

"It's a dirty green truck. I went back upstairs to wake Jack and we both looked out of the bedroom window. We saw two men loading Bo's sheep into the back of the truck..."

"Do you recognise the men?"

"Yes."

"Do you know their names?"

"Yes."

"What are their names, Jill?"

"One was Wee Willie Winkie, and the other was John Dumpling. John was carrying a little lamb. It was a sweet little lamb and..."

Another interruption by Harry to bring Jill back on track. "Who was driving the truck, Jill?"

"John Dumpling. Willie ran off towards the hill when Bo Peep came out of her cottage. The truck had gone by then."

"Did you see where the truck went?"

"No."

"Did you see which direction the truck went?"

"Yes - towards the farm."

"Okay. You're doing really well, Jill."

"Can I go to sleep now?"

"No, Jill. Not yet. Stay with me for a few more minutes. I won't be long. I promise."

Jill smiled.

The Sergeant also smiled. He had now got the evidence he needed to confirm who had stolen the sheep. Harry continued to press Jill for answers.

"Jill, shall we now go to the hill? What happened there?"

There was a pause as Jill recovered the information from the rècess of her mind.

"Jack forgot to fill the pail of water. We'd had a letter from the water company..."

"Concentrate, Jill. Did you see anybody going up the hill in front of you?"

"Yes, briefly, but we couldn't see who - only that he was wearing a dressing gown."

"What time would that be?"

"Eight forty-five-ish."

"Okay, let's now jump forward to the time you were at the top of the hill. Do you remember that time?"

Another pause, then, "Yes! Yes! That's when we were pushed!" Jill became a little agitated.

"Okay, but shall we take it slowly, Jill? What did you see before you were pushed?"

"We saw a commotion down in the village. We couldn't hear what was going on…"

"What time was it when you saw that?"

"Umm, I think it was about nine-fifteen."

Jill had settled down, once more.

"Move on Jill. What happened next?"

"As we walked towards the drop, a man suddenly appeared out of the bushes."

"What was he wearing?"

"A grey dressing gown and wellies… dirty wellies."

"Go on…"

"We told him that we recognised him. Told him that he was the man we saw loading the sheep into the truck."

"Did he say anything back to you?"

"Yes… I think he said *'Nobody was supposed to see that.'*

"Then what?"

"He ran forward hit Jack and pushed him over the edge."

"And what happened to you?"

"The man turned, grabbed me by the shoulders and pushed me over the edge."

Jill was now highly agitated and Harry decided that she had had enough.

"Okay, Jill. It's alright. You're quite safe now. You're in the hospital, remember?"

Jill held her brow in her hands for a few seconds, then sat back into her pillows.

"Do you know who it was that pushed you and Jack?"

"Yes."

"Wee Willie Winkie."

Harry looked up at the Sergeant. "Does that give you what you need?"

"More than enough," answered the Sergeant. "Thank you Doctor, for your assistance."

Harry turned back to Jill to bring her out of her hypnotic trance.

"Can you see the feather on the floor, Jill?"

"Yes."

"Pick it up and put it in your pocket. Then you can sleep. When you wake up you will feel refreshed, and your memory will be refreshed and you will feel fine. Now go to sleep. We'll wake you at tea time."

Jill took a deep breath, let it out slowly and by the time she breathed in again she was fast asleep.

After being handed the tape recording, the Sergeant left Jill's room and got straight on the radio.

"Slack. Round up PC Griller from where he is hiding and meet me back at the station. We've got some criminals to catch!"

CHAPTER 34

Week 1. Saturday, 5.30 p.m.

After consolidating all their notes and obtaining appropriate search and arrest warrants from Judge Fairly, the Sergeant briefed his team. Armed with their search and arrest warrants, they were instructed to bring all the suspects in the stolen sheep case back to the station for questioning.

The Sergeant split his team up. PC Griller was despatched to John Dumpling's address, PC Peecie was dispatched to Little Boy Blue's address and PC Slack and the Sergeant went to Wee Willie Winkie's address.

*

NEWS FLASH! From Chatty Chaste on the news desk at Rhyme Place TV station.

Chatty - "We interrupt today's programme to bring you some breaking news about activity that is disrupting traffic in Rhyme Place Village. We've just heard that police have closed off all roads to and from Rhyme Place so that they can carry out a search and arrest operation safely. All inhabitants are asked to stay indoors while the police carry out their duties in the area. Our chief crime reporter, Nosy Nolan, is on site now and we'll go over to him to see what he can tell us... Nosey, what can you tell us about activities in Rhyme Place?"

Nosey Nolan - "Hello Chatty... Well, as you can see, I'm standing at Hot Cross looking down the high street towards the castle. The road has been blocked off to all traffic by the police, so I haven't been able to get a closer view of the police activities. However, I've got the Mayor of Rhyme Place here, with me, who was on his way back from the fair when the road block was put up… [*Turning to the Mayor*]. Mayor, what can you tell us about the activity taking place down at the village?"

Mayor Reform - "I can't go into the details of this police operation, because I don't know them. I'm on my way back from the fair… And this road block is a bloody nuisance!"

Nosey's camera quickly pans away from Mayor Reform back to Nosey.

Nosey Nolan - "Thank you Mayor. Well, Chatty, from what I understand, the police are raiding three addresses in Rhyme Place Village with the intention of arresting suspects in the stolen sheep case…"

Mayor Reform is heard in the background, talking to his driver. "How did he know that? I didn't know that. Nobody tells me anything around here…"

Nosey Nolan continues his report - "… Three men are presently suspected to be the individuals involved with the theft of Bo Peep's sheep on Monday morning. These men are Little Boy Blue, John Dumpling and Wee Willie Winkie…"

Mayor Reform [*in the background*] - "Look! He's done it again. See that? He's giving out information that I haven't got. Who the Hell is giving him this information? Why haven't I been told…?"

Nosey Nolan - "… I'm told that Wee Willie Winkie has gone on the run. This person is considered to be a dangerous man and should not be approached by anyone. If anyone has any information regarding the whereabouts of Wee Willie Winkie, Sergeant Argent, or any of his staff at Rhyme Place police station, will take your call. Back to you, Chatty, in the studio."

Just before Nosey Nolan's microphone is switched off, Mayor Reform is heard complaining, "Bloody TV reporters - why was he told about this before me…?"

Back to Chatty Chaste on the news desk - "Well, there you have it. Police are raiding three addresses in Rhyme Place Village to gather information on the theft of Bo Peep's sheep on Monday. Any information you have about the theft of Bo Peep's sheep or, indeed, the whereabouts of Wee Willie Winkie, should be given to Rhyme Place police as soon as possible. I'll just repeat that Wee Willie Winkie is considered to be dangerous and should not be approached by anyone except the police. That's all we have on this news report, for now, but we'll keep you informed of developments as they take place. We'll re-join today's programme, 'Bouncing Billy', but we'll be back for an update on this incident during the evening's news."

*

Little Boy Blue came quietly to the station, accompanied by his mum and PC Peecie. He was put in one of the interview rooms to await the Sergeant. His mum sat in the reception, patiently.

John Dumpling was a different matter. Mrs. Dumpling opened the door for PC Griller to enter and called John downstairs. In the hallway, as soon as PC Griller tried to caution him he exploded and tried to fight his way out of the door, but he was no match for Griller. Laying on his stomach with the PC's knee holding him down, he was fitted with the PC's handcuffs before being dragged back onto his feet. Mrs. Dumpling sobbed in the kitchen while Griller finished cautioning John.

The Sergeant and Slack were not so lucky. There was no response from Slack's hammering on Willie's front door. The Sergeant went round the back to see if Willie had taken this route, but couldn't see any evidence of Willie running away. The back door was, however, unlocked. The Sergeant entered the cottage, shouting Willie's name, and he made his way through the kitchen and hallway to the front door.

After letting Slack in, they both started a search of Willie's cottage. A thick roll of ten pound notes was found in the cottage, tucked away inside a sock inside a drawer inside a bedroom. A photo was taken of this with Slack's mobile phone, and the money was put into an evidence bag and sealed.

Downstairs, the Sergeant found a set of keys inside a fruit bowl in the kitchen. The key fob confirmed that one of these was the ignition key to the truck. Into an evidence bag, these went.

A significant find was the pair of green wellies standing inside a cupboard under the stairs, still covered in sheep shit. These, also were put into an evidence bag and sealed… Actually, *two* evidence bags were used for each welly, both individually sealed because of the stink from the sheep shit.

The Sergeant and PC Slack returned to the station to see if the other two suspects had been apprehended. On their way they met contrary Mary.

"Hello, the Sergeant. Fancy a cup of coffee?"

"I do, Mary, but I'm tied up at the moment. I've got to get back to the station to hand in these evidence bags."

Slack piped up, optimistically, "I'll have a coffee…"

Mary looked him up and down, then returned her look back to the Sergeant.

"Later, then. About seven-ish?"

"Okay."

*

Week 1. Saturday, 6.00 p.m.

Back at the station, the Sergeant gave his approval for the road blocks to be removed.

The TV Crews packed up all their gear and disappeared over the horizon, no doubt in search of another news flash. Rhyme Place residents continued to mingle in the street for a while, gossiping about today's events, but eventually the village slowly returned to normal.

The Mayor returned to the town hall, constantly complaining that "...nobody ever tells me anything."

The Sergeant had a quiet word with Boy Blue's mum.

"Mrs. Blue, it's late and I'm sure you're tired of sitting here, waiting for something to happen. I'm going to release Boy into your custody, but I'd like him to be brought back here first thing in the morning for me to take his statement. Will you bring him?"

"Yes, of course," answered Mrs. Blue, looking worried. "Is he in a lot of trouble?"

"Quite honestly, I don't know that, yet. A lot depends on what he has to say for himself, but he is implicated in the theft of Bo Peep's sheep, so we must get to the bottom of his involvement."

"I see," surrendered Mrs. Blue. "I'll bring him in at 10.00 a.m., if it's okay?"

"Yes, of course. Whatever is convenient for you."

"Thank you Sergeant."

Boy Blue was released from the interview room and he and his mum departed from the station. He will, no doubt, be given a hard time by his mum when he gets home.

The Sergeant opened the flap in Dumpling's cell door and peered in.

"You'll be spending the night in here Mr. Dumpling and I'll interview you first thing in the morning," he said.

"Get knotted!" was Dumpling's reply.

The door flap was noisily closed.

The policemen finished writing up their reports. Following a briefing about tomorrow the PC's departed from the station to go to their homes.

The Sergeant went to contrary Mary's cottage for a cup of coffee…

CHAPTER 35

Week 1. Sunday, a.m.

PC Slack arrived at the police station early to make John Dumpling's breakfast and give the Sergeant a wake-up call.

Getting no response from the Sergeant, Slack went upstairs to knock on the Sergeant's bedroom door and poke his head inside. It was apparent that the Sergeant hadn't slept in his own bed last night…

Returning to the kitchen, Slack finished making Dumpling's breakfast, a bowl of porridge and a cup of station tea, and took the tray to the holding cell. Lowering the cell door flap he looked inside and shouted Dumpling's name to wake him.

With a grunt, Dumpling responded, "What!"

"Breakfast, John. I'll leave it here. Don't let your tea get cold."

"Sod off!"

Slack left the tray on the door shelf, an integral part of the cell door's viewing hatch, and returned to the reception desk.

PC Griller strolled through the station door and smiled at Slack. "Mornin'," he said as he entered. Slack reciprocated the greeting. "How's our guest?" Griller asked.

"I've woken him with his breakfast and left him to it. He's as grumpy as ever."

"Yeah, well, we'll see how grumpy he gets when the Sarg starts his interview. Do you know if he's got a solicitor, yet?"

"I phoned Mrs. Dumpling. She gave me the number of a solicitor she uses whenever John gets into trouble. A chap called Fleeceham, from Fleeceham, Greedie & Crooks. I called him straight away. He was none too pleased at being woken up, but he says he'll be in at about nine-thirty. He ordered no interview with Dumpling without his say-so."

"Better let the Sarg know. Where is he, anyway?"

"Don't know. His bed's not been slept in."

"Ah, if he doesn't turn up before nine I'll nip round to contrary Mary's place to let him know what's happening."

"Contrary Mary? Is that who he's with? No wonder she was a bit off-hand with me yesterday."

"Why? What happened yesterday?"

"She offered us a coffee and when I said yes she just blanked me out, although she agreed to meet the Sergeant later in the day."

With a chuckle, Griller opined, "There you go, then. Now you know why he's not in yet."

Griller went to see how Dumpling was getting on with his breakfast. The tray had been removed from the door shelf and Dumpling was looking at it, sat on the table in front of him. He looked up at the door flap to see who was watching him and picked up the bowl of porridge. Griller closed the door flap.

The two PC's busied themselves with paperwork until the Sergeant arrived at 9.00 a.m. Slack brought him up-to-date on the morning's activities.

"Okay," responded the Sergeant, "Make sure the interview room is ready for the solicitor's arrival, and make sure there are fresh tapes in the recorder."

Slack went off to check the interview room, the Sergeant went to his office and Griller manned the desk. At 9.15 a.m. the solicitor arrived.

Immaculately dressed, and carrying his briefcase, he introduced himself and asked, "Where is my client, now?"

Griller answered, "He's in the holding cell, sir. I'll let Sergeant Argent know you've arrived."

Griller pressed the undercounter bell button, ringing a bell in the Sergeant's office to summon him.

"Release my client from the cell immediately, unless you've charged him."

"No, no charge yet, but he has been cautioned."

"How long is this going to take? I haven't got all day, you know!"

"No, sir. We didn't know. A lot depends on your client, Mr. Fleeceham. If he co-operates it will be over quickly. If not, then it could take some time... you know?" A bit of mischievous repartee always lightens the conversation, don't you think?

The solicitor huffed and sat down on one of the visitor chairs to await the Sergeant's arrival. Two minutes later the Sergeant emerged from his office. Without waiting for the pleasantries of an introduction the solicitor immediately went on the attack.

"Sergeant, I've been kept waiting long enough! When can I see my client?"

The Sergeant looked at his PC's, both shrugging their shoulders at the solicitor's ill-mannered approach and then answered, "Oh! Sorry, sir. I've left my pen in my office," he lied. "Would you mind waiting for a moment while I go back to get it?" More mischievous repartee...

The Sergeant turned and went back into his office. With another huff, the solicitor sat down again and tapped his impatient toe on the ground. His neck was now beginning to swell and his face was turning red with anger.

The Sergeant waited several minutes, to let the silence of the reception sink in, then he returned.

Ignoring the solicitor's bounce up from the chair, he asked Slack, "Is Mr. Dumpling in the interview room?"

"Not yet, Sarg. We're waiting for your instructions."

"Oh. Okay. Perhaps you can go and collect him and take him to the interview room?" He turned to the Solicitor. "This will only take a few moments, sir."

The solicitor was now fuming at being kept waiting. He wasn't going to wait a few moments. When Slack went down the corridor towards Dumpling's cell the solicitor dashed off, to follow him.

Now, this was a wrong move - as the solicitor will find out in about fifteen seconds.

At the cell door, Slack noisily opened the door flap to look into the cell. He called out to Dumpling, advising that he was going to take him (Dumpling) to the interview room. Closing the flap, Slack asked the solicitor if he wished to speak to his client in the cell, or in the interview room. The solicitor demanded to see Dumpling in his cell.

"You sure, sir? It's more comfortable in the interview room."

"Of course I'm sure. For goodness sake, open the door!"

After shrugging his shoulders, Slack unlocked the cell door and opened it for the solicitor to enter the cell. The solicitor got as far as the door jamb when his Armani suit got splattered all down the front with the bowl of porridge that Dumpling had thrown, thinking that it was Slack who was entering the cell. The bowl bounced off the solicitor's copious stomach and dropped down to the floor and smashed. The solicitor looked down at his suit and Slack looked down at the solicitor's shoes - to hide his grin. What the solicitor didn't know was that Slack had seen Dumpling raising the bowl of porridge to throw at him when the door flap was first opened...

Slack closed the cell door and nonchalantly asked, "Would you like to go to the interview room now, sir?"

The Solicitor growled and stormed off, back to the reception.

Griller's and the Sergeant's faces were a picture when the solicitor emerged, porridge all over his face and immaculate suit and shiny shoes.

"I see you've spoken to your client," mused the Sergeant.

"I'll be back later," was all that the solicitor growled, and he departed from the station to change his clothes.

The Sergeant turned to his PC's and ordered, "Get a bucket and water, and get Dumpling to clean up his mess before the solicitor returns."

Laughing loudly, the two PC's went about their business.

CHAPTER 36

Week 1. Sunday, 9.55 a.m.

As promised, Mrs. Blue brought Boy Blue in for his interview. Slack showed them both into a spare interview room and made sure they were comfortable before going to let the Sergeant know they had arrived.

The Sergeant entered the room and thanked Mrs. Blue for bringing her son back to the station.

Turning to Boy Blue the Sergeant said, "Protocol demands that I caution you, Boy Blue, under the Criminal Justice Act, 2003."

Boy Blue and his mother looked nervous.

The Sergeant continued, "Don't worry, Mrs. Blue. This is just what is referred to as a simple caution, but I must let Boy Blue know what his rights are while we interview him."

"I see," answered Mrs. Blue, still a little nervous.

"Okay. Now, Boy Blue, you do not have to say anything but it may harm your defence if you do not mention, when questioned, something that you later rely on in Court. Anything you do say may be given in evidence. Do you understand?"

Boy Blue nodded his head.

"I must ask you to speak up, Boy, for the tape."

"Yes, sir, I understand what you said."

Mrs. Blue interrupted the Sergeant. "Sergeant, does my son need a solicitor?"

"Well, he can have a solicitor, if that's what either you or he wants, but at this stage I don't think a solicitor is necessary… Unless he has performed a criminal act.

Do you think you have done anything that can be considered as a criminal act, Boy?"

"A criminal act?" questioned Boy.

"Do you think you have done anything you should not have done?"

"I don't know, sir."

"Do you know why we've asked you to come here today?"

"Yes, sir. Bo Peep's sheep."

"What about Bo Peep's sheep?"

"I didn't steal them, sir." Boy turned to his mum. "I didn't steal them mum. I was just doing what I was told by old MacDonald."

The Sergeant could see that Boy Blue was now quite agitated. Perhaps even frightened. So he decided to calm things down a notch. "Do you want a drink of water, Boy? How about a cup of tea, Mrs. Blue?"

"Yes, please," answered Boy, and Slack disappeared to fetch Boy a glass of water.

The Sergeant continued, "We're not accusing you of anything, Boy. We just want to get to the truth. How about you start at the beginning and, in your own words, tell me how you came to be involved with the sheep?"

Boy Blue looked at his mum for some encouragement. She prompted, "It's okay, Boy. Just tell the truth and you'll be alright."

Boy turned back to face the Sergeant.

"I wanted some extra pocket money for the fair, but Mum can't afford it, so she told me to ask old MacDonald if he needed any help around the farm."

"When did you ask him?"

"On Saturday, last week. He told me to come back on Monday, so I did."

"Go on…"

Boy was now relaxed, and the Sergeant perceived he was telling the truth.

"Well, I went back on Monday morning at about eight thirty, and he told me to get one of the barns ready to take in some livestock."

"Ready?"

"Yes sir. Tidy it up, move some bales of hay around, sweep up. You know? Get it ready."

"Okay, go on."

"Well, at about nine o'clock MacDonald's truck backed into the barn while I was sweeping up. It nearly ran into me. As I stood to one side, John Dumpling gets out of the cab holding a lamb, and he tells me to put the lamb into the pen inside the barn, so I did. John then opened the back of the truck and four sheep jumped out of it, into the barn. John helped one of them out of the truck because it's only got three legs. He told me to get out and he followed me and closed the barn door behind him."

"You're sure it was nine o'clock?"

"It was about that time, sir. I don't know exactly 'cos I don't have a watch, but I heard the village bells chime."

"And you're sure it was MacDonald's truck?"

"Yes, sir. I've seen it around and about whenever he's in it, driving to the village. It's his, alright. It's got a teddy bear tied to the front."

"On Thursday afternoon you were heard being shouted at by MacDonald. What was that all about?"

"Well, sir, somebody had left the barn door open and the sheep escaped. It wasn't me, sir. I was inside another barn when MacDonald shouted for me to come to the sheep barn. He was really mad about the sheep escaping. He told John and me that we would have to pay for them out of our wages. He told us to *'get out and find those sheep,'* so we did."

"What happened to the truck?"

"Don't know, sir. I saw Wee Willie Winkie collect it on Tuesday afternoon, but I don't know where he took it."

"Did you find the sheep?"

"No, sir. We searched everywhere, for ages, but there was no sign of them at all. John and myself decided to forget the sheep and go home. He told me not to go back to the farm, ever again. I was a bit angry, because MacDonald had not paid me for my work. I know he paid John because on Tuesday, after work, I heard him tell MacDonald that he was going down to the pub. He didn't have two brass farthings to rub together before then, so he must have been paid."

The Sergeant rubbed his chin while looking into his file of papers, then asked, "Is there anything else you want to tell me about the sheep? Anything at all?"

"No, sir. That's all I know. I didn't steal them, sir. I was just doing what I was told."

"It's okay, Boy. You're not in any trouble. I believe what you've told me."

The Sergeant turned to Mrs. Blue.

"Would you both mind waiting in the reception while PC Slack types up Boy's statement? Once he's signed it he can go."

"No, not at all. Thank you, Sergeant."

The Sergeant smiled and opened the interview door to let Mrs. Blue and her son leave.

As they approached the door he turned and asked, "Please don't speak to anyone about your involvement with the sheep, Boy. Don't say a word about it or you might prejudice my enquiries."

"No sir."

Boy Blue and his mum sat patiently in the reception while Boy's statement was typed up. After reading through it, and being satisfied at its veracity, Boy signed on the dotted line.

A photocopy was made and given to Mrs. Blue and they both departed from the station.

CHAPTER 37

Week 1. Sunday, 10.45 a.m.

Mr. Fleeceham, of Fleeceham, Greedie & Crooks, entered the police station, this time wearing another Armani suit. Griller looked up from the desk and welcomed him.

"Good morning again, sir. I'll just let the Sergeant know that you have arrived."

"Make sure you remind him to bring his pen this time. I'm in a hurry to get this over with," demanded the solicitor.

"Yes, sir. Right away."

Griller pressed the undercounter bell button, ringing a bell in the Sergeant's office to summon him. The solicitor didn't sit down, this time, he just stood propping up the desk, tapping impatient fingers on the countertop. The Sergeant entered the room.

The solicitor quickly prompted, "Have you got your pen with you, this time? I asked this oaf to remind you but he didn't."

Griller chipped in, sarcastically, "I'm not the oaf that got covered in porridge, sir..."

The solicitor chose to ignore Griller's remark. "Can we now interview my client?" he demanded.

"Of course, sir," replied the Sergeant, turning to Griller. "Has Mr. Dumpling been escorted to the interview room?"

"Not yet, Sarg. We were just waiting for your instructions."

Slack piped up, "I'll go and get him now, Mr. Fleeceham. Would you like to accompany me?"

The solicitor's reply was quick, made without any thought whatsoever, "No… No. I'll wait here until he is ready for me."

Slack smiled and said, "As you wish, sir."

Dumpling and the solicitor were both shown to the interview room. The Sergeant permitted the solicitor about ten minutes of private time with his client before entering the room with PC Slack and sitting in the chairs across from the interview desk.

The solicitor started the interview by asking, "Is it necessary for my client to wear handcuffs?"

The Sergeant replied, "I'm afraid it is, sir. More for your safety than ours…"

"Oh. Yes. Can we get on?"

The Sergeant cautioned Dumpling. "Mr. Dumpling, you do not have to say anything but it may harm your defence if you do not mention, when questioned, something that you later rely on in Court. Anything you do say may be given in evidence. Do you understand?"

"Drop Dead!"

The solicitor answered the question for his client. "My client understands, Sergeant. Has he been charged with anything, yet?"

"Not yet, sir, but it's early days."

"Then why is he being held?"

Argent opened his file and read a few pages of data, much to the annoyance of the solicitor. "Couldn't you have read that before we started the interview, Sergeant?"

"I could have, sir, but you may recall that you were particularly anxious to start the interview."

"Get on with it, then."

"Mr. Dumpling, where were you at eight forty-five a.m. on Monday, this week?"

"Driving."

"What were you driving?"

"A truck."

"What truck?"

"A green truck."

"At that time, where were you driving the truck?"

"No comment."

"Does that truck belong to you?"

"No."

"Who does the truck belong to?"

"Old MacDonald."

The solicitor tapped his pen on his pad loudly to remind Dumpling not to answer the questions.

"Do you have a full driving license?"

"No comment."

"Are you insured to drive MacDonald's truck?"

"What's it got to do with you?"

"Just answer the question."

"No comment."

"Did MacDonald know you were driving his truck?"

"No comment."

"What was in the truck?"

"Me."

"Not who, Mr. Dumpling, WHAT?"

"No comment."

"Am I right in assuming that you were driving the truck at eight-fifty a.m. the same morning?"

"What? Five minutes later?" asked Dumpling.

"Five minutes later…" prompted the Sergeant.

"Why?"

"We have witnesses that confirm you almost knocked some pedestrians down at that time."

"Did I hit him?"

"Who said it was a him, Mr. Dumpling. I just said that it was some pedestrians."

The solicitor decided to give Dumpling some well paid for advice. "Keep your mouth shut, John. I've told you - don't answer any questions!"

The Sergeant gave the solicitor some free advice. "Your client isn't helping himself by answering 'No comment', Mr. Fleeceham. I'm sure a jury will take his silence to be the silence of a guilty person, don't you think?" He said this more to Dumpling than the solicitor.

No comment from the solicitor or Dumpling.

The Sergeant continued.

"After the truck almost collided with the pedestrians, did you stop to see if any of them had been injured?"

"I… [*a sideways glance at the solicitor*] … No comment"

"Do you remember where this accident…"

The Sergeant was interrupted by the solicitor. "Alleged accident, Sergeant, and there was no accident. My client didn't run anyone down."

"My apologies, sir - Incident, Mr. Dumpling… Do you remember where this incident took place?"

"Somewhere."

The solicitor huffed loudly.

The Sergeant continued. "So you do recollect the incident? What was in the back of the truck, and where were you taking it?"

"Nowhere."

The solicitor closed his notepad and demanded, "It's time to take a break, Sergeant. I'd like to ask my client some more questions."

"Of course, sir. Will ten minutes be enough time with your client?"

"Yes, and what about providing my client with a drink?" actually meaning, 'Can **I** have a cup of tea?'

"I'll see to it right away, sir."

*

The two policemen returned to the reception, where the Sergeant asked Slack to put the kettle on for a pot of tea. The door to the station opened and Little Tommy Tucker entered.

At the reception desk he faced the Sergeant. "Mum's told me to come down to the station to give you a message."

"Hello, Tommy. What's the message from your mum?"

"Well, she got off the train from the city, earlier today, and she thinks she saw Wee Willie Winkie lurking down in the railway yard. She said that she remembered that you were searching for him, so she told me to come and tell you what she thinks she saw."

"Well done, Tommy. Thank your mum and let her know that we'll look into it later today."

"Yes, sir… And she also said to ask Mr. Slack if he would like a cup of coffee while I'm at the fair?"

The Sergeant turned to look at Slack. Slack shrugged his shoulders.

The Sergeant answered, "Tell your mum that PC Slack will let her know about the coffee."

"Yes, sir." Tommy turned round and left the station.

Griller asked the obvious question. "Do you want us to go down there to see if it was him?"

"Yes, you go. If he's there, don't let him know you're watching him. Slack and I will join you this afternoon. Stay on your radio. There are no more trains leaving Rhyme Place today, so he can't get far if he's thinking about doing a runner. He might just be laying up to wait 'till the first train out, tomorrow."

Slack and the Sergeant returned to the interview room with the tea tray. Griller made his way to the railway station yard.

*

Before entering the interview room, the Sergeant peered through the small window in the door.

The solicitor appeared to be reprimanding Dumpling about something. Without knocking, the Sergeant entered the room. Silence descended.

"Shall we continue, Mr. Fleeceham?"

The solicitor eyed the tray of mugs and sat down. Slack passed the glass of water to Dumpling and put both mugs of tea in front of himself and the Sergeant. The solicitor face took on a surprised look as his eyes oscillated between the mugs and the Sergeant. The Sergeant decided to take some more wind out of the solicitor's sail.

"Oh, sorry… Did you want a cup of tea? You didn't say…"

The solicitor just stared back.

"I'll take that as a 'No', then."

Taking a long and noisy sip of tea, the Sergeant resumed the interview.

"Where did we leave off? Oh, yes. What was in the back of the truck, and where were you taking it?" he asked Dumpling.

With a worried look at the solicitor, he answered, "No comment."

"I see," said the Sergeant. "Well, we have another witness that suggests that you unloaded the truck inside one of MacDonald's barns. Is that true?"

This angered Dumpling. "Did Boy Blue tell you that? I'm going to punch his lights out when I see him!"

"So it was you that unloaded Bo Peep's sheep from the back of the truck?"

The solicitor jumped in. "My client admits that he drove the truck to the farm, but he was unaware that it contained the stolen sheep until he got there. He was acting under orders from MacDonald, that's all."

"Well, sir, I'd like to know where your client got Mary's lamb. Can you answer that, John?"

"No comment."

"Let's turn to Tuesday night, shall we? Where did you go on Tuesday night, John?"

Dumpling looked at the solicitor, who nodded his approval.

"I went to the pub. There's nothing wrong with that, is there?"

"No, not at all, John. Where did you get the money for this night out?"

The solicitor jumped in, once more. "My client is entitled to socialise with a couple of drinks with his friends, Sergeant. Where is this going?"

"Well, sir, We know that John didn't have any money that night. We checked with his Mum and she confirmed that he was broke, so where did you get the money to socialise, John?"

"No comment."

The Sergeant took a long look at Dumpling and the solicitor and continued, "The problem here is that Mrs. Dumpling called me out to her place on Wednesday morning because she couldn't wake John up. It turns out that he was in a drunken stupor from his pub visit on Tuesday night. If he was broke on Tuesday, confirmed by his Mum, where did he get the money to get so drunk that his Mum couldn't wake him on Wednesday?"

The solicitor thought about that question and made a few notes. He then turned to the Sergeant and answered, "Unless you have sufficient grounds to charge my client with something, I think it is time for us to leave, don't you?"

The Sergeant dropped his pen onto his pad and summarised his thoughts to the solicitor.

"We know that John was driving the truck. He has just admitted it and we have witnesses that saw him drive the truck. We know that he off-loaded Bo Peep's stolen sheep at MacDonald's barn and we have a witness to confirm that. We also know that he almost knocked some pedestrians down at Hot Cross, and we have witnesses to confirm that. Now, what we think is that MacDonald paid John and somebody else to steal the sheep and take them to the farm in the farm truck. We think that he was handed Mary's lamb by the same person that helped him steal the sheep, and we suspect that John used the payment from MacDonald to get drunk on Tuesday night. Isn't that right, John?"

Dumpling looked at his solicitor for an answer.

The solicitor replied, "My client has nothing to say."

The Sergeant stood and instructed Dumpling to stand. "John Dumpling, you are charged with handling stolen goods under section 22 of the theft act 1968. You are also charged with using a vehicle without reasonable consideration for other road users under section 3 of the Road Traffic Act 1988, with driving without due care and attention under section 3 of the Road Traffic Act 1988 and also with dangerous driving under section 2 of the Road Traffic Act 1988. You are also charged with using a motor vehicle without there being in force a relevant policy of insurance under section 143 of the Road Traffic Act 1988, and also of driving without a valid licence under section 87 of the Road Traffic Act 1988. The time, now, is eleven forty-five, a.m. Do you have anything to say?"

An emphatic "No comment!" from the solicitor.

The Sergeant looked at Dumpling and demanded, "I must ask you to answer the question, Mr. Dumpling. Do you have anything to say to these charges?"

From Dumpling, a feeble, "No comment."

"Well then," continued the Sergeant, "I think your solicitor *is* correct, in that it is time for us to leave. We'll deal with the theft of the sheep later. Take him back to his cell, Slack."

Before Slack could take Dumpling's elbow, Dumpling asked, "What about the factory? I need to make arrangement for someone to take charge while I'm away."

The Sergeant coldly replied, "I'm sure that your solicitor will make the appropriate arrangements for you if you let him have the details."

With that, Dumpling and his solicitor were escorted to Dumpling's cell by PC Slack, and the Sergeant returned to his office to write up his report.

CHAPTER 38

Down by the station early in the morning,
See the little pufferbellies all in a row.
See the engine driver pull the little handle,
Puff, puff, Toot! Toot!
Off we go.
(USA, first seen in a 1931 Recreation magazine)

Cut back to Sunday, early a.m. (Week 1).

Wee Willie Winkie knew that he was a wanted man.

He had been seen stealing Bo Peep's sheep, he had abducted Mary's lamb, he had pushed both Jack and Jill off the top of the hill, and his name had been well and truly publicised by the TV station's news channel. Everyone must be looking for him, by now, so he had to find a place to lay up until he could leave Rhyme Place.

He thought about stealing MacDonald's truck to drive away to some distant town, but he would need to return to his cottage to retrieve the keys. Too risky… The police might have already searched the cottage and found the keys, and the police might even still be there, so the cottage was now a no-go location.

What about his den at the top of the hill? He knew that this was a reasonably safe place to hide because neither Jack nor Jill had spotted him when they arrived. On second thoughts, it was possible that there may be a police presence there. After all, the top of the hill was now a crime scene. No, not an option right now.

There was certainly nowhere to hide in, or near, the bun factory, and the fairground is full of people, all of whom would undoubtedly have seen his face splashed all over the TV screens.

The castle grounds and surrounding forest will definitely be well guarded by now.

There was, he thought, only one place left for him to hide - the railway station's goods yard. This would be a convenient place to hide. There were many nooks and crannies behind the pallets of goods waiting to be picked up and, being a Sunday, nobody would come to collect the goods before tomorrow. By then the early milk train will have arrived, early tomorrow morning, and he could secrete himself on that.

Yes, the Railway station's goods yard is the place to disappear overnight.

As he furtively climbed the yard gates to find a hiding place, a train from the city pulled into the station, and he didn't see Tommy Tucker's mum eye him climbing over the gates. Who would have thought that *anyone* from Rhyme Place would have been on that train?

*

Week 1. Sunday, 11.15 a.m.

PC Griller cautiously approached the gates to the railway station's goods yard.

He reasoned that *if* Wee Willie had already entered the yard he (Griller) would probably be seen by Willie as he climbed the gate.

He decided to work his way round to the back of the yard where there was a convenient access point through the chain link fence. He knew there was a loose segment of fence that the teenagers of Rhyme Place used to access the privacy of the yard - to do those things that their parents did when they were their age, but have told their kids not to do now.

Quietly squeezing through the gap, he knelt down and looked around the yard. From this location he couldn't see any sign of Willie, but there were numerous places to hide so Griller cautiously crept to a nearby stack of timber. Looking over the top of the pile, he scrutinised each pallet for signs of movement. There was none.

As quietly as the gravel covered ground would allow, he made his way to a nearby stack of three pallets, all loaded with bricks. There was quite a distance from here to the next vantage point and it was possible that his size thirteen boots would be detected reaching it. An idea came to him.

There is a gap under all pallets' platforms, a gap formed by the pallets' joists. Providing the pallet joists had not sunk into the gravel, there may be a chance to see Willie's feet through the gaps of these, and other, pallets. Griller lay on his stomach behind the stack of bricks and, with his cheek pressed firmly to the gravel, he peered along the ground at each of the distant pallets.

He heard a muffled cough…

Scanning the underside of each pallet he hoped that he would see where the cough came from. Then he heard a sneeze…

This time he could detect the direction of the sneeze and he scrutinised the pallets in that area. He saw the slightest of movement from under a tarpaulin covering some boxes, and through a gap in the bricks he was hiding behind he concentrated his eyesight on that pallet.

The tarpaulin bulged, clearly indicating that something, or someone, was under it. Then there was the noise of someone noisily blowing a nose. It could only be

Willie. *'Who else,'* thought Griller, *'would hide under a tarpaulin in a railway station's goods yard?'*

Griller sat with his back to the stack of bricks and radioed the Sergeant. When the Sergeant answered he whispered, "Willie's here alright. I've just seen where he's hiding. How long will you be getting here?"

The Sergeant answered, "Keep your eyes on him for the time being, and let me know if he moves to a different location. We'll be finished here, soon, and we'll get straight down there."

"Okay Sarg. Use the back entrance. You know, the gap in the fence - and make your way to a stack of brick pallets. He won't see you arrive. I'll wait for you here, and be quiet. Fresh gravel has been laid on the ground."

"Okay, thanks for the heads up."

The call was terminated and Griller sat back to wait for his backup.

CHAPTER 39

Oh, where have you been, Billy Boy, Billy Boy?
Oh, where have you been, Charming Billy?
I have been to seek a wife, she's the joy of my whole life,
But she's a young thing and cannot leave her mother.
(Traditional folk song and nursery rhyme
from the USA, c.1912)

Week 1. Sunday, 12.30 p.m.

The Sergeant and PC Slack squeezed through the gap in the fence at the back of the rail station's goods yard.

They both lowered to one knee and the Sergeant whispered, "Can you see him?"

"Who? Willie?"

"No - Griller."

"Oh, him. No Sarg. He said he was hiding under some tarpaulin."

"Who, Griller?"

"No, Willie."

"CAN YOU SEE GRILLER?" emphasized the Sergeant.

"No Sarg. Wait here and I'll go to that pile of wood."

Slack carefully made his way to the nearby stack of timber and cautiously peered over the top. He spied Griller sat with his back to a pallet of bricks. Ducking down, he gestured to the Sergeant to come to his location.

When the Sergeant arrived, Slack whispered, "He's sat with his back to a pallet of bricks, just in front of us."

"Who, Willie?"

"No, GRILLER!"

"Oh, right," answered the Sergeant, and both men peered over the wood stack.

Griller had turned round and was peering through a gap in the bricks.

The Sergeant attracted his attention. "Psss!"

Griller looked back and waved the two policemen forward after holding his finger over his lips to remind them to be quiet. Slack and the Sergeant slowly approached Griller's location and joined him with their backs to the bricks.

Griller reported, "Look at one o'clock. You'll see a large pallet of something covered with a tarpaulin."

Slack and the Sergeant gingerly poked their heads above the wood stack and ducked back down.

"See it?"

"Yeah," answered the Sergeant, "and he's still under it?"

"Yep. I've been watching through this gap in the bricks. The tarpaulin moves occasionally, but nobody has come out from under the tarpaulin while I've been here."

"Good. Okay, here's what we'll do. Slack, you make your way left, towards the pallet next to the tarpaulin. Griller, you go right. When you're both in position I'll blow my whistle and we'll all pounce on the tarpaulin from three sides. Any questions?"

Slack held his hand up. "Is that one blast on the whistle, or two?"

The Sergeant and Griller glanced at each other, then the Sergeant answered, "I'll just blow the bloody whistle, Slack. I'm sure you'll hear it, and when you do, pounce. Got it?"

"Yes Sarg. That's one blast, then."

The other two policemen both took a deep breath and let it out slowly.

"Go!" prompted the Sergeant and the PC's slowly made their way to their separate locations.

After making sure his team was ready to pounce, the Sergeant gave a blast from his whistle and all three policemen converged on the tarpaulin. Griller was the first to reach it and he grabbed a corner and threw it back. Like a pack of lions, all three policemen pounced onto the person now exposed to the elements.

A girl screamed and the three policemen froze and looked up from the man that they had pounced on. After looking back at themselves, they looked down at the man whose body was squashed under them.

It was Billy Postlethwaite, a young resident of Rhyme Place, shouting, "Get off me! Get off me!"

The three policemen suddenly rolled off the boy. The Sergeant stood and surveyed the scene. Billy was dressed in his underpants, only, and the girl just sported her bra and knickers. She was trying to hide her body behind her folded arms.

"What's going on here, then?" asked the Sergeant, as if it wasn't obvious.

The boy and girl sat looking at the ground, silently.

After a pause, the Sergeant ordered, "Get dressed, you two," and watched as the kids began pushing on socks and donning their clothes.

Slack suddenly alerted everyone by shouting, "LOOK! HE'S THERE!" whilst pointing towards the main gates.

Wee Willie Winkie had heard the kerfuffle caused firstly by the whistle blast, then the girl's scream and finally the scuffle of the three policemen and Billy on the gravel. He looked around and saw the scrummage taking place over by the tarpaulin, and he made a dash out of his hiding place, the gate house, to climb the gates.

Seeing Willie jump down onto the road, the Sergeant ordered, "Get after him!"

Slack dashed off towards the gates. Griller dashed in the opposite direction towards the gap in the fence.

Turning to Billy and the girl, who were now both fully dressed, he angrily ordered, "Get off home, you two… And I'll be having a word with both your parents the next time I'm in the village."

Heads down, Billy and the girl made their way towards the gap in the fence. The Sergeant followed.

The Sergeant met up with Griller and Slack. Griller was the first to speak.

"He got away."

"You don't say?" answered the Sergeant. "We'll get him," he said, more to himself than his PC's. "He'll make a mistake, and we'll get him…"

The Sergeant gave his PC's the remainder of Sunday to rest and recuperate.

He went for a cup of coffee at contrary Mary's cottage, Griller went for a cup of coffee at Mrs. Lamb's cottage, and Slack decided to take up Mrs. Tucker's offer of a cup of coffee at her place.

None of the policemen drank much coffee… Neither did they get much rest!

CHAPTER 40

Wee Willie Winkie runs through the town,
Up stairs and down stairs in his night-gown.
Tapping at the window, crying at the lock,
Are the children in their beds, for it's past ten o'clock?
(Scotland/UK. A pre-existing nursery rhyme,
popularised by William Miller (1810-1872)

Week 2. Monday, a.m.

PC Peecie is now a new member of Sergeant Argent's team, having been permanently posted to Rhyme Place police station this morning. He was manning the desk while the Sergeant, Griller and Slack were busy catching up on paperwork.

Because Peecie was new to the village he had some catching up to do with regard to people's names and addresses. He had not yet been briefed about all the goings-on in Rhyme Place Village, but the Sergeant had promised him a complete update when all the outstanding paperwork had been completed. Peecie studied the map of the village, pinned to the wall behind the desk. The station door opened and Humpty Dumpty walked in.

"Good morning, sir. What can I do for you?" asked Peecie.

"Is Sergeant Argent in?"

"He is, sir, but he's a bit tied up at the moment. Will I do, for the time being?"

"You're new here, aren't you?"

"Yes, sir, posted in this morning. How can I help?"

"Well, I've come to complain about someone creeping around my shed. I saw him out of my bedroom window, this morning."

Peecie sharpened his pencil on the rotary pencil sharpener attached to the desk, opened his pad of writing paper and licked the end of the pencil while Humpty waited patiently for Peecie's reply.

I'm sure I've mentioned this before, but licking the end of a pencil does NOT enhance one's writing.

Anyway, Peecie started his questioning.

"What time would that be, sir?"

"Early. The noise of the dustbin being moved woke me up at about eight, a.m."

While making a note, Peecie asked his next question. "Did you recognise this chap?"

"No. He kept his head down."

"Can you describe him for me?"

"No, not really."

"Oh? And you didn't see his face?"

"No, but he was wearing a grey dressing gown."

"Okay, sir. I'll let the Sergeant know when he's finished what he's doing. Is there anything else, sir?"

"No. Are you going to send someone round?"

"I'll see what the Sergeant says. It's probably nothing, sir. As long as chummy doesn't threaten you in any way, or cause any damage, I'm sure he'll leave you alone, but we'll look into it, anyway."

Humpty shrugged his shoulders, turned and exited the police station.

Peecie closed his note pad and watched Humpty leave, making a mental note of Humpty's name for future reference.

*

Week 2. Monday, p.m.

The rest of Monday was quiet. The Sergeant finished writing up his reports for Judge Fairly just before lunchtime. Slack and Griller also completed their reports, shortly afterwards. All the policemen congregated in the reception area. The Sergeant stood facing the three PC's who were behind the desk.

"Okay," looking at Slack and Griller, "This is PC Peecie, posted in from Jingle Town station this morning. Slack, will you fully brief him while Griller and myself do the rounds? With a bit of luck, we'll find out where Willy is hiding."

"Yes Sarg," answered Slack.

Peecie had forgotten his conversation with Humpty Dumpty, earlier…

The Sergeant and Griller departed from the station to patrol the streets of Rhyme Place.

Slack extracted the file on Bo Peep's sheep from the filing cabinet and began his briefing. When he got as far as explaining about Humpty Dumpty's involvement, he was stopped by Peecie mid-sentence.

"What?" asked Slack.

"I've just remembered something," replied Peecie, opening his note pad. "That bloke came in this morning to report a snooper lurking around his shed. I should have told the Sergeant about him, but I forgot."

"Catch the Sergeant when he gets back in," advised Slack, and continued his briefing.

*

Week 2. Monday, tea-time.

The Sergeant and PC Griller returned to the station.

PC Peecie had clocked off, for the night, and Slack was manning the desk. Slack hadn't associated Peecie's snooper with anything else, so he, too, had forgotten about his conversation with Peecie.

Locking up the station, the Sergeant and the policemen all retired to their homes for the night.

Wee Willie Winkie was never far from the Sergeant's mind, but he just knew that Willie would be caught. All Willie had to do was make just one mistake.

*

Week 2. Monday, 10.15 p.m.

The Sergeant was particularly tired from last night's late night, so he went to bed early and was asleep by 9.45 p.m. He was rudely woken by the telephone on his bedside cabinet at ten-fifteen.

"Argent," he answered, sleepily.

It was Bo Peep. "Sergeant," she whispered, "there's a man creeping around the cottages, looking in all the windows. I saw him go into the old woman's shoe cottage and come out a couple of minutes later. He's obviously up to no good. He's just looked through Tommy Tucker's cottage window."

"Do you recognise him?" asked the Sergeant.

"Yes. It's Wee Willy Winkie..."

CHAPTER 41

Week 2. Monday, 10.16 p.m.

The Sergeant suddenly sat up in bed, startled by Bo Peep's comments.

"You're sure it's him?" he asked.

"Absolutely. He's now snooping around Jack and Jill's place."

This was, maybe, the mistake that the Sergeant had been waiting for.

"Okay. Don't go out! I'm on my way. Don't let him know you've seen him."

The Sergeant was, by this time, out of bed and pushing on his socks and trying to get dressed with one hand while holding the telephone handset. Terminating the call he put the phone down until he had his trousers on and zipped up. Sitting on the side of his bed he stabbed the quick-dial button for PC Griller's telephone number.

Mrs. Lamb's answer took the Sergeant by surprise.

"Hello?" was all she said.

"Err, is PC Griller there?"

The Sergeant heard a shuffling around and a muffled "It's for you," as the phone was passed over to Griller.

"Griller? Is that you?"

"Yes Sarg."

"Oh, right. Sorry to disturb you, but I need you to get dressed if you're not already dressed, and get to Humpty Dumpty's end of the village. I'll be at the opposite end."

"Oh? Why?"

"Willie has just been spotted snooping around the cottages. If you quietly start a search from your end, while I start a search from my end, optimistically, we'll catch him somewhere in the middle."

"On my way, Sarg."

*

Week 2. Monday 10.30 p.m.

The Sergeant and Griller started their search of the village. The night was warm and silent, except for the screech of an owl somewhere near the castle. There wasn't a cloud in the sky and the moon was full. The two policemen silently and covertly crept from garden to garden, their eyes peeled for any sign of movement.

Griller heard the noise of a dustbin lid rattling to the ground. The sound came from the back of Boy Blue's cottage. The policeman silently tiptoed down the side of the cottage and peered round its corner. Nothing.

Then he heard a rustling sound at the back of the bin. Quietly approaching the bin he pushed it to one side and shouted "GOT YER!"

A cat yowled and dashed out from behind the bin, making the hairs on the back of Griller's neck stand up in surprise. After a couple of choice words, he returned to the street at the front of the building.

*

Cut to the Sergeant.

He was prowling around Bo Peep's cottage. He was half way down the side of the cottage, in a shaded part of the path, when heard the commotion created by Griller's surprise on the cat, and he heard Griller shout *'GOT YER!'*

The Sergeant froze and turned, thinking that Griller had caught Willie. He was about to run back down Bo Peep's path towards the street when he was suddenly pushed from behind with such force that he was propelled forwards, landing on his stomach.

Willie had also heard the clatter of a dustbin and Griller's shout. He had been lurking next to the back door of Bo's cottage, trying the door handle to see if the door was locked, and hearing the commotion he had decided that the police were too close for comfort. His next decision was the wrong one to make. Not knowing that the Sergeant was just around the corner of the cottage, Willie made a run for it.

The Sergeant had turned to face the street when Willie rounded the corner and he bumped into the Sergeant's back, immediately giving the Sergeant a colossal push. As the Sergeant tumbled to the ground Willie jumped over him and dashed towards the street.

The Sergeant shouted, "HE'S HERE, GRILLER! GET HIM!"

Griller had, by this time, returned to the street. Seeing Willie appear from the side of Bo's cottage he shouted "Oi, YOU! STOP! POLICE!" and chased after Willie.

The Sergeant got to his feet and chased down the path after Willie. Meeting Griller the two policemen chased after their quarry. All three men were rapidly approaching Hot Cross. At the same time as Willie arrived at the cross, the pie man, carrying a big tray of pies, collided with Willie.

Willie, the pie man, the tray and the pies all scattered as the two men collided. Willie and the pie man bounced off each other and both ended in a heap on the ground. The tray landed on top of the pie man and the pies rolled down the road.

The two policemen pounced on top of Willie. There was a fight as Willie tried to escape and Griller took a left hook to his chin. The Sergeant grabbed Willie's head in a head lock and wrestled him back down to the ground. Griller jumped on top, winding Willie to the extent that he had no fight left in him. The Sergeant quickly fitted his handcuffs onto Willie's wrists while Griller hung onto his feet to stop the Sergeant being kicked.

Realising that he was well and truly caught, Willie gave up the fight. With Griller's arm hooked around his, he stood looking at the Sergeant. A breathless Sergeant cautioned him.

"Wee Willie Winkie, I'm going to charge you with attempted murder. You do not have to say anything but it may harm your defence if you do not mention, when questioned, something that you later rely on in Court. Anything you do say may be given in evidence. Do you understand?"

"Get Knotted!"

"I'll take that as a 'Yes,' then. Griller hold him there while I help the pie man."

The Sergeant helped the pie man back onto his feet. "Are you alright, sir," he asked.

"Yes, but look at the state of my pies." He turned to face Willie and said, with some venom, "That's something else you owe me for…"

The two policemen didn't place any credence on the pie man's outburst. They were more concerned with getting Willie to the cells.

As the pie man was picking up his broken tray, Griller asked, "Just out of interest, sir, where were you going with those pies at this time of the night?"

"I was taking them to the fair. They always like a fresh batch around this time. I'm going to have to make some more, now. That'll keep me working 'till midnight."

The policemen began their walk back to the station. They didn't see the pie man picking up the scattered pies and dusting them off. It was doubtful that he would do any more baking tonight…

The punters at the fair will be eating grass with their pies, tonight, but the pie man couldn't care less.

CHAPTER 42

Week 2. Monday, 10.55 p.m.

Wee Willie Winkie was locked up in a cell at the police station. The police now had Willie and John Dumpling in custody.

As the station was being locked up for the night the Sergeant asked Griller, "How come Mrs. Lamb answered your phone tonight?"

With a smile on his face, Griller replied, "'Cos I was round at her place."

"Oh? Doing what?"

"Having a cup of coffee."

The Sergeant decided not to ask…

*

Week 2. Tuesday, a.m.

PC Slack unlocked the police station and manned the desk. He opened the incident book to refresh his memory on events that had taken place, and read the entry that the Sergeant had written before locking up last night.

PC Peecie entered the station with a cheery "Mornin'."

Slack looked up from the incident book and replied, "Mornin'. Looks like the Sergeant and Griller were busy last night."

"Why?"

"Wee Willie Winkie is locked up. That's two breakfasts you need to get ready. Be careful with John Dumpling - he has a habit of throwing his food at people."

"Oh? Why?"

"Read up on it in the incident book after breakfast."

"Is the Sarg in yet?" asked Peecie.

"Not yet, but…"

Slack's sentence was cut short by PC Griller entering the station. "Mornin'," he chirped.

A chorus of "Mornin'." answered back. PC Peecie disappeared into the kitchen to make the detainee's breakfast.

Slack said, "You two were out late last night."

"Yeah. The Sarg disturbed me just as I was getting in the zone."

"In the zone? Doing what?"

"Having a cup of coffee round at Mrs. Lamb's place," smiling.

"Oh… Right. I just read about Willie's arrest in the incident book."

"Yeah. He's in cell three," informed Griller.

"Peecie's just gone to make breakfast for him and Dumpling."

"Okay, I'd better find out who Willie's solicitor is and give him a ring to let him know that Willie has been arrested," said Griller.

The Sergeant entered from the door behind the desk.

"Mornin'."

Another chorus of "Mornin'" returned.

"How's your chin?" asked the Sergeant.

"A bit sore, but I've had worse," replied Griller.

The Sergeant continued, "Has anyone phoned Willie's solicitor to let him know that we've got him in here?"

"Just about to do that," replied Griller.

*

Week 2. Tuesday, 10.00 a.m.

Mr. Greedie of Fleeceham, Greedie and Crooks entered the station and introduced himself, handing over a business card decorated with a gold border and flowery writing. He's another solicitor who is highly respected and important… According to himself.

"I trust you have not spoken to my client yet?"

"No sir. We're just preparing the interview room for you, unless you would prefer to discuss matters with him in his cell?" replied the Sergeant.

There was a pause while the solicitor recollected a particular conversation he had had with his partner, Mr. Fleeceham. A conversation about why Fleeceham had returned to the office with porridge all over his suit, shoes and face.

"Er, no, no thank you. I'll wait until he is in the interview room."

"As you wish, sir. Would you like a cup of tea?"

"No, thank you."

The policemen busied themselves until Slack returned from the interview room, having checked there was a fresh tape in the recorder and that the camera was working.

"Interview room one is ready for you, Sarg. Peecie, will you help me get Wee Willie Winkie out of his cell and into the interview room?"

"Will do."

The two policemen made their way to the cells while the solicitor made himself comfortable in the interview room.

*

Week 2. Tuesday, 10.30 a.m.

Mr. Greedie has been afforded some time to discuss matters with his client in private. The Sergeant started to interview Willie.

"Willie, I'm sure you don't need reminding that you're still under caution. Is there anything that you want to tell us?"

The solicitor jumped in. "My client has nothing to say."

"Is that right, Willie?" asked the Sergeant.

The solicitor jumped in, again. "Yes that's right."

"Mr. Greedie, I'm sure that your client is capable of answering my questions. Would you be so good as to let him speak for himself?"

Silence descended until the Sergeant's next question.

"Willie, why did you push Jack and Jill down the hill?"

"I didn't."

"That's not what we've been told."

"Who said what?"

"Doesn't matter. Why did you push them?"

"I've just told you - I didn't."

"Okay, why did you steal Bo Peep's sheep?"

"Who?"

"Bo Peep."

"Who's she?"

The Sergeant paused while he read the file.

"You know… Why did you steal Bo Peep's sheep?"

"I didn't. She gave then to me."

"So you admit to being in possession of Bo Peep's sheep?"

The solicitor jumped in, once more. "Being in possession is not sufficient proof that my client stole the sheep."

"We have witnesses to confirm that Willie was seen loading the sheep into the back of old MacDonald's truck. It's an offence to handle stolen goods."

"My client has nothing to say," looking at Willie, reproachfully.

"Yeah, no comment," chipped in Willie.

"Were you given permission to drive the truck?"

"I didn't drive it. Dumpling was the only person to drive that truck."

"Shut up!" demanded the solicitor to Willie. Willie looked a bit sheepish.

"While searching your cottage, we found a roll of ten pound notes. Where did you get all that money?"

"No comment."

"Let's turn to Thursday morning, last week, Willie. Where were you on that morning?"

"In bed."

"Do you have anyone to confirm that?"

"No."

"My client has NOTHING to say, Sergeant." The solicitor stared at Willie with angry eyes.

"What were you doing at the hospital, Willie? We have a witness to say that you were seen leaving the hospital. Your shit covered wellies gave you away."

"She's wrong."

"My client has NOTHING TO SAY!" bellowed the solicitor into Willie's ear.

"Who said the witness was a 'she', Willie? I didn't."

"No comment."

A breath of relief was heard escaping from the solicitor.

"Okay, Why did you throw Lucy Locket's purse into the bush?"

Silence.

"Answer the question, Willie."

"No comment."

"You say that you didn't drive the truck. Why were the truck keys found in your cottage?"

"Somebody planted them there."

"I don't think so, Willie. You used the keys to hide the truck which, I might add, was found in the forest. Why did you hide the truck?"

"I didn't. Somebody else hid it."

The solicitor looked as if he was ready to punch Willie on the nose. "Look, Sergeant, it doesn't sound as if you have anything to charge my client with. So, with, or without, your permission I think we are ready to leave." He stood and turned to Willie. "Let's go, Willie."

Willie stood, but the Sergeant took back control of the interview.

"Sit down, Willie. Let me tell you what we have on you, then your solicitor can decide whether we have anything, or not."

Willie and his solicitor sat back down.

The Sergeant continued, "I believe that we have sufficient evidence to charge you with several crimes."

He read from the file while listing Willies crimes.

"One - both Jack and Jill are willing to testify that you pushed them down the hill. You did this because they both saw you loading Bo Peep's sheep into the back of the truck. Two - forensics have proved that you drove the truck. Yours and John Dumpling's fingerprints are all over the door handles, gear stick and steering wheel. Three - I found a handwritten map of the area in the truck, handwritten written by you. I believe that you used this map to locate the sheep. Four - sheep shit covered wellies, your wellies, were found inside your cottage, the same wellies that witnesses, including my PC, saw you wearing at the hospital. We believe that you went to the hospital to further harm Jack and Jill…"

"I only went there to warn them off. I wasn't going to do anything to them," interrupted Willie.

"SHUT UP!" demanded the solicitor, now banging the desk in frustration.

"Five," continued the Sergeant, "other witnesses saw you loading the sheep into the back of the truck with John Dumpling. Six - you were witnessed running away from Bo Peep's paddock after you had loaded the sheep into the truck."

By now, Willie was leaning on the desk with his elbows, holding his head in both hands.

"Seven - we believe that the money we found at your cottage was payment for stealing the sheep and hiding the truck, using the keys that we found inside your cottage. Eight - we believe that you abducted Mary's lamb and gave it to Dumpling to take away. Nine - we have a witness who will testify that you threw Lucy Locket's purse into the bush. We believe that you stole that purse from Lucy, took the money out of it then threw the purse away. Now do you think we have nothing on you? Either way, I'm going to throw the book at you for the crimes that we know you committed. Has your memory returned to you yet, Willie?" asked the Sergeant, angrily.

The solicitor stood and spoke to the Sergeant.

"May I have a word with you in private, Sergeant?"

The Sergeant calmed down and walked out of the interview room, followed by the solicitor. Griller continued to guard Willie while Slack went to make a cup of tea for everyone.

In the Sergeant's office, the Sergeant sat behind his desk and opened up his note pad. Calmly, he advised the solicitor, "Mr. Greedie, what we say now will be recorded by me."

"No need for that, Sergeant. I just want to make a suggestion."

"Okay…"

"Well," continued the solicitor, "allow me a little time to speak with my client, and I'm sure he will give you a statement. However, he will need some assurances before doing so."

"What assurances will he want?"

"Well, for a start, he will need to be convinced that you will provide a good reference for him if… *when* he goes before the judge."

"I can't answer for the judge, as you know, but depending on the value of Willie's statement I'm sure that Judge Fairly will look favourably upon him. What else?"

"I'm sure my client will testify the names of those he was working for… For a lenient sentence."

"Again, that will be up to the Judge, but I can let the Judge know how helpful Willie has been if I'm called as a witness."

"This charge of attempted murder - perhaps this can be reduced to, say, reckless behaviour?"

"It's a possibility. I'll think about it while you have a word with your client. Willie must appreciate, though, that there are other charges for him to answer to."

The solicitor thought about the Sergeant's comments for a few moments. "Alright," he said, eventually, "Let me see what my client says."

The Sergeant led the way back to the interview room, where Willie and Griller were supping from mugs of tea.

"Griller," suggested the Sergeant. "let's give Willie some more time with his solicitor, shall we?"

CHAPTER 43

Week 2. Tuesday, 10.45 a.m.

It took Mr. Greedie, of Fleeceham, Greedie and Crooks, some time to persuade Wee Willie Winkie to co-operate with the Sergeant on the question of causing harm to Jack and Jill. Eventually, he begrudgingly acquiesced in the optimism that his jail sentence *might* be reduced if he co-operated more fully. The solicitor called the Sergeant and PC Griller back into the interview room.

"My client is now ready to answer your questions, Sergeant," Mr. Greedie advised, and sat down next to Willie.

"Shall we start off with Jack and Jill, Willie?" prompted the Sergeant.

Willie shrugged his shoulders.

"Why did you push them off the top of the hill?"

Willie looked at his solicitor, who nodded to encourage Willie to answer.

He took a deep breath in, let it out slowly and answered, "Because they saw me stealing the sheep."

"We'll come on to the sheep in a moment, but firstly, I'd like to tie up a few loose ends with Jack and Jill."

"Okay…" another shrug of the shoulders in submission of the questioning.

"We know you were at the hospital because we have witnesses that saw you. Why did you go to the hospital? To harm Jack and Jill?"

"After I pushed them over the top, I looked down and saw they were both lying there. I thought they were dead…"

"So you did try to kill them?" interrupted the Sergeant.

"No... I just wanted to frighten them. I didn't think they would be so badly injured."

"Okay, so tell me why you were at the hospital."

"Once I heard that they were alive I felt relieved that I hadn't killed them. That would have been too much for me to bear..."

"The hospital, Willie, the hospital."

"Well, I didn't want them blabbing that they saw me steal the sheep, so I just went there to warn them off, that's all. I wasn't going to do anything to them - just warn them off."

"Shall we now turn to the sheep? Why did you steal them?"

"Because me and Dumpling were paid to steal them."

"And Mary's lamb."

"Yes. That, as well."

"Who paid you, Willie?"

Turning to his solicitor, Willie asked, "Do I have to answer that? I don't want to get anybody into trouble."

"Yes," replied the solicitor.

Willie took a little while to think about the question, then declared, "No, I can't tell you that."

"Why not, Willie?"

"Because he'll do me in. He'll make sure that I never walk again."

"Oh? what makes you think that?"

"He's evil. He's a nutter. I've seen him stick one on a cows' head, and that cow just dropped to the floor. He had to shoot it, and he made me and Boy Blue dig its grave. No... No way. I'm not answering that question."

"I presume you're talking about old MacDonald, seeing as he's the only person in Rhyme Place that owns cows."

Willie took on that *'Oh, no!'* look, eyes tightly shut and jaw tightly locked, in the knowledge that he had inadvertently answered the question.

"Okay, Willie. Why did you try to hide the truck?"

"Because MacDonald told me to."

"Are you insured to drive the truck?"

"No."

"Do you have a valid license to drive the truck?"

"No."

"I want to now discuss Lucy's purse…"

The Sergeant was interrupted by Willie. "Yeah, yeah. I stole it from her and threw it into the bushes," a resigned sigh escaping from him.

"Why did you do that? Wasn't the payment from MacDonald enough for you?"

"You can NEVER have enough money."

"One final question, Willie, before I charge you with your solicitor present. Why do you always wear that dressing gown?"

Willie looked down at his tatty old dressing gown and answered, "Because I don't have a coat. MacDonald promised to have a sheepskin coat made for me with the hides from the stolen sheep, but I don't suppose he'll do that now, will he?"

"I doubt it," answered the Sergeant, standing up from the table. "Please stand up Willie while I formally charge you."

Willie and his solicitor stood. Willie looked down at the floor.

The Sergeant continued, “Willie, I’m going to reverse the charge of attempted murder, but you will be charged with a lesser crime.”

Willie’s head jerked up and he took on an optimistic smile on his face.

“Wee Willie Winkie, I’m charging you with the Misdemeanour of Reckless Behaviour, in that you unlawfully and maliciously inflicted grievous bodily harm upon Jack and Jill by deliberately pushing them off the top of the hill. I’m also charging you with theft of Bo Peep’s four sheep, theft of Mary’s lamb, and theft of Lucy Locket’s purse. Further, you are charged with driving whilst uninsured and also with driving without a valid licence to drive the truck. Do you understand all the charges against you?”

“Yes.”

“Do you have anything more to say?”

“No.”

“Okay. I’m going to hold you in custody until such time as Judge Fairly can make a date for you to appear before him.” Turning to Griller, the Sergeant ordered, “Lock him in his cell, Griller.”

“Wait!” ordered the solicitor.

Willie and Griller stood their ground.

“Is there any possibility of bail, to allow my client to get his affairs in order?”

“I’m afraid not, sir.” replied the Sergeant. “Willie has already tried to do a runner and he is now considered to be a flight risk. Carry on, Griller.”

Once Griller and Willie had left the room, the solicitor turned to the Sergeant and thanked him for his consideration towards Willie’s charge of attempted murder. “No doubt you will let me have a copy of the charge sheet, indicating the relevant laws associated with Willie's charges, in due course."

"Of course," replied the Sergeant.

Tidying up his pile of papers, the solicitor left the station to begin preparing Willie's defence.

After securing a search and arrest warrant from Judge Fairly, the Sergeant ordered Slack and Griller to bring old MacDonald in for questioning.

CHAPTER 44

Week 2. Tuesday, p.m.

Somebody… I won't say who, but he and Chatty Chaste sometimes get together for a cup of coffee… Somebody phoned Rhyme Place TV station to report a potential story.

NEWS FLASH! From Chatty Chaste on the news desk at Rhyme Place TV station.

Chatty - "This news, just in… We've just had news of an arrest being made at old MacDonald's farm. Our roving reporter, Roaming Ronnie, is on site right now and we'll go over to him for this story. Ronnie, it's always good to talk to you. What can you tell us about this incident?"

Roaming Ronnie - "Hi Chatty. Yes, as you can see behind me there is a lot of activity centred around old MacDonald's farmhouse. The police made a forced entry to the farmhouse at about twelve-fifteen today and we can see them taking several bags of what might be evidence to the police van. Wait a moment… Yes, we can now see old MacDonald being escorted to the police van under a blanket to hide his face."

Chatty - "Ronnie, do we know, yet, what this police raid is all about?"

Ronnie - "As yet, Chatty, we don't have any details about it. We do, however, have Mayor Reform here and I'll asked him for a statement. Mayor, What can you tell us about this police operation?"

Mayor Reform - "Absolutely nothing! I was just on my way for a quick… Err, cup of coffee, with Mrs. Blue, when this crowd blocked the road. I'm sick to the high teeth about all these road blocks and I'll be raising the subject at the next council meeting."

Ronnie - "So you don't have any information about the police raid?"

Mayor - "No, and I'd like to know who told you people about it! You got here long before me. Nobody EVER tells me what's going on around here. I'm fed up with being left out of the loop. I'll be raising that at the next council meeting as well, because…!"

The camera quickly pans back to Ronnie without letting the Mayor finish his sentence.

Ronnie - "Well, Chatty, there you have it. Nobody seems to know why this raid is taking place, but there is a strong rumour that it may be connected to the theft of Bo Peep's sheep."

Mayor Reform can be heard in the background. "See that? He cut me off! Look! He's done it again! Who told him that? What about Bo Peep's sheep? Nobody tells me anything around here…"

Ronnie - "We'll keep an eye on things here at the farm for now but in the meantime, Chatty, back to you in the studio."

Chatty - "Thank you Ronnie… We'll now return you to our documentary, 'Two weeks in the life of Rhyme Place,' and we'll let you know if anything new happens at the farm. For now, goodbye."

*

Old MacDonald came quietly.

Before being placed in the cell he demanded to see his solicitor. "I'm not saying a word until my solicitor is present."

The Sergeant ordered PC Peecie to get in touch with MacDonald's solicitor and invite him to the station to be present during MacDonald's interview.

CHAPTER 45

Week 2. Tuesday, 2.00 p.m.

Mr. Crooks, solicitor of Fleeceham, Greedie and Crooks, entered the police station. You will, by now, have gathered that Fleeceham, Greedie and Crooks are the *only* solicitors in Rhyme Place village.

"Good morning, sir," welcomed PC Peecie. "How can I help you?"

"I've come to see my client, Mr. MacDonald. Has he been charged, yet?"

"Not to my knowledge, sir. Would you like to take a seat while I let the Sergeant know that you're waiting?"

"No, I would like to speak with my client."

Peecie ignored the solicitor's demand and pressed the undercounter bell push to alert the Sergeant, then continued with his paperwork. Actually, he was doing the crossword.

The solicitor tutted and growled, "When you've finished playing games would you mind taking me to my client?"

"The Sergeant's on his way, sir."

Crooks was about to give Peecie a tongue lashing when the Sergeant emerged from his office. Approaching the desk, Peecie introduced the solicitor.

"Good morning, sir," welcomed the Sergeant. "How can I help you?"

With a look of exasperation, the solicitor angrily demanded to see his client once more. The Sergeant answered by informing him that the visitor book needed to completed before he could be anywhere near his client.

"Peecie, help Mr. Crooks to fill in the visitor book, please," and the Sergeant disappeared back into his office.

The solicitor dumped himself into one of the visitor chairs, an angry expression darkening his face and muttering, "I've got better things to do than to follow this bureaucratic claptrap with you clowns."

Peecie replied, indifferently, "Just following procedures, sir."

"Get on with it, then!"

Peecie took his time sharpening his pencil, opening the visitor book to the correct page, licking his pencil point, and taking in a deep breath before asking, "Name?"

"I've just told you my name, you oaf!" irritation in his voice.

"Name?"

With a huff the solicitor repeated his name.

"Company?"

"What!? I've told you that. It's clearly shown on my business card, fool!"

"Company?"

The solicitor was now almost in tears, shaking with frustration, steam shooting out of his ears. To expedite matters he shouted out his company name.

"Who are you visiting?"

The solicitor just gave up, dropped his shoulders, took in a deep breath, let it out and stared at Peecie with a pleading look on his face. The Sergeant was now leaning on his door frame and had listened, with interest, to this verbal pin-pong and had watched the rapport between the two men deteriorate. He decided to put the solicitor out of his misery.

"Will you step into my office, please, Mr. Crooks?"

Crooks stood and furiously followed the Sergeant, carrying his brief case under his arm. Once inside the office, the Sergeant invited Crooks to sit in the chair in front of his desk.

"Mr. Crooks," began the Sergeant, "I don't like my staff being abused, and neither do they. I'm sure that PC Peecie would have dealt with matters more quickly if you had just shown some respect towards him. He was just doing his job."

The solicitor thought about the Sergeant's comments for a moment and appeared to calm down after taking a breath.

"You're absolutely right, of course, Sergeant. I apologise."

"Now," continued the Sergeant, "before I let you interview your client I'd just like to say that we have sufficient evidence to charge him with conspiracy to steal sheep. However, I'd like to get to the bottom of precisely why he stole the sheep, and your help in this matter would be very much appreciated. I'm sure that Judge Fairly will look favourably towards Mr. MacDonald's sentence if he co-operates with us as fully as possible. What do you think?"

"Surely, conspiracy to steal sheep doesn't merit him being held in custody, Sergeant?" pleaded the solicitor.

"That's true, sir, but if he refuses to answer our questions we will charge him with theft and he will remain in our custody until he does co-operate."

"Okay, Sergeant. I'll have a word with him and see if he is willing to co-operate. That's the best I can do at this stage."

"Thank you, Mr. Crooks. If you would be so kind as to wait in reception I'll prepare the interview room and get your client from the cells."

The two men shook hands and returned to the reception.

“Peecie, would you mind showing Mr. Crooks to the interview room and preparing it for Mr. MacDonald’s arrival?”

“Yes Sarg.”

The Sergeant turned to PC Griller. “Will you get Dumpling out and bring him here, please?”

“Yes Sarg.”

The Sergeant then turned to PC Slack. “Slack, do you want to sit in on this interview and take the notes?”

“Yes please, Sarg.”

Griller reappeared with John Dumpling.

The Sergeant addressed him from behind the counter. “Mr. Dumpling, you’ve been charged, and I’m going to bail you to appear before the Judge at a later date. Now, you’re not going to do anything stupid, like disappearing before your trial, are you? You know that we will find you, if you do, and you will be returned to the cells until your trial date. Going missing will not look good for your sentence. Is that clear?”

Dumpling nodded.

“Off you go, and keep your nose clean, or you’ll feel my bracelets around your wrists.”

Dumpling turned, headed towards the door and left the station. Slack and the Sergeant waited for MacDonald and his solicitor.

*

Week 2. Tuesday, 3.00 p.m.

PC Peecie lightly tapped on the interview room door, opened it and ushered MacDonald and his solicitor to the waiting chairs.

When everyone was sat, the Sergeant opened the conversation.

"Mr. MacDonald, would you like a drink? Tea, or maybe a glass of water?"

"Nope."

"I assume your solicitor has informed you why you have been brought in for questioning?"

"Yes."

"Do you have anything to say?"

"Nothing."

"Take him back to the cells, Slack."

The solicitor jumped to his feet and said, "No, wait…" he turned to his client. "Mr. MacDonald, we spoke earlier and you agreed to co-operate. If you now feel that you cannot co-operate, then I will have to advise you to find another solicitor to handle your case."

MacDonald rubbed his brow, puffed out a long, slow sigh then said, "Okay, what do you want?"

The solicitor sat down again, and the Sergeant continued his questioning.

"It's unusual for you to want some sheep, sir. I thought you were entirely a dairy farmer?"

"I am, but I was asked to get some sheep. At first, I wasn't interested, but the guy offered a lot of money, so I agreed."

"Now, we have statements from both John Dumpling and Wee Willie Winkie that you paid them to steal the sheep. Is that the case?"

"Yes."

"And we have a statement to show that you kept the sheep in one of your barns. Is that true?"

"Yes. I didn't have room for them in my lounge…" a sarcastic smile appearing on his face.

"So what happened to the sheep?"

"That damned fool, Boy Blue, let them escape. I never saw them after that. I told the guy who'd agreed to pay me to steal them, and he went ballistic. He threatened to burn my farmhouse down if I didn't get them back, but I couldn't find them - anywhere."

"Did you give Willie permission to use your truck?"

"Yes."

"Why did you tell him to hide it?"

"No, I didn't. I told him to take it away and get it cleaned up. I didn't want the back of it stinking the place out with sheep shit."

"I see. What about the lamb?"

"What about it?"

"Why did you get Willie to steal that?"

"The guy said he would pay me a premium to get lamb - mutton didn't pay as well."

"So what were you supposed to do with the sheep? Was he going to collect them?"

"No. He said that I wasn't going to get a penny until I had prepared them."

"Prepare them?"

"You know, skin 'em and chuck out all the offal. Then de-bone the meat."

"What did he want them prepared for?"

"I don't know - I don't suppose he wanted to do it himself."

"Who was it, Mr. MacDonald? Who agreed to pay you to steal the sheep?"

"It was the pie man…"

CHAPTER 46

Week 2. Tuesday, 3.30 p.m.

Old MacDonald has just admitted to arranging for Bo Peep's sheep and Mary's lamb to be stolen and delivered to the farm. He had been contracted by the pie man, but having now pointed the finger at the pie man it was doubtful that MacDonald would receive any payment.

Notwithstanding MacDonald's confession, payment to him was cloaked in a lot of doubt in any event because the sheep had escaped and MacDonald was unable to fulfil the contract. This annoyed him, immensely, because he had already paid Willie and Dumpling for their part in this fiasco, so he was out of pocket. What's more worrying for MacDonald was the fact that the pie man had threatened to burn the farmhouse down if the sheep were not found.

MacDonald stood in front of the reception desk, his head bowed, eyes looking down at the floor. His solicitor was stood next to him.

"Mr. MacDonald," declared the Sergeant, "I'm charging you with conspiracy to steal Bo Peep's sheep and Mary's lamb under the Criminal Law Act, 1977. You're not obliged to say anything but it may harm your defence if you do not mention, when questioned, something that you later rely on in Court. Anything you do say may be given in evidence. Do you understand this charge?"

"Yes."

"I'm going to bail you to appear before Judge Fairly on a date to be decided by the Judge. Now, Mr. MacDonald, you're not going to leave the country, are you?"

"Leave the country? I've got a bloody farm to manage. No. I'm not going to leave the country," answered an angry MacDonald.

"Okay, sir, but be advised - if you fail to attend the court when ordered to do so you will be re-arrested and jailed. Is that clear?"

"I'll attend. Just let me get back - my cows need milking."

"Off you go, sir. I advise you NOT to talk to the pie man about today's interview. I don't want him to do a runner before we've arrested him."

MacDonald and his solicitor left the police station. The Sergeant requested yet another search and arrest warrant from Judge Fairly.

*

Week 2. Tuesday, 4.00 p.m.

Armed with the warrants, the Sergeant and Griller's first port of call was the Hot Cross bun factory reception.

As they approached the reception desk, the receptionist repositioned the lump of chewing gum inside her mouth and advised, "Good afternoon, officers. Sales, this way…, [*pointing*] and order pick-up that way… [*pointing in the opposite direction*].

"No, we've not come for any buns, we've come to interview the pie man. Is…?" The Sergeant was interrupted before he could finish his sentence.

"Ahh! I'll just phone for the duty officer. In the meantime, would you like a bun?"

The two policemen looked at each other then back at the receptionist, without answering. The receptionist picked up the telephone handset and dialled the duty officer's number, then continued to ruminate her chewing gum until her call was answered. Taken by surprise, she attempted to speak but instead projected the chewing gum out of her mouth.

She dropped the telephone as she tried to save the chewing gum from bouncing off the desk onto the floor. Trying to multi-task by picking up the telephone *and* prevent the chewing gum falling to the floor she got tangled in the phone cable and dropped the phone, once more. The chewing gum disappeared off the top of the desk.

The Sergeant leaned over the counter and cut off the call to the Duty officer.

"When you've got yourself sorted out, just let the pie man know we are on our way to his bakery. We know the way."

The police officers made their way towards the door to the bakery just as the duty officer appeared out of the bun factory door.

He started his sentence to the receptionist. "Julie, have you just tried to phone me? We got cut off..." then he saw the policemen. "Oh, good afternoon officers. Have you come to place an order for the station?"

"No," answered the Sergeant. "We've come to see the pie man. Is he available?"

"Erm, I don't know. Are you sure you won't place an order? We've got a good offer on for today - *three* buns for a penny."

The Sergeant just stared at the duty manager and waited for a reply to his question.

The manager took the hint. "I'll take that as a no, then," he said. "You know the way to the bakery, but first I must ask you to wear some protective clothing. Please, follow me," and the manager walked towards the door he had just used to enter the reception.

The two policemen followed. On the way past the receptionist, this time, PC Slack did not mime for any buns… he didn't have his wallet with him.

The policemen entered the bakery reception. They faced the same identical receptionist as the last time they came to the bakery.

"Good afternoon, officers. Sales, this way…, [*pointing*] and order pick-up that way… [*pointing in the opposite direction*]," chirped up the receptionist.

The policemen didn't enter into any conversation. They just went through the bakery door, unannounced, to seek out the pie man. Startled, the pie man turned from an oven door to look in their direction.

"Good afternoon, officers. What brings you here today?"

"Pie man, we've come to ask you to accompany us to the station to answer some questions about Bo Peep's sheep."

"Oh?… [*a long pause*]. What about them?"

"We'll explain down at the station, sir. Please turn round and put your hands behind your back," ordered Griller, taking his handcuffs out of their pouch to install around the pie man's wrists.

"What? What's all this about? Why am I being arrested?"

The pie man was turned to face the Sergeant. The Sergeant cautioned the pie man.

"Pie man, I'm going to arrest you for crimes connected with theft of sheep. You're not obliged to say anything but it may harm your defence if you do not mention, when questioned, something that you later rely on in Court. Anything you do say may be given in evidence. Do you understand?"

"No, I don't understand. What theft? When?"

"We'll talk at the station, sir. Do you wish me to contact your solicitor?"

No reply.

At the police station the pie man was asked, once more, if he wanted a solicitor to be present at his interview.

"What for?" he asked. "I've done nothing wrong. I haven't got one - and anyway, you still haven't answered my question. When am I supposed to have stolen Bo Peep's sheep?"

"Who said anything about Bo Peep's sheep?" asked the Sergeant.

The pie man didn't answer.

The Sergeant ordered Slack to take the pie man to the interview room. Ten minutes later, the Sergeant decided it was time to interview the pie man.

As soon as he and PC Peecie entered the room, the pie man demanded, "I want a solicitor!"

"Yes, of course, sir," replied the Sergeant. "If you had indicated that you wanted a solicitor when I first asked you, things might have taken a lot less time, sir. As it is, I must ask you to wait in the cells until I can find the duty solicitor."

"Wait! I use a guy called Rippemhoff. He's based down in Jingle Town."

The pie man was escorted back to his cell, complaining bitterly that there was no reason for him to be arrested and emphasising his innocence. The Sergeant ordered PC Peecie to contact the pie man's solicitor.

*

Week 2. Tuesday, 5.25 p.m.

NEWS FLASH! From Chatty Chaste of Rhyme Place TV Station, reporting from outside Rhyme Place bun factory. The background shot shows a flurry of activity by firemen around the bun factory and bakery. Two fire tenders can be seen, with hoses being pulled from them.

Chatty [*standing next to Hot Cross Monument*] - "I'm bringing this news flash to you from outside Rhyme Place bun factory. Earlier, today, the fire brigade was called to attend a fire at the bakery. As you can see, [*turning to face the bun factory*] there is a pall of smoke hanging over the factory and I understand that the firemen's activities are centred around the bakery at the rear of the factory building. As yet, we have not heard how, or why, the fire started but a fireman has suggested that the seat of the fire may be one of the bakery ovens. Currently, the fire seems to be contained to the bakery area, and it appears to be under control, although the bun factory personnel have all been evacuated from their workplace as a precautionary measure. Hot crossed bun production, therefore, has been paused until the bakery fire is fully extinguished and there is no danger of it spreading to the factory. So far, we have not heard of any fatalities or injuries, but we'll report any updates on this fire as and when we receive them. For the time being I'll return you to your afternoon's programme."

*

Week 2. Tuesday, 5.30 p.m.

News of the fire travelled at the speed of light to the police station. Leaving PC Griller in charge, the Sergeant and PC Slack cycled down to the bun factory as fast as their bikes could take them.

Slack homed in on Chatty Chaste.

"What we got?" he asked.

"A fire at the bakery," she answered.

"Yeah, we got that from the fire brigade's notification. What else can you tell me?"

"Nothing. We've been kept outside the fire brigade's cordon. As far as we can tell, the fire started in one of the bakery ovens. The bun factory doesn't seem to have been affected, but everyone's been evacuated from it."

"Oh. Right. I'll join the Sarg."

"See you later?"

"Seven-ish?"

"I'll have the coffee ready."

Satisfied that there was nothing for them to do, the Sergeant requested a report from the leading fireman and made his way out of the cordon to meet up with PC Slack. He was approached by Mayor Reform.

"What's all this about, Sergeant?"

"Well, sir, we were informed of a fire at the bakery at approximately five-thirty this afternoon. I've spoken to the leading fireman, who confirms that the fire is now under control and that he will be sending his report to my office first thing tomorrow. From what they can see, the fire appears to have started in one of the bakery ovens. All personnel from the bun factory have been evacuated, but the firemen anticipate allowing them back to work shortly."

"Why wasn't I told about this. My car's got a radio, and my driver has got a mobile phone. *Somebody* could have let me know before now. What's PC Slack doing talking to the TV people?"

"I think he's just getting some background information from her, sir."

"Background infor.nation? I should have been notified of this. I'm NEVER told what's happening around here. Nobody ever keeps me in the loop. What the Hell is wrong with everyone?"

"Don't know, sir. You'll have to take that up at the next council meeting. I must go, sir. I've got a suspect to interview about Bo Peep's sheep."

"And why haven't I been kept up-to-date on that incident?"

"You have, sir. My most recent report was handed in to your office this morning."

"Oh, sorry. Not had time to read it. I've been busy showing my face around town, shaking hands with mothers and kissing babies."

The Sergeant excused himself. "If you'd like to come to the station some time I'll bring you up to speed on everything. I must go, now, sir. I have a suspect waiting to be interviewed."

The Sergeant met up with Slack, and the two policemen cycled back to the station.

The mayor continued to argue with the firemen about not being told about the fire.

CHAPTER 47

Pat-a-cake, pat-a-cake, baker's man,
Bake me a cake as fast as you can,
Roll it, pat it, and mark it with a B,
Put it in the oven for Baby and me.
(The earliest recorded version of this rhyme appears in Thomas D'Urfey's play 'The Campaigners' 1698)

Week 2. Tuesday, 5.55 p.m.

Entering the police station, the Sergeant and PC Slack noticed Mr. Rippemhoff, from Rippemhoff & Smurk, solicitors in Jingle Town, sitting in one of the visitor's chairs.

Mr Rippemhoff didn't look up from the file of papers that was hidden inside his briefcase, with its open lid facing the desk. The Sergeant went straight to his office, motioning Griller to follow him.

"Who've we got in reception?" asked the Sergeant.

"That's Mr. Rippemhoff, the pie man's solicitor. He's been sat there for about fifteen minutes. Other than introducing himself, he hasn't said a word."

"Has he been to speak with his client?"

"Nope. Didn't ask."

With a furrowed brow, the Sergeant considered if the solicitor was playing some kind of game. Solicitors usually demand to see their client immediately they arrive at the station, so why didn't this one do the same?

"Do you think he's up to something?"

"Don't know Sarg. He's not caused us any problems while he's been sat there. He just reads his files."

"Show him into my office," instructed the Sergeant after thinking for a moment.

Griller nodded and left the office, leaving the Sergeant to think about a strategy for discussing matters with the solicitor. After a few minutes, Griller poked his head into the office and introduced the solicitor. The two men shook hands, amiably.

"Good afternoon, Mr. Rippemhoff. I'm surprised you haven't asked to see your client yet."

"Oh, he'll wait. He's not going anywhere, anyway, locked in his cell."

"I'll be honest with you, sir. Contrary to what I expected you seem unusually laid back and relaxed that your client is being held in custody. You've not even asked why."

There was a slight pause as the solicitor opened his briefcase and took out an enormous file. It was at least two inches thick.

Placing the file on the desk, the solicitor smiled and said, "I've known the pie man for several years, Sergeant, and I am aware that he has sailed very close to the wind on many occasions. I assume you have not yet run a background check on him?"

"No, sir, we haven't. We've only just arrested him. What is it about him that's made your file so large?"

"Well, you'll no doubt find out soon enough, so there's no harm in giving you a few details. He's been arrested for several misdemeanours. Usually they're nothing serious… [*reading from the file*] Overcharging, not putting enough meat in his pies, not putting enough of *anything* in his pies, that kind of thing. He's been charged with disorderly conduct and threatening behaviour a couple of times, but nothing has ever stuck to him, so he usually gets a fine, a smack on the wrist and he's let go, although I have to add that much of his freedom is due to my learned intervention."

The solicitor smiled as he conveyed his last comment to the Sergeant. "He keeps my firm in bread, so to speak - no pun intended - so I don't mind spending a lot of time with him. Now, has he been charged? If not, why not, and what is he charged with?"

The Sergeant opened up his own file on the pie man - a measly file compared to the solicitor's thick wad, with just a few of sheets of paper inside.

"He's been arrested for crimes in connection with the theft of Bo Peep's sheep and Mary's lamb. He's been cautioned, but not charged. I've left the charge open until I've interviewed him."

"So he's not been interviewed yet?"

"No, sir. We thought it prudent to await your arrival."

"That's very thoughtful of you, Sergeant. Shall we go and interview him now?"

"Of course, sir."

The Sergeant showed the solicitor to the interview room, on the way there asking Griller to extract the pie man from his cell.

As they waited for Griller to appear with the pie man, the Sergeant advised the solicitor, "I should let you know that the bakery has burned to the ground this afternoon."

"Yes," replied the solicitor, "I heard about it on the way here. Would you like me to inform him?"

"That would be most helpful, sir. Do you think he will take it badly? I'll have Griller on standby just in case."

"I don't think he'll do anything stupid. He'll probably instruct me to deal with his insurance claim."

*

Week 2. Tuesday, 6.15 p.m., in the interview room.

When everyone was settled, the Sergeant opened the conversation.

"Pie man, I must advise you that you are still under caution. Do you require anything? A drink? Something to eat?"

"I'm okay, thanks. A glass of water would be nice."

Griller left the room to fetch the water. The Sergeant continued.

"Before we start, Mr. Rippemhoff has some bad news to give to you. Mr. Rippemhoff…?" indicating for the solicitor to speak.

"Yes," facing the pie man, "I'm afraid that the bakery was burned down at about five-thirty this afternoon. There's not much of it left."

The pie man's face turned a thunderous dark colour, but he just sat there, lips tightly shut.

"Would you like me to inform your insurers?" continued the solicitor.

The pie man looked down at the floor and nodded. With a resigned sigh, he looked up and, with an angry, accusing look at the Sergeant, said, "I forgot to take my pies out of the bloody oven when you guys turned up and brought me here." His chin returned to his chest.

The Sergeant broke the silence that had descended on the interview, once more. "I'll repeat why you have been arrested, pie man. We've brought you here to discuss your involvement with the theft of Bo Peep's sheep and Mary's lamb. Do you wish to make a statement?"

The solicitor answered. "Perhaps I can speak with my client in private, Sergeant. Can you give us, say, half an hour together?"

The policemen left the interview room to return to the reception. A little later than the half-hour requested by the solicitor, Mr. Rippemhoff poked his head round the corner of the reception door and let the policemen know that his client was ready to be interviewed. Everyone trudged back to the interview room, sat back down, scraped their chairs forward and placed their elbows on the desk.

The solicitor spoke first. "Sergeant, my client and I have prepared a written statement for you to save time. May I read this out to you?"

"Please, do," came back the reply.

The solicitor coughed, shook the statement and laid it on the desk in front of him. Reading from the written statement, the solicitor narrated the pie man's account of his involvement with the stolen sheep.

STATEMENT BY PIE MAN, ASSISTED BY MR. RIPPEMHOFF OF RIPPEMHOFF & SMURK, SOLICITORS, JINGLE TOWN.

Today is Tuesday at 7.00, p.m.
I, the pie man, make this statement of my own free will and without any coercion from the police, or my solicitor.

I bake pies and cakes for Rhyme Place and surrounding towns. My bakery ~~is~~ - was - situated at the rear of Hot Cross bun factory. I have owned the bakery for about fifteen years, and I am contracted to provide pies and cakes for a variety of clients. I do not employ anyone to help me.

Approximately one and a half weeks ago, the fairground manager called into my bakery to ask about pies for the fair. He wanted a large selection of beef pies, pork pies and lamb's meat pies, and a contract was signed for me to provide these. The contract was for a sum of money that would have paid my bills for about six months, so it was too good to pass up. If I hadn't taken the contract it would have gone to someone up country.

This was on Friday, the week before last, and the fairground wanted the pies on Wednesday of last week. This meant that I had five days, only, to source the meat, bake the pies and deliver them to the fairground. At the time, I had the idea of using cheaper cuts of mutton for the fairground pies and charging them for lamb. They wouldn't know the difference between mutton and lamb if their faces were smacked with it, and I thought it a good way of making some extra profit.

Normally, providing the pies would not be a problem. I had an ample supply of beef from old MacDonald's farm and the pig farmer in Jingle Town regularly delivers pork to the bakery for my pork pies. However, I was unable to source any lambs without having to get them from Balladshire, a few hundred miles away. I didn't have enough time to go that far, so I knew that I had to get some lambs locally.

The next day, the Saturday, I was asked to go up to the castle to speak with the King. He wanted me to supply two dozen beef pies and two dozen pork pies, all for his banquet, together with a special order of a dozen lamb's meat pies. The king said he would pay me a handsome sum for the pies, but they must be delivered in time for his banquet on Friday, this week. He also insisted that the lamb's meat pies had to be lamb, not mutton. The king warned me that the queen can taste the difference between lamb and mutton, and as lamb was her favourite she insisted on lamb's meat and not mutton. The lamb pies were for her, and only her. This put me between a rock and a hard place. There was no way that I was going to let the King down, but I was unable to source lamb locally.

Having discussed matters with old MacDonald he suggested that as he was providing the beef, ready prepared for cooking, he would source and prepare the sheep and lamb. I had calculated that I would need just four sheep for the fairground but only one lamb for the Queen's pies. He told me that that was no problem, and we signed a contract for supply and preparation of the meat. I didn't let on that the payment I had in mind for him was about a quarter of the amount I was being paid by both the fair and the King.

Contract signed, I left it to MacDonald to deliver the meat to me on Tuesday, last week. That would give me twenty-four hours to bake the pies for delivery to the fairground. The King's pies would have been delivered on the same day.

MacDonald failed to deliver the sheep. He told me he had lost them, so I never paid him anything. I did, however, deliver some apple pies to the fairground on Monday of last week. On the way there I got help, to carry my tray of pies, from young Simon, although I couldn't deliver as many as I expected because some got too damaged in an accident. We were both almost run down by one of MacDonald's trucks. I didn't see who was driving, but I made a statement for Sergeant Argent shortly afterwards.

I never knew where MacDonald sourced the sheep from. I never asked.

I did, however, hear on the TV that Bo Peep had had her sheep stolen. I wondered if that was connected to my contract with MacDonald, but I decided not to say anything at the time - just in case it was. I didn't want to be implicated in any way.

I did not steal Bo Peep's sheep or Mary's lamb.

This statement is, to the best of my recollection, a true and honest account of my actions in connection with Bo Peep's sheep and Mary's lamb.

Having read the statement out aloud, the solicitor asked the pie man to sign it in front of the policemen and he, himself, signed as a witness. He gave the statement to the Sergeant and requested two copies; one for himself and one for the pie man.

The solicitor then asked, "Is there anything else, Sergeant, or can my client go, now."

The Sergeant looked at the pie man and said, "You could have told us all that when we first discussed this matter with you earlier. You've wasted a lot of police time pie man."

There was no response from the pie man.

The Sergeant continued. "Mr. Rippemhoff, can we have a word outside, please?"

The two men left the interview room and continued their discussion in the reception.

"I think now is the time to charge your client," declared the Sergeant. "I'm not going to hold him in custody, so I'm going to trust that you will persuade him to attend court, when summoned."

"I think he will co-operate, Sergeant. What about the charge?"

"Well, he's certainly perverted the course of justice by not giving me the full story. He also attempted to fraudulently pass off mutton pies as lamb. As far as the theft of sheep is concerned, we'll never know if he knew that they were going to be stolen, but he certainly knew after the event and didn't come forward with any information at the time."

"So you're not going to charge him with theft, then?"

"Let me think on that one as we return to the interview room."

The two men made their way down the corridor, back to charge the pie man.

Entering the interview room, the Sergeant spoke to the pie man.

"Stand up, please, pie man."

The order was obeyed.

"Pie man I believe you knew that the sheep and lamb were going to be stolen. You must have discussed where to get them from when you discussed your deal with old MacDonald, so I'm charging you with conspiracy to steal Bo Peep's sheep and Mary's lamb. I'm also charging you with perverting the course of justice.

"I'm going to hold, on file, a charge of attempting to fraudulently pass off sheep pies as lamb's meat pies, and likewise, a charge of wasting police time. These charges will be resurrected when, or if, you are arrested again in the future. Now, you are still under caution, so I assume that you will co-operate if we need to call you in again for more questioning. Do you understand these charges?"

"Yes." Turning to the solicitor he angrily growled, "You're useless. My cat would have done a better job than you!"

The Sergeant finished with, "I'm not going to hold you in custody, sir. I'm going to bail you to appear before Judge Fairly at a time that is convenient to him… You can go."

CHAPTER 48

As I was going to St Ives,
I met a man with seven wives.
Each wife had seven sacks,
Each sack had seven cats,
Each cat had seven kits:
Kits, cats, sacks, and wives,
How many were there going to St Ives?

(This version of a riddle in the form of a rhyme was found in a manuscript dating from about 1730. However, the earliest known published versions of this rhyme omit the words 'a man with' immediately preceding the seven wives (i.e. 'I met seven wives'), but he is present in the rhyme by 1837).

Do you know the answer to this riddle?

Week 2. Wednesday, a.m.

The Sergeant was pleased with his team's work in solving the mystery of the stolen sheep and missing lamb and, indeed, the missing tarts. First thing, when all the PC's had arrived for work, he mustered them in the reception area to give them some much welcomed good news.

"Men, you've all worked hard to help me solve the recent crimes that have taken place, and I'm proud of every one of you. Well done."

The three PC's - Slack, Griller and Peecie - smiled from ear-to-ear.

The Sergeant continued. "I've had a word with Judge Fairly, and he's agreed to get a couple of men from

Jingle Town to stand in for us while we take the day off, tomorrow, to celebrate our success."

The PC's shook hands with each other, slapped each other's backs and chatted happily. They all shared the Sergeant's pride that they had done a good job.

"Okay," interrupted the Sergeant, "listen in... We'll all go down to the fair with our other halves and have a good time there. The candy floss is on me." Cheers from the men. "I would have paid for some pies but, as you know, the bakery no longer exists you'll have to make do with candy floss and hot cross buns..."

More laughs from the men.

"What I want you to do, today, is complete all your reports on the stolen sheep, the missing lamb and the missing tarts. These must be ready for submission to Judge Fairly by close of play today. Okay? Any questions?"

With that the men went to their respective corners of the station to prepare their reports.

*

Week 2. Thursday, a.m.

All the policemen met outside the station to go to the fair.

Sergeant Argent had contrary Mary dangling from his arm, PC Griller took Mrs. Lamb - there could be something long term in this relationship - and PC Slack invited Chatty Chaste, who came with a camera and microphone just in case there was anything to report. PC Peecie turned up with one of the pretty maids from contrary Mary's garden. The pretty maid was a surprise guest - Peecie must have worked fast to capture that one...

Now, I'm going to digress, for a moment, to explain that the name of the fair is not, as you might think, Rhyme Place Fair, but it is St. Ives Fair. This is because it is a travelling fair with its home base during the winter months in St. Ives, Cornwall. Rhyme Place is just one of the fair's many summer stops around the country. Ballad Village, in Balladshire a couple of hundred miles away, is another of the fair's stopovers. Okay…? Okay.

On the way to the fair the policemen met a chap jovially chatting to a group of women. Seeing the policemen approaching, he excused himself from the group and approached the Sergeant and his men.

"Good morning, Sergeant. Is there a problem?"

The Sergeant chuckled. "No, sir. We're just on our way to the fair to enjoy ourselves."

"Oh," answered the man. "We've just come from there - it's got some fantastic rides. We're now on our way home to feed the cats," pointing to the group of women.

"Cats?" enquired Slack.

"Yes, cats. They're in the sacks. Want a look?"

The man bolted off to ask the women to open their sacks for the policemen - not that the policemen were all that interested in looking at cats. The group of women approached and busily chatted to the policemen, telling them their names and opening their sacks to show off their cats.

"What's all this about, then?" enquired Griller.

One of the women stepped forward to explain.

"We're all from the wives' knitting circle in Jingle Town and we've knitted those woolly jumpers that the cats are wearing."

The policemen had already noticed that each cat had a woolly pully wrapped around it, but they hadn't asked why.

The woman continued. "We've just been to the fair to show off our knitting and to take some orders for more cat woolly jumpers."

"Oh. Right," answered Slack.

Okay… Now, we all know that some cats just don't like other cats. They don't have to have any reason to dislike other cats, they just hate the sight of them.

All the women had put their sacks on the floor to open them, and two neighbouring cats looked at each other and took an instant dislike to what they saw. Who knows what there was to dislike? Perhaps one of the cats thought the other was ugly, or perhaps they both had a long standing grudge about something. Anyway, up shot the hackles, back went the ears, out came the claws, and with teeth bared the two cats started yowling profanities and throwing punches at each other. Now this took the women holding those cats' sacks by surprise. Both let go of their sacks to prevent their hands from being shredded to the bone by the cats' razor sharp claws. The cats escaped and continued their private brawl. The other women in the group all let go of their sacks to try to part the two fighting cats, and *all* the cats, with their kittens, escaped and manically dashed off in all directions. Some even joined the brawl.

The Sergeant, with his men and their partners, joined the women to chase after the cats to retrieve them, but as soon as a couple of cats were sat back in their sacks, they started a brawl of their own. The two cats who had originally started brawling had decided that distance between them was probably a better bet than fighting and they, too, joined the other cats dashing around the undergrowth. When they were eventually seated back in their sacks they sat there, madly eyeing each other, displaying their teeth with ears pointed backwards and growling more profanities.

About an hour later, all the cats and kittens were eventually retrieved and put back in the sacks. The two original brawlers continued to growl unrepeatable words at each other from inside their sacks.

When order had been established, the women and their chaperon continued their journey back to Jingle Town.

Dabbing their bloodied hands with well used hankies, the policemen and their partners continued to the fair, laughing and joking at the brawl that they had just supressed.

A brawl not in the usual sense, but a brawl of cats!

Oh! And in case you're wondering, the answer to the riddle is one (1) - 'As ***I*** was going to St. Ives…'

CHAPTER 49

Several weeks later. Monday, a.m.

The day of sentencing.

To cut a long story short, the perpetrators have attended their pre-trial hearings and they were sent away to attend court at a later date for their trials. Every one of them adhered to their bail conditions and they all attended the court when ordered.

At their trials, they all pleaded guilty to the charges brought by Sergeant Argent and so the Judge didn't find a need for them to repeat their stories in front of a jury. They were all bailed, once more, to appear in front of Judge Fairly again, today, for their sentences.

*

NEWS FLASH! From Chatty Chaste of Rhyme Place TV Station:

Chatty - "The headlines, this morning… Residents of Rhyme Place are asked not to park in the village on Wednesday because this year's carnival procession will be travelling to Jingle Town on that day. The usual convoy of floats and acts will be out, headed by The Grand Old Duke of York and his men. The village's Morris Dancers will be dancing round the Mulberry Bush this afternoon. A good attendance is required or you might miss the wielding of the handkerchiefs, sticks and swords. The dance organiser, Mr. Maurice Morris, has informed us that all money taken at this event will be donated to the King's Charity Fund. The King's Charity

Banquet is being held on the same night. Everyone is invited. Make sure you…"

Chatty suddenly stopped mid sentence and put a finger to her ear. "I've just heard that the men responsible for stealing Bo Peep's sheep and Mary's lamb are about to be sentenced at the court, with Judge Fairly presiding. We'll go, live, to the court to listen to Judge Fairly's summing up and sentencing of Wee Willy Winkie, John Dumpling, old MacDonald and the pie man. These men, you will recall were charged by Sergeant Argent several weeks ago with offences related to the theft of the sheep. All the men pleaded guilty at their trials. The Judge is about to start his summing up, so we'll go there now."

*

The court was packed. Friends, relatives, wives, children and policemen were all squashed into the few bench seats available for the public.

"All rise," ordered the Court Clerk as Judge Fairly entered from his chamber door. After the Judge made himself comfortable in his padded and buttoned chair, the Court Clerk bid everyone to, "Be seated… Today's session will be presided over by the 'orrible… Er, 'onourable Judge Fairly."

First up was the pie man.

"Pie man, I have read the reports submitted by the police and your solicitor," began the Judge. "To your credit you have pleaded guilty to the charges of conspiracy to steal sheep and to perverting the course of justice. Both these charges should not be taken lightly. Do you have anything more to say before I sentence you?

The pie man shook his head and meekly answered "No."

"I am aware of the strain you are now under, in view of the fact that you have lost your livelihood until the bakery is re-built and you are able to earn a living once more, so I'm not going to fine you. I don't believe that you have the means to pay a fine, in any event, so I am going to sentence you to sixty days community service, to run concurrently with sixty days probation. I sincerely hope that you will reflect on the harm that you might have caused Bo Peep if her sheep had been processed into pies by you. Luckily for you, no harm was done to the sheep. If any of the sheep had been harmed, your sentence would have been far more painful than the one I've bestowed upon you. In future I hope you will do the right thing by making sure that the meat you buy comes from a suitable source. You can go. See the Court Clerk for your instruction regarding your sentence."

The pie man left the dock and departed from the courthouse, his head bowed, trying to think of what he could do to retrieve his once good name.

Next up was John Dumpling.

"John Dumpling, I have read the reports submitted by the police and your solicitor and I have listened and noted your mother's character reference. You have pleaded guilty to all of the charges brought by Sergeant Argent. Your charge of driving whilst uninsured and driving without a valid licence merits a fine of one hundred pounds, and you are banned from driving for a period of twelve months. The charges of dangerous driving and inconsiderate driving are a little more serious, as you very nearly injured two people carrying a tray of pies as they walked along the road on their way to the fair. These charges carry an additional fine of one hundred pounds and a further ban from driving for period of six months, this ban to run consecutively to the ban for driving whilst uninsured. You will also pay for a new shirt for Simon because the one he was wearing at the time got torn. I am not entirely satisfied that a charge of handling stolen goods is serious enough for the crime you committed. In my books, you should have been charged with theft of the sheep, but your mother's testimony of your previously good character went a long way to mitigating your sentence for this crime. I award you eight months community service. I will not fine you, in this case, because I have it on good authority that your mother is unable to finance such an award, but heed my words, John Dumpling. The next time you are brought before me, you will face a period in jail. Is that clear?"

A nod and a weak, "Yes, sir. Thank you," from Dumpling.

"You can go," declared the Judge. "See the Court Clerk about the terms of your community service."

John Dumpling left the dock and departed from the courthouse, followed by his mother who constantly smacked the top of his head.

Following Dumpling was old MacDonald.

"Mr. MacDonald, you have been charged with conspiracy to steal Bo Peep's sheep and Mary's lamb, and you have pleaded guilty to these charges."

The Judge turned to MacDonald's solicitor and asked, "Are there any more mitigating facts before I award this man's sentence?"

"No, sir. I believe that you have all appropriate reports in front of you, so I will not waste any of your time repeating what's in them."

"That's very good of you, Mr. Crooks, and, if I may say, a pleasant change from your usual acerbic attacks. Are you feeling unwell?" The Judge smiled a friendly smile, revealing his sense of humour."

The solicitor replied, "The last thing on my mind today, sir, is making life difficult for you." The solicitor smiled back - a false, sarcastic smile.

"Good," continued the Judge and turned back to face MacDonald. "You say, Mr. MacDonald, that you were unaware of where the sheep came from. Frankly, I don't believe you. I think you colluded with the men that stole the sheep and that they informed you of how, and where, they intended to get the sheep. You even loaned your truck to one of those men. But I must take your comments, in this respect, at face value and I must also take account of your guilty plea when sentencing you. You could have gone to Ballad Village to buy the sheep and lamb that you intended to sell on to the pie man, but you didn't. Instead, you chose to steal the sheep and a lamb from local inhabitants - people who regard these animals as their pets. People who have fed and watered their pets, and kept them well looked after. People who would never have thought that their beloved pets would be so heartlessly taken from them and sold on so cheaply for the meat that could be harvested from them. You are a callous and heartless man, Mr. MacDonald, but I have to consider that you have a farm to run, and animals to feed. However, in view of the seriousness of your crime, and the outcome that might have taken place had the sheep not escaped, I have no difficulty in sentencing you to twelve months in prison, suspended for a period of twenty four months pending reports on your future behaviour. You are also sentenced to twenty four months probation, with a fine of two hundred and fifty pounds.

You will also pay Bo Peep a sum of two hundred pounds as compensation for the pain and suffering sustained upon her. Do you wish to say anything?"

MacDonald just stared an angry stare at the judge.

"You can go, Mr. MacDonald, but be advised - If you do not attend your probation officer, as ordered, or you break the law again, you will be returned to this court to complete the sentence awarded to you today. Is that clear?"

More angry stare from MacDonald. The Judge turned to MacDonald's solicitor.

"I trust, Mr. Crooks, that you will fully brief your client on his responsibilities from now on?"

"Yes, sir," answered the solicitor. "I'll brief my client the moment we leave the court."

"Good," declared the Judge. "Next?"

Old MacDonald left the dock and stormed out of the courthouse. His solicitor followed. The solicitor attempted to lecture MacDonald, but the farmer was having none of it, oblivious to the solicitor's rhetoric.

The Court Clerk announced, "Bring in Wee Willie Winkie."

Willie entered the courtroom a changed man. He was clean shaven, had had his hair cut, and he was wearing a suit and tie. After being placed in the dock he waited to be told to sit and looked nervously at the Judge. The Judge inspected Willie closely, inwardly summing up his opinion of the criminal.

"Wee Willie Winkie, you have been brought in front of me before. You have a crime sheet almost as long as my arm, full of misdemeanours and violations of the laws. Have you got anything, at all, to say in mitigation of the crimes for which you have been brought before me today?"

Willie sighed a big sigh, folded his arms, shrugged his shoulders and said, "Get on with it," in an unconcerned, offhand manner.

The Judge stared at Willie for a long time, as if he was thinking hard about the sentence he was about hand out.

Reading from the file in front of him, the Judge listed Willie's charges. "You have been brought before me this time on the multiple charges of theft of Bo Peep's sheep, theft of Mary's lamb, theft of Lucy Locket's purse, reckless behaviour, driving while uninsured and driving without a valid licence. Do you have anything, at all, to say in your favour?"

"Any chance of a cup of tea?"

The Judge sat back and held his chin while he read through the volume of papers before him. Looking up, he declared, "You now face my charge of contempt of court. Are you sure you don't want to say anything to mitigate your sentence?"

"Two sugars, nice and milky."

"Okay, Willie. Which of these charges do you want me to deal with first? The theft charges, reckless behaviour, or the driving charges?"

"Take your pick, Judge. Either way, I'm going down, so let's get this over with, shall we?"

Judge Fairly turned to Willie's solicitor.

"Mr. Greedie, have you fully briefed your client on his attitude towards this court?"

"Yes, sir. If I may say a few words in mitigation?"

The Judge nodded.

"Well, sir, my client fully appreciates the distress he caused the owners of the sheep and lamb, and he is deeply sorry for this and, indeed, his attitude towards yourself and this court. He is deeply sorry for his actions.

His… uncharacteristic behaviour is merely a culmination of the poor treatment he received from the police during his arrest and…"

The judge interrupted the solicitor's flow. "Sit down, Mr. Greedie. Your mitigation is having about as much effect on me as your client is having."

Willie piped up, "Yeah. He's about as useful as a soggy bread bun."

There were titters of laughter from the spectators. When silence once more prevailed the judge spoke up.

"Wee Willie Winkie, I'm not going to waste any more of the court's time in listing all your sentences…"

"Good," interrupted Willie.

"… For the charges of theft, you will be confined to Balladshire Correction Facility for a period of two years for each of the charges put to you, these terms to run consecutively from the first charge of theft of Bo Peep's sheep because I consider you to be a dangerous person, unable to accept authority in any way. You will, therefore, be jailed for a period of six years for these offences. I order that the minimum period of incarceration is that which is equal to your sentence. Hence you will remain in prison for the full six year period. The charge of reckless behaviour is a serious one. Had things turned out differently you could have been facing a charge of murder but, as it is, both Jack and Jill have recovered from their injuries without too many side effects - although Jack still has a short term memory problem that, in time, may return to normal. For this, you will spend a period of three years in Balladshire Correction Facility, to run concurrently with the periods awarded by the charges previously mentioned. For the remaining charges of uninsured driving and driving without a valid licence, you will be fined a sum of two hundred pounds and banned from driving for a period of twelve months from the date of your release from prison. You will also pay a sum two hundred pounds each, to all three parties you have wronged, this being compensation for the pain and suffering you caused. I won't ask if you have anything further to say because I doubt that you can say anything to make me change my mind. Take him down."

Shouting profanities at the Judge, and anyone else that comes to his mind, Willie disappeared out of the dock and down the stairs to his cell to await the vehicle that will take him for a long holiday at His Majestie's pleasure.

With no-one else in the cells, the court closed for the day and Sergeant Argent and his men finished writing up their reports.

The telephone in the station reception rang. The Sergeant, being the duty desk policeman, picked up the receiver.

"Rhyme Place police station," he said.

"Sergeant? This is contrary Mary. Do you fancy a cup of coffee…?"

EPILOGUE

Now are you convinced that the characters in nursery rhymes exist?

No? Can't be fooled, eh?

Think back to your early child years. I bet you thought they were real then, when you sat on Mum's knee and listened to her telling you all about Baby Bunting, or Goosey Gander, or Looby Loo.

It is believed that the term 'nursery rhyme' emerged in the 1820s, although the first known book containing a collection of these texts was Tommy Thumb's Pretty Song Book, published by Mary Cooper in 1744. Since then, scholars and collectors such as Iona and Peter Opie, Joseph Ritson, James Orchard Halliwell, and Sir Walter Scott have helped by documenting and preserving the lyrics.

It wasn't very long before the words were put to music to create lullabies, or cradle songs, usually played for, or sung to, children, but did you know that the purposes of nursery rhymes and lullabies vary. Generally, they were originally used to pass down cultural knowledge or tradition, but educated people put lots of slants on then to demonstrate stuff like 'development of communication skills', or 'maintenance of infants' undivided attention', or 'regulation of behaviour'. That lot is too highbrow for me. I prefer to think of lullabies and nursery rhymes as a sleep aid for children. They worked that way for my kids, anyway.

Lullabies have existed since ancient times, so I'm pretty sure that when they first started to be used, nobody gave 'development of communication skills' a thought… They just wanted their kid to go to sleep so that they could get back to bed and try to retrieve some of their own lost sleep time.

Anyway, the more you think about it, the more you will come to agree that the stories in nursery rhymes contain real life experiences. So, if the stories have been appropriated from real life scenarios, it follows that the people in the nursery rhymes are real.

Aren't they…?

europe
books